Midnight,
CHRISTMAS EVE

Andy Clapp

FIREFLY
SOUTHERN FICTION
LIGHTHOUSE PUBLISHING OF THE CAROLINAS

Firefly Southern Fiction is an imprint of LPCBooks
a division of Iron Stream Media
100 Missionary Ridge, Birmingham, AL 35242
ShopLPC.com

Cover design by Elaina Lee
Author photo by Jaime L. Pike

Scripture quotations marked HCSB are taken from the Holman Christian Standard Bible®, Used by Permission HCSB ©1999, 2000, 2002, 2003, 2009 Holman Bible Publishers. Holman Christian Standard Bible®, Holman CSB®, and HCSB® are federally registered trademarks of Holman Bible Publishers.

This is a work of fiction. Names, characters, and incidents are all products of the author's imagination or are used for fictional purposes. Any mentioned brand names, places, and trademarks remain the property of their respective owners, bear no association with the author or the publisher, and are used for fictional purposes only.

Library of Congress Control Number: 2021940363

ISBN-13: 978-1-64526-297-8
eBook ISBN: 978-1-64526-298-5

PRAISE FOR *MIDNIGHT, CHRISTMAS EVE*

Andy Clapp's story-writing captures the heart of readers with this powerful account of love and redemption. The perfect addition to anyone's holiday collection. The storyline of joy. pain, and the tenacity of waiting for God's perfect timing hooked me from the first chapter.

~ **Tez Brooks**
International speaker and award-winning author of
The Single Dad Detour

Midnight, Christmas Eve is a heart-warming, touching story from author Andy Clapp. I firmly believe it will touch lives and have a lasting impact on everyone who dives into this literary treasure. Andy has a true gift from the Lord to tell stories and this wonderful Christmas piece will not only brighten your holiday season, but also your life.

~ **Del Duduit**
Award-winning author of *Buckeye Believer*

Andy Clapp's *Midnight, Christmas Eve* ignites, in just the first few chapters, a spark of hope that true love never ends. It then fans the flames of undying love with each fast-moving chapter. Clapp masterfully brings to life the biblical account of Hosea and Gomer with modern-day characters, causing the reader to ponder God's redeeming, never-ending love for His children, while turning pages to find out if love triumphs in the end. An excellent read!

~ **Julie Lavender**
Award-winning author of *365 Ways to Love Your Child*

With *Midnight, Christmas Eve*, Andy Clapp has woven a poignant tale of faithfulness and dedication. His deep, rich characters are nearly tangible. And despite the hardships they face, there is a thread of hope that tugs the reader through. Clapp's keen understanding of scripture and of people is on full display in his debut novel.

~ **Aaron Gansky**
Author of the Hand of Adonai series, *Who is Harrison Sawyer*, and *Heart's Song*

For all those who have ever felt broken beyond hope, *Midnight, Christmas Eve* shares the spirit of enduring love. Author Andy Clapp presents a story of a soul who doubts her worth and the faithful friend who refuses to give up on her. Pastor Clapp weaves a subtle reference to deeper truth as he wraps this heartwarming tale in the ribbons of Christmas.

~ **Tina Yeager**
Award-winning author, therapist, speaker, and Flourish-Meant Podcast host

The plot and characters of Andy Clapp's *Midnight, Christmas Eve* are not trite or gimmicky. There are such things as heartache, forgiveness, and endurance. Brady and Sarah experience these and more on their way to finding each other again, amidst years of obstacles. Filled with relatable experiences and memories that could easily be our own, Clapp takes the reader on a journey of broken dreams, discovery, and a greater understanding of true love. This is not a book to be put on a shelf, but read repeatedly, throughout the year.

~ **Molly Jo Realy**
Author of the romantic location-mystery *NOLA*

Be prepared to quickly slip into the seasons of Brady and Sarah's story. Moments after reading the first few sentences, I was ready to turn down the AC and wrap myself in a comfy throw, and by the end, I was wishing for a second cup of hot chocolate.

~ **Bethany Jett**
Author of *The Cinderella Rule* (and sucker for an angsty love story)

Andy Clapp has combined two things that I adore—a touching love story and my favorite holiday—with his first novel *Midnight, Christmas Eve*. This author masterfully shares God's unwavering love for us through his believable and likeable characters, and if you're like me, you'll be up all night reading page after page because you simply can't put this book down. This is an amazing novel guaranteed to entertain, make you think, and maybe even change your life. Hurry and grab your own copy of *Midnight, Christmas Eve* because I'm not sharing mine.

~ **Michelle Medlock Adams**
Bestselling author of more than 100 books including
Dachshund Through the Snow and *Dinosaur Devotions*

Many have captured the magic of Christmas, but Andy has done more than that with *Midnight, Christmas Eve*. Along with reminding us of the wonder of Christmas, *Midnight* reminds us of the incredible magic of friendship, romance, and faith. In *Midnight, Christmas Eve*, Andy Clapp has created an instant classic that seizes the magical wonder of Christmas while allowing old-soul biblical values to shine with the same enchanted glow of a snow-frosted Christmas classic inspiring all but especially a new generation to embrace the joy and life-giving attributes of Christ-centered living and principles. Readers will be left with a smile, a hot chocolate warmth in the heart, likely a tear, and the desire to be a better person.

~ **Jake McCandless**
Award-winning author, pastor, and executive director of Stand Firm

In *Midnight, Christmas Eve*, author Andy Clapp gives us amazing characters in Brady and Sarah, a warm and real southern setting in West Jefferson, and a story that tells us that faith can guide us through heartbreak and tragedy. And what love is all about.

~ **Britt Mooney**
Author of *SAY YES: How God-sized Dreams Take Flight*

ACKNOWLEDGMENTS

I THANK THE LORD FOR the opportunity to write this book and see it published. May all the glory be His because without Him, it would not be possible.

I would also like to thank my wife, Crystal, and my kids – Cheyenne, Autumn, and Brady. The patience you showed as I spent long hours away working on the novel amazes me. I am thankful for my church, Mt. Zion Baptist Church in Liberty, NC, for allowing me to write and for your support of the North Carolina Christian Writers Conference each year. I wish I could list all of you because your love and support mean so much.

A special thank you goes to my friend and agent, Cyle Young, who took a chance on me. You told me it would happen one day. I also want to thank the Serious Writer family for their support. Thank you to Bethany Jett because without her, my career would not be where it is now. Thank you, Michelle Medlock Adams, for the positive support always and to Del Duduit, a true friend and inspiration. A special thank you to Victoria Duerstock, whose guidance continues to help me grow.

I am eternally thankful to Eva Marie Everson, someone who deserves more recognition than I can ever give. Her impact in my life cannot be expressed in a few sentences. Thank you to Ramona Richards and all those at Iron Stream Media, Lighthouse Publishing of the Carolinas, and Firefly Southern Fiction who made this dream a reality. This experience has been wonderful and uplifting.

Also, thank you to Steven James. Steven and I sat at a coffee shop at the Blue Ridge Mountains Christian Writers Conference and at a restaurant in Burlington and talked about books. He showed an interest and a belief in me that pushed me to never give up.

I want to thank the residents and business owners in West Jefferson, NC. Meeting many of you, spending time in your town, and the welcome you extended me made this an even bigger thrill to write.

Thank you to JT, Shea, Alexis, and Bethany Turney for your friendship and constant support. I cannot do life without Cliff, Kelli, and Kyndall Foley, so I thank them. To Bryan and Elizabeth, Renee, and Eddie – thank you, guys, that we do life together. I appreciate greatly the support of Heather and TJ Paschal, Brian and Kristyn Lowe, Joni and Tim Clayton, Sam and Tyler Brown, Melissa and Jon Cole.

I would also like to thank Edie Melson and DiAnn Mills for their work on the Blue Ridge Mountains Christian Writers Conference. Attending their conference helped me develop relationships and grow in the craft. Thank you to Alton Gansky, Aaron Gansky, and Molly Jo Realy – Firsts in Fiction Podcast paved the way for this novel. Also, thank you to Word Weavers, a great organization for authors from all genres. I am so thankful for my Page 11 friends.

Thank you to my mom, Rickie, for believing in me and to my dad, Wayne, for putting a love of literature in my life. Thank you to my sister, Angie, and brother-in-law, Bobby, for your support. I also thank Ron and Melinda, Dave and Nicole, Nana and Papa, Aunt Sissy and Uncle Jim for their support. Thank you also to the Southern Alamance Class of 1995 and my University of Mount Olive family – you are part of everything I do.

Thank you to all my friends and to you, the reader. I deeply appreciate all of you.

Andy

In Memory of Noah Tate Foley – We love and miss you.
And of my great-grandparents, Slocum and Marcia Johnson
because they loved West Jefferson.
and
To Crystal
You gave me the encouragement to chase a dream.

Chapter 1

BENEATH THE GLOW OF AN old streetlamp, a bench held a single visitor on a freezing Christmas Eve night. The place knew the visitor well, his arrival at the same time each year and his departure equally predictable. What had begun as hopeful and romantic could now be seen as desperation. Or even denial. Nonetheless, Brady Jameson sat in the biting North Carolina winter as a light snow drifted around him, years of hopes dashed. This year would be no different.

A blanket of white covered the streets and trees that had long stood barren. The breeze was enough to cause the branches to crackle, the sound easily mistaken for that of a heart breaking. But lights and wreaths—the town's attire for the season—told that something greater was coming.

The streets were desolate, stores all closed, as the busy townspeople had made their way to their destinations with intentions of slowing down for Christmas. Children had long since been put to bed, their excitement about the next day's morn finally losing the battle to bodily exhaustion. Those who remained awake did so only for a final unwinding or a last gift-wrapping before the flurry of activity on the morning's horizon.

Yet, Brady sat in the cold and alone. Wondering if this might be the year. Going home was the most logical choice, but logic and reason were not valued when it came to matters of the heart. Love had driven him to the bench, even if it meant his heart might shatter with another rejection.

Everything had begun at the bench, beneath the glow of that

streetlamp. She had been there that night, and, over time, Brady had grown convinced that God had also put him there on that Christmas Eve night when he was seventeen for a reason, their worlds colliding as their souls intertwined. Perhaps, though, Brady had taken this too far. Perhaps this was not meant to be.

Brady glanced at his phone. Fifteen minutes stood between him and Christmas Day. For fifteen more minutes, he could hold on to a hope that began to seem nonsensical, even to him. The clock of his life had him nearing twenty-seven now and he longed for a family. His friends, his family, and nearly everyone who knew the story implored him to move on. To forget about her. To enjoy his life. But the past has a way of imprisoning a soul.

His spiritual confidant, Todd, saw things through a different lens, and now, even the faith leader of his life had concerns. Though the woodworker knew the voices of concern were probably right, the words of a recent sermon seemed to resonate. The situation was vastly different, but the core message was the same. So, here he sat again.

What Brady held on to was unconditional love, the very type that forgives hurts, hopes for the best, rejoices in triumphs, cries in the pain.

And waits.

No one from their gang of friends had seen Sarah in at least a year and a half, since the day she exited the Christmas in July event. Brady had spent time with her then. She said she would call but those words became just another broken promise. Even when she'd said them, he'd doubted she'd live up to them. Maddie, Sarah's best friend, rarely heard from her these days and when her name was mentioned, Maddie always changed the subject.

So, he sat on this frosty Christmas Eve, reading a passage of Scripture with two cups of hot chocolate next to him. He relived the history of that place, of that person, of that promise.

And each passing second was a moment closer to another letdown.

Chapter 2

AT SEVENTEEN, BRADY HAD AN adoration for Christmas. He saw the season as nearly magical, creating a joy in people that was lacking throughout the year.

"Mom," he softly called out to his mother, who sat cross-legged on the living room floor wrapping the last of the gifts, the tree lights casting a crown of colors around her. "I'm going out for a walk downtown. I'll be back in a little bit."

His mother's love for Christmas had been instilled in his life as a boy. Brady served as her little helper as she transformed the house each year into a winter wonderland. From her, he learned how to wrap the garland down the staircase handrail, how to meticulously decorate the mantel, and how to keep the candles centered in each window. His mom, Lauri, ensured that the traditions of the holidays were understood by her son so they would carry on after her life had come to an end. His sister, Chelsi, didn't care as much for traditions, but Brady—an old soul in a young man's body—embraced them.

"Okay, son, but be careful," his mother said, her attention on applying ribbon to the gift in her hand. But then she looked up and instructed, "And don't stay out too late."

"I won't."

"Make sure you bundle up, Brady. Freezing out there." There was a momentary pause before she added, "Are you meeting some friends or something?"

He sighed. Although he was seventeen, she still seemed to treat him as though he were seven, but his father had taught him early on that this was her way of showing she cared."No. Just want to see the lights, get some hot chocolate, and get out of the house. You know me. I can't just sit around."

Going for walks in the evenings and during the season highlighted his routine. As the days grew shorter, his work outdoors ended early. Too early. He needed something to do.

"Like I said, not too late. I will not have a grumpy teenager, that being you, ruining our Christmas tomorrow."

By now, Brady sat on the stairs that led upstairs to put his boots on, tying them tight to keep the snow from getting in and soaking his feet. "I promise," he said with a grin. "But I'm not the one you have to worry about. I'm always joyful, Mother. Your daughter, however, is grumpy even after twelve hours of sleep." He cut his eyes upward.

"Leave her alone, Brady." His mother chuckled as she paused in her wrapping. "You do have a point, though."

With a laugh and retrieval of his coat, he headed to the front door. "Love you, Mom."

"Love you, too."

He closed the door with a gentle click. The farmhouse door creaked if not closed just so. His father believed that no one needed to be out after nine o'clock, something Brady had heard all his life, but the family joked that his dad said this because he wanted to go to bed at nine. At fifteen, his sister normally wanted to go wherever Brady went. Being the older brother, he liked having Chelsi around . . . sometimes . . . but every now and then he wanted to get away by himself. While only twenty-two months separated them, they were worlds apart; he had grown closer to leaving home while she was still adjusting to high school.

The walk from the front door to the road where his father had erected a cross to show the world where they stood on faith was a good quarter mile, and downtown was a little over a half mile from their farmhouse. Easy enough; Brady decided to walk. Between playing baseball for his school team and his work on the farm, he stayed in good shape. Walking was better than driving anyway.

While walking, he could take in the details of the landscape that passed by a car window too quickly to appreciate. After a glance at his phone, he picked up the pace, hoping to get to Bohemia, the local coffee shop, before it closed at nine. The warm promise of the hot chocolate completed the atmosphere for him—lights, snow, Christmas Eve, and near silence.

As he walked, Brady reflected on the message he had heard at church that Sunday evening. Pastor Todd taught them about the Light of the world. He said, "The light of the world came to Bethlehem that night, forever piercing the darkness. As the gospel of John says, 'Life was in Him, and that life was the light of men. That light shines in the darkness, yet the darkness did not overcome it.' As Jesus is the Light of the world, we also remember that He said that we are to be the light of the world. Remember why the lights shine this Christmas season, and remember the light is to shine in our lives in every season."

Lessons with images on display all around were lessons that Brady would not easily forget. Amazing how the lights made such an impact at Christmas. Everything seemed to be brighter when the lights were shining.

Brady arrived at the coffee shop moments before closing, both for the night and for the holiday. He kicked the snow off his boots before stepping inside, then took note of the tree that stood near the front. Inside, the coffee shop had been transformed with snowflake ornaments hanging throughout. White Christmas lights adorned the front window. Luke stood behind the counter, grinning as his best friend made his way to place an order. "Final customer of the night," he announced. "Better make it quick."

"*Best* customer of the night," Brady fired back. "If you could remember anything, you would already know what I want."

"Merry Christmas. What are you in the mood for?"

"Hot chocolate as always."

"Haven't you ever heard of Swiss Miss? You do know that you can make your own hot chocolate at home," Luke chided.

"If I made it myself, what would you do for a job? I'm just trying to keep you employed."

"I need a large hot chocolate for my friend," Luke called out to one of their classmates who was busy wiping down the end of the counter.

"Thanks, man," Brady said. Then, to Erica, "Thank you, Erica."

"No problem, Brady."

"What are you doing out so late?" Luke asked. "Shouldn't you be at home? In bed?"

"Nope. Needed to get out of the house. I've been stuck inside most of our break, so I jumped at a chance."

Erica finished making his drink and handed it to Luke. Luke passed the hot chocolate over to Brady as Erica resumed cleaning up.

"Here's one large hot chocolate for you." He jutted his chin toward the door. "And I'll see you on Friday night."

Brady wrapped his hands around the warmth of the cup, then raised it in a salute. "Sounds good. Merry Christmas, *Lucas*." Brady grinned as he turned toward the door.

"Don't call me Lucas, *Bradford*. You know I hate that."

Brady walked out the door with a smile. He and Luke had been friends since first grade and now, in their junior year of high school, they were more like brothers. Luke followed Brady to the door, turning the lock and flipping the "Open" sign to "Closed."

Three inches of fresh powder blanketed much of the sidewalks as the foot traffic had thinned considerably since six o'clock. Brady made his way across Jefferson Street, admiring the lights and the silence. A glance over his shoulder told him that the coffee shop now rested in darkness. Bohemia and the gas station had been the last two businesses to close.

The gas station now stood alone.

Chapter 3

Brady made his way past Town Hall, walking a bit farther than the bank at the bottom of the hill. He was in no hurry. He could survive on a few hours of sleep. Crossing back over Jefferson, he strolled down the main strip of town. West Jefferson knew how to make Christmas come alive. Outsiders drove from Virginia, Tennessee, and other parts of North Carolina just to see the streets, to absorb the magical atmosphere, to immerse themselves in the season. Growing up here, one could not avoid Christmas; they were surrounded by a declaration of its impending arrival.

When he drew close to the Old Hotel, he spotted a girl sitting alone on an outside bench beneath the glow of a streetlamp, her brokenness audible. No one had been there when he'd passed by on the other side of the street after leaving Bohemia. She sat bent over, her sobbing too painful to be ignored.

He approached from behind. "Hey . . . um . . . are you okay?" As soon as the question left his lips, he realized the ridiculousness of it.

"I'm fine," she answered, but her words didn't match the sounds emanating from her only seconds earlier. All Brady could see was the back of her black coat and the dark-brown, nearly black hair that lay along her shoulders, flowing from underneath a jet-black toboggan.

"Are you sure?"

"Yeah," she said as she sniffled, her finger brushing her cheekbones. "I'll be okay."

"Do you need help or something? Is there . . . some way I can help you?" He made his way around to the front of the bench. Brady didn't want to leave her alone, but he also didn't want to irritate her if she wanted to be left alone.

"No. I'm all right." The girl sighed deeply. "Just a bad day." When she looked up, their eyes locked. He knew her. Sarah Ashford, the head cheerleader at their high school, the girl everyone knew would be crowned Prom Queen eventually. Mascara streaks marked her cheeks, her hazel eyes bloodshot from the tears that had come from the depths of her soul.

"Sarah," Brady said, astonished not only by who sat in front of him, but also by the fact that he had spoken to her. He'd never once uttered a word to her. He wanted to know her, but her appearance—even her presence—gave him anxiety.

"Hi, Brady."

She knows my name. How does she know who I am?

"Hi . . . what's going on? Something seems wrong."

She swiped at her cheeks, this time with her thumbs. Sighed deeply again, then shook her head as if she couldn't believe what she was about to say. "My dad left my mom today."

Brady dropped to the bench beside her. "On Christmas Eve?"

"Yep," she said, her tone sharp. "On Christmas Eve."

Brady realized his reaction didn't help matters. He always seemed to state the obvious and, definitely, this was not the time to do so. "I don't know what to say. I mean, what happened?"

"Mom and I went shopping early this morning up in Boone. When we came home, he was putting some stuff in the car." Her voice cracked and she drew in a deep breath. "We thought it was gifts or something. But then he followed us inside, sat us down at the table, and said he wasn't happy anymore." One brow rose and she looked at him. "He told Mom he had met someone else." Another tear trekked toward her jawline. "And then, he was gone."

Brady slid back on the bench, his cupped hand cradling his hot chocolate, and silently prayed for the right words to say. "How's your Mom?"

She threw gloved hands up that landed in her lap. "Devastated.

They've been married for twenty years."

Brady's heart hurt for a girl he barely knew. He tried to imagine what it might be like, to have his father walk in on Christmas Eve and make such a declaration. He couldn't. "I really don't know what to say."

"There is nothing anyone *can* say." But then she sobbed, "Brady, this hurts *so bad*." Unexpectedly, she shifted to lay her head on his shoulder. He placed his barely touched hot chocolate on the cold bench beside him, then wrapped an arm around her. For the next few minutes, he rubbed her shoulder while she sobbed on his. Finally, he said, "I'm here, Sarah. I don't know if that helps, but . . ."

She nodded. "That's what I need right now."

For over two hours, they sat and talked. Brady tried his best just to listen without saying anything he would later analyze as stupid. He pledged support when he had no other words. As midnight drew near, Sarah stood to go home, thanking Brady for being there before she left. He wanted to walk her home, but she insisted she was fine. Still, he watched until she was no longer a speck in the darkness.

Brady made his way home, his mood anything but what he had anticipated when he left the house earlier that night. Mainly his heart broke for a girl whose Christmas—not to mention her whole life—had been turned upside down.

Chapter 4

THE SUN CAST SPARKLES ON the new-fallen snow—the majestic sight of an early Christmas morning. Normally, the teenage boy who loved Christmas was the easiest to awake but the previous night had kept him up late.

"Brady, Momma said you need to get up." Chelsi's voice disrupted the little sleep he enjoyed.

"Go away, Chelsi."

But she didn't. One thing stood in the way of her opening her gifts and that one thing wouldn't get out of the bed.

"It's Christmas. People mighta waited for Baby Jesus but ain't nobody waitin' on you."

"I'll be down in a minute."

He knew she wasn't going to leave. He rolled over and tried to cover his head with a pillow to drown out the voice of his younger sister, the one who was eager for the family to get through breakfast so she could open her gifts. Nothing could drown her out.

"Momma said to hurry it up. She said she told you to come home early last night."

"It wasn't my fault."

"Oh, here we go. The devil-made-me-do-it excuse."

"Chelsi, shut up and go away."

"I will when you get up."

Without looking, Brady reached toward the floor for one of his discarded shoes, then threw it. It landed with a thump against the wall. "I'm telling!" she said before racing down the stairs. Within seconds, his father yelled for Brady to get up.

Reluctantly, he slid on his flip-flops, threw on a Wake Forest hoodie and hat, then made his way down the stairs to the kitchen. He could hear Chelsi describing the earlier trauma of the shoe incident to their mother. Despite the warm and inviting aromas blanketing the kitchen, he really wanted to go back to bed . . . but it was Christmas.

"I told you that nobody was going to be grumpy on Christmas Day," his mother said sternly as she placed a plate of bacon on the table, one brow raised for emphasis.

"I'm not grumpy, Mother."

"So, what mood would you call it that leads one to throw a shoe at his sister on Christmas?" his dad asked. He'd dished up a bowl of fluffy scrambled eggs, which he placed next to the bacon.

Brady plopped into his chair at the table and responded without hesitation. "A giving mood."

"Giving mood, huh?" Dad responded, now sitting back in his chair, pointing with the serving spoon at his son.

"Yes, Dad." Brady grinned. "I was *giving* her a chance to live to next Christmas."

His father tried not to laugh, but Brady's wittiness cracked him up. It always had.

"Well, issuing threats and throwing shoes is not what we are celebrating today, Brady," his mom said as she took her seat at the table, placing a basket of biscuits in the middle.

"I know, Mom. Just had a long night last night."

"I thought you said you wouldn't be home late," she noted, a subtle reminder of her instructions from twelve hours earlier. She motioned for him to pour orange juice from the pitcher into the four short glasses near his plate.

"Hadn't planned on it," he said, pouring juice into the first glass. "I ran into someone who was upset and crying, and I felt like I couldn't just walk on past her."

"Anybody we know?" His mom took her glass of juice as he poured the second and handed it to his father.

"I doubt it. I hardly know her. She's the head cheerleader at our school."

Chelsi's eyes widened as she reached across the table for her own glass. "He's talking about Sarah Ashford."

"Chelsi, please," Brady shot back, wanting the subject dropped as quickly as possible. He reached for a biscuit to start breakfast and hopefully kill the questions.

"Sarah is the most popular girl at school. Every guy drools over her when she walks by," Chelsi continued, a smug look on her face.

Dad looked at Brady, shrugging his shoulders as if to say he had no control over what was coming, then grabbed some bacon and allowed the ladies to begin the inevitable interrogation.

"Was something wrong with her?" Brady's mom asked. She also reached for the bacon, then passed it to Brady.

"Rather not say," Brady said, taking the platter while brushing aside the question as well as the direction the conversation was beginning to take.

"Is she on drugs?" Chelsi asked.

Brady glared at his sister. "No."

"Is she pregnant?"

"No . . . I mean, I don't know," Brady fired back. His sister was far from finished.

"Did Aiden break up with her?"

"Chelsi, I don't know. Just let it go. She was having a bad day. You really need to quit watching so much TV. You turn everything into an episode of *Dr. Phil*."

"So, what is it, Brady?" his father asked. "Is the girl in trouble?"

Brady bit into bacon that crumbled in his mouth. "I don't want to talk about it," he said around it. "It's none of my business and none of anyone else's business. She's just going through . . . something." He reached for his glass of orange juice. "But I'm not going to talk about it. Just let it go, please."

Dad agreed and led the prayer for their breakfast and for the Christmas Day that had come again. He thanked the Lord for peace and prayed that those who needed peace would be able to find it, especially on that day. Brady silently prayed for the girl across town whom he knew was suffering on a day of celebration.

After breakfast, the Jamesons celebrated the day, complete with gifts and a visit to their grandparents. As much as he tried to enjoy it all, Brady could not let the events of the prior night go. Sarah was broken. Her world was engulfed in a darkness she never wanted nor had she invited, and he was in the place to be a light in her darkness.

But how?

Chapter 5

FOUR DAYS PASSED.

Though Brady thought he should do something, he wasn't sure how to approach Sarah again. He called his youth pastor to see if Todd could help (should the opportunity arise), an invitation that Todd readily accepted and prayed with Brady over the phone about.

Brady's phone lit up around ten o'clock Friday morning—a text from a number he didn't know.

Can I talk to you tonight?

He sat on the edge of the bed, hesitated for a moment, then texted back: *Not sure whose number this is.*

Within a minute, a reply came through. *Sarah.*

Sure. What time and where?

Same bench. Nine?

I'll be there.

Brady set his phone down and wondered why she had texted. They knew of each other but, other than the two hours they'd spent on Christmas Eve, that was all. He knew more about her than he thought she knew of him. He also wondered why she didn't just talk to Aiden about her parents.

Before he could ponder the thought any further, his phone lit up again. *Don't forget me tonight.*

Brady hung his head. He had completely forgotten the promise he'd made to be at Luke's. Now he either had to back out on Luke or on Sarah. Luke would forgive him. Sarah needed him.

Can't tonight. Something came up. he texted back.

It's all good. You okay?

Yeah, all good.

You're going to miss an epic bonfire tonight.

Next time, Luke Skywalker, Brady texted and then laughed, visualizing Luke's face.

I hate you.

Facing the unknown made the day long. Endlessly, he checked the clock as minutes took hours to pass. A multitude of scenarios played like a movie with an ending that left the viewer hanging. Brady wanted to know what she wanted, though he knew the topic was most likely the situation with her parents. He began a text to Sarah to ask why she wanted to see him, only to delete it before sending.

He paced.

As eight thirty arrived, he grabbed his coat and headed toward the door.

"Going out, Mom. I'll be home later."

"Not too late. Are you meeting up with Luke?"

"Not tonight. Something else came up." He refused to lie to his mother but wasn't about to mention Sarah; he'd be standing there until New Year's Day answering questions.

His mom raised one brow as she looked up from the couch. "Oh, okay."

Brady made his break, ensuring the conversation could go no further. The biting breeze of a late December's night had him blowing on his hands and walking quickly. After a quick stop by the coffee shop, he arrived at the bench three minutes before nine with two hot chocolates, a simple act of kindness. Brady knew he could be impatient, sometimes self-centered, and mostly a people pleaser, but, despite those faults, he also thought of himself as genuinely kind.

"You came," a voice from behind said.

Just the sound of her voice took his breath away. "Yeah. I—um—I got you a hot chocolate." He raised one cup. "I don't know if you like hot chocolate but thought you might want one since it's so cold out."

"I love hot chocolate. Thanks, Brady." Sarah smiled as she sat on the bench beside him.

"Are you okay?" He shifted enough to hand her the drink. The thermometer outside the coffee shop said that the temperatures were in the upper twenties, but Brady was sweating as hard as he would on any given day in July. His question seemed awkward, even to him. If she were truly okay, would she have texted? If everything were fine, wouldn't she be doing something else on a Friday night?

She wrapped her gloved hands around the Styrofoam cup. "Not really. I still can't wrap my head around everything at home. I barely slept the last couple of days. I didn't have anyone else to turn to, so I texted you." She kept her focus on the cup of hot chocolate, then pulled the lid off. The scent of it filled the space between them.

Brady didn't know whether to be pleased or offended. "What about Aiden?' he asked, hoping for a little clarity as to why she called him rather than her boyfriend.

"Aiden is consumed with Aiden. Plus . . ." She took a sip of the chocolate. ". . . I talked to Maddie about you."

Brady and Maddie had been friends through their church youth group for years and Sarah was best friends with Maddie. "What did Maddie say?" He took his own sip of the chocolate, preferring to leave the lid on.

"She told me that you're a Christian. She said you are like one of the leaders in the youth group. So . . ." She raised the cup to her lips again. "Can you help me understand why God let this happen?"

She took a long sip, but her voice had begun to break again. Brady assumed she had tried to hold everything together at home, but in the asking of the question, she showed her vulnerability. He slid back on the bench, knowing he had no answer to her question. Nervously, he flicked the lid of his hot chocolate with his thumb; the clicking noise penetrated the silence. "Sorry," he said sheepishly when he noticed that she now watched the repetitious movement. The question opened the door of possibilities for guidance, but it was an opportunity that Brady felt ill prepared for. "I'm not sure I can answer that."

"I know," she said as she wiped tears from her eyes. "Impossible question with an impossible answer."

Another sip of hot chocolate bought him time. "Do you *believe* in God?" he asked, winging his line of questioning to come up with some answer.

"I don't know. My mom goes to church at Christmas and Easter, but my dad is an atheist. I don't know if I have ever thought about what *I* actually believe. I hoped you might have an answer and . . . to be honest . . . I knew you wouldn't judge me."

"I believe in God," Brady responded, "but I don't know how to answer that." He flicked at the lid of his cup once more, then added, "Why don't you come to church with me and talk to my youth pastor? Todd is easy to talk to and he knows more about stuff like this than I do."

Sarah looked away, but only for a moment. "I guess so."

Brady's heart smiled. "Cool. Wednesday night is the best night to come. You want to come with me next Wednesday?"

She paused again, this time slightly longer than before. Looking over in the direction of the Old Hotel Tavern, she took a long drink from her hot chocolate, as if it were giving her the answer.

Had he jumped the gun? He looked away. Maybe he had pushed the issue too hard, too quickly. His desire to help may have put more pressure on her, which was the very thing he didn't want to do.

With a deep sigh, she placed the cup on the bench. He looked down at it; it was nearly empty.

"All right," she said, bringing his attention back to her. "I'll go." She turned to him with a slight grin; a pin-prick pierced the tension that had built inside him during the pause.

He smiled, careful not to allow the curling of his lips to become a grin. Her acceptance of the invitation brought a relief that warmed him more than hot chocolate ever could. He didn't have all the answers, but Pastor Todd might.

Brady pulled back the lid from his cup and peered inside. Though the cup was nearly empty, his heart overflowed. "I'll pick you up at six."

"Thanks, Brady." She smiled again, picked up the discarded lid to her drink, and snapped it back over the rim. "I'll see you next Wednesday. I can text you my address."

She stood, then started toward Jefferson Street. When she reached the curb, she looked back at Brady. Smiled and held up her cup. "Thank you again for everything. Not just the hot chocolate . . . for being there, you know?"

"I told you I would be . . . and I meant it."

Sarah turned fully then and walked away, Brady's gaze never leaving her until she disappeared in the distance. He couldn't imagine why he had been put in this position. When she was well on her way home, he started the walk back to his house, calling Pastor Todd to explain what had taken place. He shared his frustration as Todd shuffled through what Brady felt sure were the pages of his Bible. Then Todd read Romans 8:28 to Brady. "This could be that moment for Sarah, where something good comes from something tragic. She needs someone. God sent you, Brady. Now, what was broken has a chance to be put back together."

Chapter 6

Wednesday night brought twenty-four teenagers to the Baptist church at the end of downtown. Joy filled the air, especially with the students still out of school on winter break. The worship set for the night included "Amazing Grace, My Chains Are Gone." Without meaning to, Brady glanced over at Sarah, keeping a careful watch over her demeanor. He hoped the song of worship and her broken heart would easily collide and prepare her heart for a message from God.

"Okay, guys, let's have a seat," Todd called out.

Brady sat beside Sarah, not too close to be awkward, but not too far away to make her feel alone. Brady measured such things. The analytical side of his mind nearly drove him and everyone around him crazy.

"Tonight, I want to talk to you about a man named Job. So, open up your Bibles to the book of Job. It's in the Old Testament, right before Psalms," Todd began. His eyes scanned the room for a moment, then locked eyes with Brady. By the way Todd looked at him, Brady knew the message was going to address something about the situation with Sarah. He looked down, found the book of Job in his Bible, then placed his Bible on the table between him and Sarah.

"How many of you have ever gone through a hard time?" Todd asked, setting the stage.

Everyone raised their hands.

"How many of you wondered why?"

Brady nodded and out of the corner of his eye, he saw Sarah nodding, though just barely.

"Anyone want to share?" Todd asked, looking to get the group involved in the discussion.

"Trying to convince my parents to buy me a truck was horrible. In fact, it still is. I have struggled to convince them that I *need* a truck," one of the guys, Micah, joked, trying his best to portray his suffering.

"Not quite sure that was where I was going with that question, Micah," Todd quipped.

"Todd, the struggle is real," he said. A ripple of laughter crossed the room, but after the laughter, a somber silence took its place. Around the tables, heads began to hang, and the students avoided eye contact. For Brady, the moment was what he'd hoped for. Prayed about. Those moments—that time when someone knows a pain, a struggle—are opportunities for hope to be shared.

"I'll give you a little bit of my story," Todd said, breaking the silence. "In high school, my father left our family. My heart was shattered, and I became so angry at God. Why did this have to happen? Why did it happen *to me?* For a lot of years, I struggled to see where anything good could come from it, but later on, I could see how God could take something bad and bring something good from it."

"I didn't know that your family was busted up, Todd," Peter said, himself a teenage boy from a broken home.

"Yeah, it happened to my family."

"How did you get through it? I mean, it's been over a year with my parents and I'm still ticked at my mom for leaving us." Peter's anger showed in his eyes and his clenched jaw.

"Just the way Job handled adversity . . . faith."

"Oh."

"All right. Let's look at this scripture together and see what we can learn."

Todd read the first chapter of Job to a group already drawn in by the initial question. While Brady tried to concentrate on the text, he was more amazed at Todd; he'd not known his story. Then again, he had never asked. When he talked to Todd, it was always about *his* life, never thinking to ask Todd what was going on with him.

How self-centered am I?

"Pretty bad, huh?" Todd asked and Brady blinked. The shocked looks on the faces of the other students gave the answer to the question.

"I can't even imagine. He lost his stuff, his kids, and a bunch of servants," Christa commented.

"And it gets worse," Todd assured them before reading again.

At the conclusion of the second chapter, Brady spoke up. "Job had to go through a lot."

"Yeah, he did. Lost his family, his wealth, and his health. All of it was a test of his faith. But look at what he said to his wife. He said, 'Should we accept only good from God and not adversity?' Having faith is not always easy but it helps us when we go through the good times and when we have to endure the bad times. Faith is knowing that God can produce good things even through the worst circumstances."

After the service closed in prayer, several of the students spoke to Todd before leaving. They also took a moment to speak to Sarah, letting her know they hoped she would return. Brady and Sarah waited for everyone to leave before they approached Todd.

"Hey, Todd, this is Sarah," Brady said, hoping his smile seemed genuine and that it wouldn't reveal feelings he was hardly ready to share with himself, much less Todd.

Todd shook her hand. "Hi, Sarah. I'm glad you came tonight."

"Thanks. It was pretty cool to be here."

"I hope you will come back again."

"I will."

Brady and Sarah turned to leave, but Todd called out before they could get out of the door.

"Hey, Sarah," he said, holding out his business card. "If you ever need anything, give me a call."

She took his card and slid it into her pocket. Tears filled her eyes, and, in that moment, Brady knew she had needed to hear the message that night. Sarah turned toward the door, but Brady lingered long enough to whisper in Todd's ear, "Thanks, man."

Chapter 7

SARAH KEPT COMING TO YOUTH group. Her friendship with Brady grew as time passed but she also continued to date her boyfriend, Aiden, who played quarterback for their high school team. Aiden and Sarah's relationship had more ups and downs than a rollercoaster and the nature of the relationship had become the talk of the group. In a righteous moment, Brady attempted to get Aiden involved in the group, but Aiden hated Brady and made no effort to hide it. From the stares across the hall at school, the comments made in passing, to deliberately making plans when Sarah intended to attend a youth event, his disdain hung in the air when Brady was around.

More than anything, Aiden despised Sarah's relationship with Brady and tried his best to put a stop to it.

As their senior year began, Sarah made an early decision to attend the University of Tennessee. She told Brady the decision was all hers, but the fact that Aiden had been recruited to play football for the Vols made Brady think she was going there for other reasons. Still, Sarah insisted it was far enough away from home to start a new life but not too far in case her mother needed her.

Brady had also considered Tennessee but knew he wouldn't be happy there; instead he decided to go to Appalachian State University, mainly so he could be close to home.

The year flew by. After Christmas, reality started to set in; everything was about to change. Aiden broke off his relationship with Sarah again during the holidays, leading Sarah to lament about another Christmas and another broken relationship and "didn't Aiden know she had planned for them to go to prom together?" Brady summoned his courage and asked if he could escort her . . . and, what do you know, she agreed.

Then Valentine's Day came, Aiden and Sarah resumed their relationship, and Brady was without a date for the prom.

"So, you decided to go alone?" his mother asked as she straightened his bowtie. "I'm sure there are dozens of girls who wanted you to ask them."

"But there was only one girl I wanted to go with and that wasn't going to happen. I'm not really sure why I'm even going."

His mother stepped back to admire her son. "Well, you will be the cutest guy there."

"Whatever you say, Mother." He gave her his best smile. "It's kind of funny. I hate dancing. I hate getting dressed up, but I am going somewhere where both are required."

"So, Sarah *is* going?"

"You know she is . . . she and her All-American jerk will be there."

His mom crossed her arms. Tilted her head just so. "Are you okay with that?"

"It's not up to me."

And then she smiled as only mothers can. "One day, she will see you for what you are, son."

Brady didn't want to get into a conversation about the situation. No more than they already were. After pulling the jacket over his arms until it rested on his shoulders, he made his way toward the door. "I've got to go. I'm going to hang out at Luke's after prom, so I'll probably just come home in the morning."

"Be careful, Brady."

Prom was what he expected it to be. The theme "This Magic Moment" became a joke at the table where Brady sat with Luke and Luke's date, Maddie, who happened to be Sarah's best friend. The prom committee had transformed the gym into a palace of silver and blue. The blue tablecloths featured silver centerpieces, and the lights on the dance floor were coordinated in the perfect shade to match.

Hanging streamers and a photo booth beckoned students to capture the magic of the night for all eternity.

After a while, Brady walked over to the refreshment area to get a glass of punch. As he neared the table, he caught his first glimpse of Sarah, nearly tripping over his feet. They had grown so close, finding a friendship that defied the norms, one that became increasingly comfortable. She went to his baseball games. He traveled to Raleigh for her cheerleading competition. He saw a side of her that most never got to see. He heard her snort when she laughed, laughed at the corny jokes she told, and witnessed her insecurity when she became her most vulnerable. In turn, she was able to see the side of him that he kept hidden.

He waited for her to see him, but she didn't, so he accepted a glass of punch, took a sip, then made his way back to the table, looking for her as he walked.

A few minutes later, Maddie convinced Brady to dance with her, which he did, but his heart wasn't in it. Throughout the night, his eyes roamed the room, catching glimpses of Sarah. He noted the blue of her dress and the way her hair was fixed. She looked like a princess. Like a dream. When she was announced Prom Queen he clapped but didn't at the announcement of Aiden as Prom King. A little while after the crowning, she spotted him, walked over, and chatted with him until Aiden escorted her away.

When he couldn't take any more, when the disappointment of what could have been his night with her became too intense, Brady stood from the table, told Luke he was going to head on home, and gave Maddie a hug. But as he turned to make his escape, there stood the princess.

"Aiden went outside. He'll be out there for a while. So . . . do you want to dance?"

Say no and go home. Dancing with her will only make all of this worse.

"Sure," he answered. "But I am terrible at dancing."

"I know," she said, her smile radiant. "It's all good, Brady. It's only right that I get to dance with the one I originally promised to go to the prom with."

For the next four minutes, nothing else in the world mattered. He held her hand in his right and placed his other in the middle of her back. She rested her head on his shoulder as they swayed to D.H.T.'s "Listen to Your Heart." And he reminded himself that, even if only for a moment, he held in his arms the one he wanted to hold forever.

"I'm so glad we got to dance together," she said, barely loud enough for him to hear.

"I am, too."

For Brady, the song's piano rhythm had been orchestrated to the beat of their hearts. He wanted to say something, but what was the end game? What good could possibly come? As the song neared its last notes, he held her a little tighter, knowing he would probably never have the chance again.

And then, the music stopped, and Aiden appeared.

The moment was over.

Brady left the dance a far different man than the one who had entered. Sometimes, a dance is just a dance. Other times, a person carries away a single song in their heart and relives the memory far beyond the moment.

Chapter 8

Over and over, the moment played in Brady's mind. Why would life ever present music that stops? Why are there endings so closely following what seems to be the perfect beginning?

He drove around for an hour, aimlessly, before going to Luke's. By the time he arrived, about forty of their friends were out by the pool. As the night wore on, they laughed and danced to the music—mostly country—that played from the pool house stereo system Luke's parents had recently installed. Brady tried to take his mind off Sarah, but the scent of her perfume had rubbed off on his shirt. With each breath of the breeze, the aroma resurrected the images from earlier that night.

He talked to those who lingered, sharing stories of the year that had passed too quickly. Some shared future plans. Some spoke only of the night. All pledged to stay connected as their seasons of life changed. But, Brady knew, such a pledge was based more on emotion than reality.

For Brady, the party was minus one; Aiden had taken her to the party he was hosting at his house. Brady had intended to stay all night at Luke's but at two o'clock, his restlessness won out.

"You okay, man?" Luke asked, as if he could sense his best friend's uneasiness.

Brady had to give an excuse. Luke knew him. "I'm good. I'm just really tired."

The expression on Luke's face said that he saw through the pathetic offering. "Tired?" Luke scoffed.

"Yeah . . . just tired . . . I think I'm going to head home. I've got to get some sleep."

"Dude, you can crash on the couch in the pool house," Luke said.

"It's all good, man. I'll see you at church in the morning."

Luke smirked. "That might not happen."

"I'm pretty certain it will. Your dad will make sure of it."

"Whatever," Luke said as he rolled his eyes.

"See ya, Lucas. Great party."

"You know I hate it when you call me that."

Brady grinned. "That's why I do it."

Brady climbed into his truck to drive home. Luke's house was on the other side of the downtown area, so Brady decided to stop downtown. He was jittery and impatient, nearly nauseated. His turmoil had no outlet and knowing he'd simply stare at the bedroom ceiling at home, he parked in front of the hardware store and began walking down the desolate, lamplight-bathed streets.

As he passed each store, he remembered something that had occurred in there. The hardware store reminded him of the day when he was eight that he and his grandfather went to pick up a Christmas tree stand. As he passed by the coffee shop, the echoes of his interactions with Luke and other friends came to mind. After crossing the street, he walked down to McB's Mercantile, remembering the younger days when what flavor of ice cream to choose was his biggest problem.

He circled back to go to his truck, giving up on the night completely, when a sob disturbed the quiet. He looked instinctively toward the bench where she sat alone, her pain as audible as it was visible by the shaking of her shoulders. He knew who it was, even if he didn't know what led her there. The girl in that dress had danced with him a few hours earlier. Slowly, he approached, the bench becoming a place of uncertainty.

"Sarah? What's wrong?"

She didn't look at him. Just kept her head down as she swiped at the tears lingering on her cheeks. "Nothing, Brady. Just a bad night. I'll be fine."

"Sure you don't need me?"

"I need you to leave. I'm fine."

Brady walked around to face her. Lowered himself on his haunches. If she could say it to him, looking him in the eye, maybe he could accept it. But she turned away.

"Sarah, what's going on? I mean, did I do something?"

"No, Brady. I just want to be left alone."

"You've never acted this way before . . . what's gotten into you?"

She turned her head enough then that Brady could see blood trickling from her lip.

"*Sarah.* What happened?"

"Brady, you can't fix this."

"Let me guess," he said. "Aiden?"

"Brady, let it go and go away."

He shook his head, the anger building. "And leave you here?"

"Yes. I'm fine. If I thought anybody else would be here tonight, I would have gone somewhere else."

Brady stood, then sat on the bench beside her. As he did, she turned her back. "Why did he hit you?"

"He didn't mean to. He was drunk."

"Not buying it. Something made him mad."

"Brady, please," she pleaded as she began to cry. "I don't want to tell you this."

"Sarah, come on. It's me."

She paused for a moment. He thought he had an idea of what happened, but he wanted to be sure.

"He thought I was going to sleep with him tonight. When I said no, he slapped me."

Brady had to bite his bottom lip to keep his mouth from flying off.

She continued, "It was my fault. I had told him that I would, but then, when it came right down to it, I said no. I know it wasn't right, Brady."

Fury rumbled in his chest, but he swallowed it down. "I don't care what you said before, he had no right to slap you."

"Please just let it go. I don't want anything to come of this. I just want it to go away."

The beauty of their dance earlier now gave way to pain. Brady could not let it go. To let it go would be to say that it was okay. Being silent in the face of abuse is a silent agreement to the abuse taking place. He sighed, trying to conceal his anger so he could keep his focus on her. Again, she needed him, and he aimed to be what she needed.

"Are you sure you're okay?"

"Yeah, but I can't go home tonight. If my mom sees this, she'll call my dad and he'll flip out and I know Maddie is still at Luke's."

"I'm headed home," he said, standing. He extended his hand to her. "You can crash in my room and I'll take the couch tonight. We'll have to be quiet, though. If Chelsi sees you like this, she's going to ask questions."

Sarah nodded.

As they took the short walk to Brady's truck, Brady shrugged out of his tux coat, then draped it over Sarah's shoulders, hoping the subtle warmth might remind her heart that there was a place where it could call home, a place where it would never experience the wrongs from an hour prior.

They snuck into the house, then crept up the stairs to his room, making sure not to wake anyone. Brady went down to get ice for Sarah's lip and one of the throws his mother kept folded on an ottoman in the living room, then hurried back upstairs. She had already curled up on his bed. He draped the throw over her, then sat on the bed and rubbed her back, saying nothing until she dozed off.

He returned to the living room and lay down on the couch. He would not sleep. He could not sleep. His anger had turned to a rage he could not contain and, for once, he was unsure about so much. Would he heed Sarah's advice and "let it go," or would he risk her trust and face someone who could easily stomp him into the ground?

Chapter 9

BRADY SAT STRAIGHT UP WHEN Sarah crept down the stairs a few hours later.

"You're up early," he whispered loud enough for her to hear.

"Can you just take me home?" she asked, never looking at him.

"Yeah. Sure."

He rolled off the couch, still dressed in his tux slacks and shirt, grabbed his keys off the key hanger by the door, and held the door for her. A silent walk to the truck was only broken by the quiet closing of the doors and the starting of the engine.

So much needed to be said. He wanted to explain why he felt the way he did, but sometimes his need to speak was overcome by the suppressive fear of what may come if the words are spoken.

"Thanks, Brady . . ." she said after a while. "For everything."

His jaw flexed. "What are you going to tell your mom?" he asked, trying to set aside his frustration.

"That I tripped. I'm clumsy so she'll believe it. Plus, with everything else going on at home, she's not thinking clearly."

"Okay."

Brady didn't like any of it, but she needed protection and security and, he figured, by keeping her secret—by staying silent—he could protect her from any further embarrassment.

The rest of the drive to Sarah's house was eerily quiet. No laughing. No sharing stories from the night before. Him, defiant. Her, defeated. Her silent staring out the window haunted Brady, unable to reclaim the girl she had been the day before. More than anything, he struggled to understand a love that had grown deeper inside him.

He pulled up to the sprawling home where Sarah lived, hoping to say the right things. When he put the truck in park, she opened the door and slipped out.

"Sarah."

She looked over her shoulder toward him, but not at him.

"I'm here for you. I always will be."

"I know," she responded, a tear making its way down her cheek.

She wiped it away as she walked toward a house that seemed so empty. He watched every step she took and resisted the urge to jump out, run to her, and tell her that he loved her, that he'd give all of himself for her. But now was not the time.

Sarah reached the front door, opened it, then stepped inside, closing the door again without looking back. Brady pulled away, exhausted physically from a lack of sleep, and exhausted mentally from the situation.

Later, after a hot shower and a change of clothes, he told his dad he was going to Log Cabin for breakfast and that he'd meet the family at church. He really didn't want to go. He wanted to sleep, but his parents had told him he had no choice before he went to the prom. He'd have to grin and bear it until just after noon, then he could go home and try to sleep.

"Long night, huh?" Todd asked when he walked into the youth room.

"You could say that," Brady replied. He spied Chelsi, already seated with her Bible open and a grin plastered on her face. His discomfort was her pleasure. The one person he'd hoped to see was Sarah, but she had obviously decided not to come.

"Why do they have to make church so early?" Luke questioned, laying his head on the table. Brady smiled. His best friend hadn't thought he'd make it, but there he was.

"To terrorize the likes of you, Luke," Todd responded with a grin.

"Well, it's working."

"You guys shouldn't have stayed up so late," Chelsi said. "Maybe you should've gone to the confessional at the Catholic church this morning."

Luke raised his head long enough to retort, "We didn't do nothing wrong last night. Besides, your brother jetted the party pretty early so he could get on home."

"Shut up, Luke," Brady shot back. Had his friend forgotten whom he was talking to?

"Okay, guys," Todd said, trying to refocus the group on the purpose of the morning. "Let's talk about God this morning. That's why we are here, right?"

Todd had written Luke 10 on the whiteboard and the students began flipping through the pages of their Bible, searching for the passage. Everyone but Brady, who just stared off, irritated.

"Today we are going to talk about what we do when we see something wrong, when we see someone hurting," Todd said, which grabbed at Brady. He looked up sharply as Todd read the parable of the Good Samaritan as most of the students followed along. No one knew the proceedings of the night before, but the Lord did. As they talked about the parable, Brady's mind began racing, and he fidgeted in his seat. He couldn't sit still. Sarah should be here.

"So, guys, you see, when someone is hurting or broken, we cannot simply go on with our lives. The Samaritan in this story understood that he had to do what he could to help the beaten man in the street."

"What if they don't want your help?" Brady interjected, dismayed by the parable and the teaching. He had seen another side, one more realistic and rawer.

"I can't imagine someone who is truly hurt not wanting some sort of help," Todd answered.

"Well, it happens," Brady responded gruffly.

A hush fell in the room and Brady felt all eyes on him. He was the peacemaker, not the instigator, and everyone knew it.

Todd walked over to the small wooden podium where his Bible lay open, his eyes never leaving Brady. He draped his forearms over it, then leaned forward. "In cases like that, Brady, no matter what it may be, you still have to do what's right," he said. "You are the one who has to be able to sleep at night, knowing what you did or chose not to do. Also, one day, you'll have to stand before God. But I know you, Brady, and I'd say that you'll know what the right thing is to do, and do it."

The bell rang to dismiss Sunday school. The class closed in prayer before a mass exodus to the sanctuary.

"Brady, hang on a minute," Todd called as the other students were leaving.

"Yeah, okay," he said, then looking at Luke, he said, "Catch you in church."

Todd waited until the last of the students, which included Chelsi who thought it her duty to hang back, had left the room. Todd walked over and closed the door. "Are you all right, Brady?"

"I'm good." He forced himself to smile. "Just tired and cranky."

Todd clearly wasn't buying the line. "You know I'll help . . . if you tell me what's going on."

Any other time, Brady would have confided in Todd. But not this time. This time, Brady wanted Todd to leave him alone. "No, Todd, seriously, I'm good. Don't worry about it."

"All right, then. If you're sure."

"I'm sure." He smiled again. "See you in the church?"

Todd nodded once, which gave Brady all the excuse he needed to turn and walk out the door.

But, if he'd known that what had been started in Sunday school would be brought to completion in the worship service, he would have somehow snuck out and headed on back home, dealing with his parents later. Every song seemed to have doubled in stanzas. Every announcement grated on his nerves. And then, as Pastor Thomas began speaking, the sermon felt tailor-made for Brady and his situation.

"Micah's prophecy includes this instruction," Pastor Thomas said as he prepared for the culmination of his sermon. "Look at verse eight. *'Mankind, He has told you what is good and what it is the Lord requires of you: to act justly, to love faithfulness, and to walk humbly with your God.'* To act justly is to do what's right. To do what is right is not always convenient. In fact, doing what's right, acting justly, can prove costly. The question is: how important is it to you to do what is right? Many have been killed, ostracized, ridiculed, and ruined for standing up for what is right. However, what was not lost in their stance was their integrity, nor did they compromise their conviction."

Brady dropped his head. Squeezed his eyes shut. Sarah had told him to let it go. Scripture said for him to do something. The bigger question was: Which voice would win out?

Chapter 10

MONDAY AFTERNOON'S BELL RANG, SIGNALING the end of the day. As was customary, many of the seniors hung out by the entrance to the football field near the parking area. Making small talk. Laughing. Brady leaned against one of the outer walls to take it all in, wondering when such a tradition had started. Lord only knew when. It could date back thirty or forty years. One thing he knew for sure: each moment together grew more precious to the seniors as their time together ran out because, deep down, they knew that, after summer, their relationships would never be the same, even if they'd sworn differently.

But what caught Brady's attention more was two of the figures—Sarah standing beside Aiden, giving the appearance that nothing had happened two nights prior.

Brady continued to hang back; he wanted to avoid all the commotion but to get to his truck, he had to walk past them.

"Hey, dude," a voice said from behind and Brady turned to see Luke, whose gaze went from the crowd to his best friend.

"Hey, yourself."

"Let's walk," Luke said.

Brady pushed off from the wall, his book bag hanging limp over one shoulder, to fall in line with Luke, who spoke of mundane things—his homework, his hours at the coffee shop—while keeping his focus on the ground, counting the steps while pretending to listen. And then . . .

"Hey, Brady," Sarah called out.

Not now. Just let me leave.

But he raised his chin to glance over and forced a smile while never breaking stride toward the truck. "Hey," he muttered, hoping she'd get the hint.

But she didn't. "Hey, wait up!" she called, hurrying to catch him.

Luke stopped and he did, too. "What's up?" he asked, keeping his voice low and even.

She cocked her head to one side. "Are you mad at me, Brady?"

"No." And to some degree, he told the truth. She wasn't the source of his anger, but her decision to stay with Aiden made his blood boil.

"So why are you acting like it?"

Brady sighed. He wanted to rip into her for her decision but he couldn't hurt someone who had already been hurt by someone else. Truth was essential and his exasperation couldn't be hidden.

"Look," he said, readjusting his book bag. "I'm trying not to get involved. You said let it go, right? I'm trying to let it go." He glanced over to Luke, whose eyes darted between Brady and Sarah. He had no idea what had happened and, as far as Brady was concerned, it was best to keep it that way.

From the corner of his eye, Brady caught Aiden walking up, an unhappy look on his face. Brady knew then that "the boy wonder" wasn't altogether sure what Sarah had told him. He also knew that Aiden had a full scholarship to play quarterback at the University of Tennessee, but his actions on Saturday night could put that scholarship in jeopardy if word got out.

"Everything all right?" he asked, his chest puffed out.

Sarah turned quickly, her faced drained of color. "Everything's fine, honey," she said as she tried to cut Aiden off from reaching Brady.

Luke tugged at Brady, pulling him by his arm. "Come on, Brady, let's just get out of here."

But by now Brady had locked eyes with Aiden.

Common sense says you should never pick a fight you know you will lose. But common sense also said not to fight with a country boy when he was in love. Still, Aiden, at six-five and over two hundred and fifteen pounds, had a shadow that engulfed Brady. Brady knew he needed to listen to Luke and just walk on, but if he did nothing, wasn't he as guilty as Aiden? Wasn't walking away the cowardly way of handling this? But one look at the plea in Sarah's eyes and he said, "Yeah, it's all good."

"Thought so," Aiden smirked.

Brady took a step toward the truck but Aiden's comment niggled and he spoke before he thought. "You know, you really are a jerk. Why don't you hit a man instead of a young woman you say you love?"

"What did you say?" Aiden started back toward Brady, veins bulging in his neck.

"You heard me, Wilkes."

"How about I knock the next words out of your mouth?"

"Go ahead," he said, dropping his book bag to the ground. "I don't care. Doesn't change the fact that you hit a girl!"

"Brady!" Sarah snapped back.

Brady could hold it in no longer. "What, Sarah? You want me not to care? Fine. I don't care! But you better know this . . . if he hit you once, he'll do it again. Jerks like him always do."

"Call me a jerk one more time," Aiden insisted while his hand balled into a fist.

Brady met his stare. "You're a jerk. You hit a . . ."

The blow came to the side of his jaw. With one punch, Aiden knocked him flat to the ground. Brady pulled himself up to his knees, trying to regain his balance, when Aiden kicked him in the ribs.

"Aiden!" Sarah screamed.

Brady's vision blurred, but not before seeing Aiden brush her aside with a swipe of his arm. Brady tried to stand again, aware that Aiden was positioning himself to strike, when Luke threw himself into the fray, taking the blow intended for Brady. His friend landed next to him, coughing.

"Get up, Brady," Aiden taunted. "Get up!"

Brady shook his head, the ringing in his ears nearly beating out the words. He staggered to his feet as Aiden took another swing, this one sending blood from Brady's nose.

"Come on, Aiden," he heard someone say. "Officer Buchanan is coming."

Brady stared through the haze as Aiden and his friends—where had they come from?—ran like cockroaches. Luckily, they could get away without anyone knowing who had done what.

Brady fell to his backside as the resource officer rushed over. "Brady, you all right, son?"

Brady wiped at the blood that had pooled along his lips. "I'm good."

"Son, you are far from good." Buchanan pulled a handkerchief from his back pocket, handed it to Luke, who now knelt beside Brady, and said, "Here. Use this and tilt your head back."

"What about you?" Brady asked Luke.

"I'm all right. Now, do it."

Brady pushed the handkerchief to his nose then looked up when Buchanan said, "Principal Cowens, we need medical assistance at the gate to the football field" into his radio.

Brady tried to play off the pain by saying, "I'm fine," even though his face and ribs throbbed.

"Brady, sit still," Buchanan instructed.

Brady looked at Luke. A bruise was already forming along his jawline. Knowing Luke, he'd be the hero in the story by dinner.

"Brady, I want to know who did this to you," Buchanan demanded, stooping down to look at him.

Brady looked around; the one person no longer there was the one who mattered most. Or, at least, she had. He didn't care anymore. He took a beating, and she ran away with the one who'd done it. "I don't know," he muttered.

"Son, you have to know who did this."

Brady shook his head. "No, sir."

"Luke?" Buchanan asked.

Brady's eyes cut over to his best friend. Luke looked from Brady back to Buchanan. "No, sir," he said. "I don't know either."

Chapter 11

Brady's phone registered Sarah's call three times that evening, but all three times, all she heard was his voicemail greeting. And, each time, he waited several minutes before listening to the same message: "Brady, please call me. I am so sorry. I didn't know Aiden would do something like that. I know you're avoiding my calls but please text me or something. At least let me know you're okay."

He wanted to answer, to call her back, but couldn't.

She'd left him bleeding. She'd chosen to go with Aiden, doing as he told her. If she didn't care then, why act like she did now?

After the third call, he eased himself up from his bed and went into the bathroom, holding his ribs, every muscle in his body aching. Right away, he caught a glimpse of himself in the mirror. His nose was swollen. Underneath his eyes, black half-moons formed. Bad as he looked—bad as he felt—even worse, he had to go back to school at some point and knew Aiden would be there. He drew in as deep a breath as he could, then groaned.

Sarah would be there, too.

A knock came at the front door. Brady walked to the bathroom door and leaned against the jamb, listening as his mother answered.

"Come on in, Todd," she said. "I really appreciate you coming over here." Her panic was noticeable in the tone of her voice, something Brady wasn't sure he'd ever heard before. "I hated to call you, but . . ."

"This is what I am here for. How is he?"

"Pretty ugly. That boy got the best of Brady and Luke today." She paused and Brady winced. "Why don't you go on up."

Brady slipped back into his bedroom and quietly closed the door. The stairs creaked as Todd came up. He knocked gently, as if he thought Brady might still be sleeping.

"Come in," Brady said, once again lying on his bed, one arm draped over his ribcage.

Todd entered and he paused just inside the door, his eyes wide and his mouth forming a silent "O."

"That bad, huh?" Brady mumbled through a swollen cheek and busted lip, forcing a smirk to appear.

"Brady, what in the world?" Todd's question was blunt. His anger unearthed. Brady had been close to Todd since he started at the church.

"Found out football players are pretty strong," Brady answered as Todd closed the door.

He pointed to the one and only chair in the room. "Mind if I sit?"

Brady shook his head.

Todd grabbed the ladderback near Brady's desk by its top rung and pulled it closer to the bed, then sat, leaned forward, and rested his elbows on his knees. "Brady, does any of this have to do with Sarah?"

"Not a big deal, Todd."

"Your face says otherwise."

"Let's just say that I learned a valuable lesson. Now, I get the pleasure of going back to the school to be laughed at."

"Did you or your parents report this?"

"No."

"I think you should."

"At this point, Todd, I don't even care anymore. I just have to get through the rest of the school year."

"Did you see a doctor?"

Brady nodded. "Dr. Nabors. He says I'm going to be pretty sore. I've got a cracked rib . . ." He held up his tee to show Todd the wrappings. "But nothing is broken." Brady attempted a smile. "I got some good drugs out of it, so all's not lost."

Todd gave a half smile in return. Laced his fingers together. "Have you talked to Sarah?"

"Don't want to."

"Do you want me to?"

"For what?"

"I don't know. Thought it might help."

"Nope. Remember that whole Good Samaritan story? Todd, this is what it looks like when someone doesn't want help. I tried to do what was right, but laying here all busted up, I can't say at this moment it was worth it."

"Well, I'm proud of you, Brady. Not so much for fighting, but for doing what you thought was right." Todd leaned back. "The bruises and bleeding are gonna heal, but I'm not so sure about your heart."

Brady closed his eyes against the pain the prescription couldn't reach. "I'll be all right."

Todd said nothing for a moment or two, then, "Can I pray for you?"

Brady nodded. As soon as Todd finished praying, his phone rang. Brady opened his eyes and looked at the face, then turned it toward Todd. "Sarah."

"Will you answer it?"

"No." He turned the ring volume off before laying the phone beside him.

"Okay, Buddy, I'm going to run. You look like you're just about to fall asleep." He returned the chair to its place. "If you need me, call me. I'm always here to help."

"Thanks Todd. I appreciate you coming by."

Todd closed the door behind him then made his way downstairs. Brady could hear the voices of his parents and his youth pastor but couldn't make out the words.

Todd was right—he was about to fall asleep. He closed his eyes as a wave of the drug's effect washed through him. The final thing he remembered was hearing the front door close and Todd's car starting in the driveway.

Chapter 12

SARAH HAD REACHED DESPERATION.

Not only was Brady ignoring her calls, but Aiden's anger had also nearly spilled over again when he drove her home that afternoon. He didn't hit her—not this time—but he wasn't speaking to her. When they'd pulled into her driveway, he'd all but ordered her out of his truck.

After the third attempt at calling Brady with no luck, she decided to try Todd's cell number. If anyone could help her, it was Pastor Todd, and she was nothing short of desperate. Brady had no reason to keep their relationship intact, and she knew it. But Todd had Brady's ear, so if their friendship was salvageable in any way, Todd would know how to put the pieces back together.

He answered on the second ring. "Sarah," he said. "Hold on. I'm getting into my car."

Sarah waited, listening as the car door slammed and the vehicle was started. "Okay, Sarah," he said. "I'm here now."

"Pastor Todd, something bad happened after school today and I don't know what to do. Can you help me?" She held her breath as Todd sighed.

"Sure, Sarah."

She started to cry. Lame, she knew, but she couldn't help it. "My boyfriend hit Brady after school today. Todd, it was horrible. Brady was bleeding and I—I left with Aiden. Aiden—he's got a temper and he's really jealous and I—I tried to call Brady to check on him, but he won't answer my calls. I don't know what to do."

There was a long enough pause for Sarah to gather her bearings. Then Todd said, "Brady is pretty banged up, Sarah. I just left his house. I think, right now, he doesn't feel like talking to anyone."

Sarah cried all the harder. "I'm sorry," she said. "I'm sorry. Give me a minute." She loved Brady—she did, he was like her best friend—but Aiden . . . and now she had to shoulder the guilt of leaving her friend behind in the condition he was in.

"Sarah, what started all of this?"

"Something stupid," she said. Though given the chance to fix the situation, or at least move in the direction of the solution, she refused to reveal what she knew others needed to know. She protected the one she knew she shouldn't protect but, in doing so, left another beaten and dejected. "It was just a misunderstanding, Pastor Todd. Brady overreacted to something and then today happened."

"Okay," Todd answered, then hesitated before asking, "What can I do to help?"

"I don't know. I don't even know what *I* should do."

"Sarah, I need to ask you a question. Is Aiden treating you the way he should? Are you in a healthy relationship?"

Sarah searched for the answer. She knew the honest answer but without spinning it, she would look like a fool. She didn't like the facts as they presented themselves, nor could she allow herself to be truthful about what had happened to her and Brady. "Well, we have our issues. But that's normal in any relationship, right?"

"It depends on what those issues are."

That much was true. What she had experienced wasn't normal. What happened to Brady wasn't justifiable. She was caught and, truthfully, there was only one right way to go—to stick by Brady—but she had chosen to run off with Aiden. Why? Because he demanded it and—when he demanded anything . . . most things . . . "Pastor Todd, I have to go. My mom just came home, so I have to help her. Thank— thank you for helping me."

"No problem, Sarah. I am always here for you, no matter what."

She hung up the phone. Had Todd bought the line about her

mother? She couldn't afford to say anything else about Aiden. She picked up her phone again to try Brady one more time, except this time she shot him a lighthearted picture, hoping to make him smile and elicit some sort of response.

It did not.

Chapter 13

Brady opened his eyes the next morning and immediately picked up his phone. Ten o'clock. He also checked to see if Sarah had called him again. She hadn't, but she had sent a cute picture of kittens.

He ached. Everything and everywhere. Even his eyelashes hurt. But a shower would do him good. He also wanted to wash off what could be washed away from the day prior.

The warm water soothed the sore muscles of his body, which was even more bruised than the day before. He turned the hot water knob until the flow ran as hot as he could stand it, which helped. But nothing in that shower and nothing in the universe would soothe the aching of his heart.

Couldn't she see she was worth more? Why couldn't she see that love was something far greater, more sacrificial, more uplifting? *Oh, God, of all the people in the world, why do I love her and why can't I just let it go?*

Normally, Brady's showers lasted no longer than ten minutes, but he stayed under the pelting spray until it ran cold; nearly forty minutes passed before he emerged from the blanket of solace he'd engulfed himself in for a temporary comfort. He wrapped his lower half in a towel and stepped onto the bathmat, reconciling that just as the warm water ran out, he would eventually have to reemerge and face the world. Face the questions left unanswered.

He pulled another towel from the rod, then gently dabbed his face, the slightest pressure causing excruciating pain. He wiped away the condensation from the mirror and glanced at his reflection long enough to see the image of one who looked to have been in a car accident. He stepped across the hall and back into his room to get dressed, first rewrapping his ribs, then pulling his tee over gently to avoid more pain. After slipping into jeans and a pair of shoes, he went downstairs to face whatever life had for him.

Inside, he was angry, but also embarrassed.

He found his mother in the living room, sitting on the sofa, folding a load of towels. "Did you sleep all right, son?" she asked, looking up when he walked in.

"Yeah. Why didn't you wake me up for school?"

"That was your dad's decision, buddy. You'll have to ask him." She stood, setting the finished load to one side. "Let me make you something to eat."

As he followed his mother, Brady's head hung in anticipation of what was to come. His father making the decision for him to stay home meant only one thing. "I'd rather be at school than sit through one of his lectures." He ambled to the table, slid out a chair, and lowered himself gingerly into it, only wincing when he thought his mother wasn't watching.

She remained silent and instead began frying bacon, keeping focused on the pieces in the pan rather than on her son. The aroma made its way to him and his stomach growled. He'd not had much of an appetite the night before. He played with the napkin and fork and glass of orange juice his mother had placed on the table in anticipation of the meal, waiting for her to say something. Anything. But she didn't. She busied herself, first with the microwave, then by removing the bacon from the pan.

Only when she brought the plate over did she speak. "I think this time could be different," she said as she put three slices of bacon on his plate, alongside a couple of biscuits and some fried eggs. "Here's some breakfast. Eat it and then you can go find him." She ran her fingertips through his tousled hair. "By the way, Chelsi was up most of the night crying about what happened. Thought you might want to know."

His mother returned to the sink to wash the dishes by hand and, while Brady ate in his own silence, he tensed each time she sniffled. His mother was crying, the worst blow of all.

He finished eating in the awkward silence. He wanted to say something but didn't know what. Usually, he wanted his mom to stop talking, to stop asking so many questions. But now, he wished she would replace her tears with words. After several minutes of staring down at his plate, of tracing the pattern within it over and over with his eyes, he broke the silence. "Mom, I'm sorry. I wish I could talk about everything, but I just can't. Trust me. I did the right thing. I may have paid for it, but I did the right thing."

His mother never turned to look at him. He knew her refusal was not out of anger but rather that she didn't want him to see the fear she had. Fear that could not be hidden.

He drank the last of his juice, reached around her to put his plate and glass in the sink, then whispered, "Mom, I love you. I'll be fine."

She only nodded.

He found his favorite ball cap hanging by the back door, adjusted it to his head, then set out to meet with his father. There was no sense in delaying the inevitable. As he reached the door, his mother broke. Not mere tears. To Brady, it sounded as if she had lost someone close to her, as if her fears had flooded over from the depths of her soul.

Chapter 14

THE WALK TO THE BARN seemed longer than normal. As spring had come, the smell of flowers and trees was strong, but even stronger was the smell of dirt in the air, fields being plowed to put seeds in the ground.

Not hearing the tractor, Brady scanned the farm, looking to make sure his father wasn't out in the field somewhere.

"Dad," he called as he approached the barn, hoping to keep from wandering around. His legs were a little shaky and his ribcage hurt enough that he figured it was time for another pain pill.

"Over here, Brady." Brady turned toward the voice. "Beside the garden," his father called as he prepared to hammer a stake into the ground.

"Need some help?" Brady asked as he approached. His ribs hurt so bad he doubted he could swing a hammer, but, for his father, he would try.

"No, I've got this. Got to get these posts up and string some wire to keep the deer out of the garden." He peered up at his son, squinting one eye. "How you feelin'?"

"I'm fine," Brady lied. "I can help."

"Brady," his dad said with a sigh, his attention returning to his work. "I didn't want you to stay home today to help."

"Okay" Brady responded, steadying himself for the lecture.

"Are you okay, son?"

"Yeah."

"You sure?"

"Yeah, Dad," Brady said, forcing himself not to sigh. "I'm sore but I'm fine."

His dad grunted, which told Brady that his father knew his boy was far from fine.

"Brady," he said as he struck the post with a hammer one last time, "I don't need to know what happened."

Brady was sure he had suffered from a concussion. Any time trouble had risen in his life, his dad would instruct Brady to tell him what happened. For some reason, this was different. "Okaaaay . . ."

His dad stood then and planted one hand on a hip. And now his father looked at him. "Somehow, I know you did the right thing. I don't know a single detail about the who or the why, but I know what you did was right. I told your mother to let you stay home today to heal up and think about what happened. Doing the right thing can often cost you, but what you gain in the long run is far greater."

Brady swallowed. "I don't know about that, Dad."

His father put his hammer down and looked at Brady, then pointed across the property to the cross he had placed at the end of the driveway, right beside the roadway.

"Do you know why I put that cross up there, son?"

"I guess for people to see when they pass by."

"I hope they see it. But truthfully, I put it there for me. That point marks the intersection of my life and the world. When I leave, that cross reminds me that I am to do what is right, regardless of how much it might cost me. It's a reminder for myself that Jesus suffered to do what's right and I have to do the same."

That cross had never stood more pronounced in Brady's eyes than it did in that moment. "I never thought about that."

His dad wiped the sweat off his brow. "I'm not going to get involved in this. You are old enough to handle it, but I promise you that if you need me to get involved, I will in a second. Remember this, son. If you do things God's way, everything will be okay in the end." His father's eyes met his own and, in them, Brady saw a reflection of himself years from that moment. Perhaps talking to his own son. Maybe his dad was right. In the end . . . everything would be okay.

"Yes, sir."

"Now, go on back inside and rest. You look like you could use another pain pill."

Brady nodded. "Yes, sir," he said again.

Brady turned, but his father's next words stopped him, although he didn't look back.

"I'm proud of you, Brady."

Brady nodded, and as he walked back to the house, tears rolled down his face. He was shocked by what had happened, and moved by the words of his father. Though his father didn't know the story, he was proud of his son, nonetheless.

His mother met Brady at the door, a glass of juice in one hand and one of his pain pills in the other. He took them without comment and his mom remained as silent as she had been earlier. Brady then retreated to his room and closed the blinds to shut out a world he wanted no part of on that day.

Around six o'clock, his slumber was interrupted with the ringing of the doorbell.

Nobody rings the doorbell.

He rolled over, hoping to be able to fall back to sleep quickly. A decision to stretch was an immediate regret as pain shot through his body, bringing tears to his eyes. He blinked them back, listening as voices mumbled downstairs. Surely, whoever it was, the visitor was a stranger. Maybe a salesman or something.

But steps drawing closer to his bedroom assured him that his solitude was coming to an end.

"Brady," Sarah said as she opened the door.

"Yeah," he said quietly, crooking an arm over his face. He didn't want to look at her, but a few seconds of silence bred an awkwardness that forced him to peer over the bend in his arm.

He caught a glimpse of the balloons in her hand before his attention was stolen by the look on her face. Like a dam that had too much pressure, she crumbled in front of him, dropping to her knees next to his bed. "I'm so sorry, Brady."

He brought his arm away from his face. "It's not your fault, Sarah."

"Yes, it is," she responded, her face buried in her hands, her chestnut hair spilling over.

"Never saw you throw a punch," he pointed out, not wanting to have the conversation at that moment, but stuck trying to console the source of the beating he took.

"Still, I'm at the heart of this. If it weren't for me, this wouldn't have happened to you."

An awkward silence settled between them. What she said was true. What she didn't know was the fullness of the feelings that had developed in Brady's heart for her.

"Look," Brady said as Sarah said, "I—"

"You first," she followed.

"Look," Brady started again, "I stuck my nose where it doesn't belong. It's your life. It's your choice, but . . . Sarah, you deserve better than that."

Brady's words hit. He could tell by the look on her face. Maybe he hadn't told her of his love for her, but she wasn't stupid. She could infer the magnitude of his feelings through what he said. And she was stunned. She played with her hair, like she always did when she was trying to think, an action that distracted him. The thickness of it. The scent of it. The way it spilled onto her shoulders.

"Brady. . . I . . ."

"What?"

She looked down. The balloons now danced over her head, slowly twisting, turning as they had only nights before. "I'm more trouble than I am worth."

"Not for me you aren't." He stared at her, willing her to look at him. He wanted her to see in him what love looked like. Love that didn't hit. That didn't break down. But she kept looking away, even as he kept his eyes trained on her face.

"Aiden has problems," she finally said. "I know that. But deep down, don't we all have our issues? They come out differently, but there are still issues. I brought this on myself and I—I know he loves me. Even though . . . even though he did this."

Her justification of Aiden's actions only made Brady's pain seem more pointless. Maybe she *was* crazy. The guy was a jerk and she had the audacity to defend him in his own house.

Brady pushed back the pain enough to sit up in the bed, hanging his legs off the side. "Sarah, I don't care if you promised him the world, he had no right to hit you. And here's the thing—that ain't love."

And just like that, she pivoted the conversation. Her face came up and her eyes met his. "But why did you say what you said to him, Brady? You had to know he was going to snap."

The turn in the conversation toward Brady being at fault made him wish she would just leave. Instead, he decided to answer her head-on. "You want to know why? Because I care, Sarah. And here is the thing about me. If I care, I can't act like it didn't happen. I'd much rather him whale on me than on you."

Sarah said nothing. She just stood, handed him the balloons, and made a turn toward the door.

"Thank you for the balloons."

"Yeah . . . well, it was the least I could do," she muttered. "Look, I have to get home. If you need anything, let me know."

And with that, she was gone. However, Brady decided as he let the balloons go, as they bounced along his ceiling, when she left she was no longer oblivious to what had started inside him. And Brady was no longer oblivious to the fact that a change had taken place in their relationship.

Chapter 15

THE SEASONS CHANGED—SPRING BECOMING SUMMER, summer slipping slowly toward autumn with all the new possibilities new beginnings held—but Sarah remained in the relationship with Aiden, and Aiden, well, he continued being Aiden. They were happy for a month and miserable for a spell. After graduation, everyone prepared for college. Sarah and Brady continued to be "friendly" but rarely saw each other outside of youth group. Texts were exchanged, the occasional call came through, but a perhaps inevitable distance seemed to be building. The stories of their lives were changing and, although one might want to hang on, the chapters would soon end.

A week before leaving for Appalachian State, Brady drove downtown. He wanted to get a few things, but even more so, he was trying to absorb the town through his current lens, knowing the days of his childhood were numbered. For Thursday night, the streets were fairly crowded, and Brady managed to speak to a few he passed along the way. His mom needed an ornament from The Third Day Gift Shop, so he ran in and made the purchase, spoke to the owner, Audrey, then left to finish his errands.

"Brady," a voice called as he neared his truck, a voice that needed no introduction. "What are you doing?" Sarah asked.

Brady turned to see her and Maddie sitting on the bench—*their* bench—Sarah, who was wearing glasses that day, smiling. Maddie's thumbs appeared busy with a text message.

"Getting finished up before taking off to App," he said, holding up the bag from the gift shop as he approached them. "What are y'all doing?"

"Hanging out before we part ways," Sarah said. Maddie finished the text she was writing before looking up and giving his a polite, "Hey, Brady."

"When do you leave?" Sarah asked.

"Next Thursday." He took his ever-present ball cap off, then replaced it. "One week left."

Maddie smiled now. "Are you ready?"

"Trying to get there," Brady acknowledged, knowing that this—seeing Sarah, talking to her—wasn't going to help his attempts at saying goodbye to his pre-college life. "Good thing is that I'm only about a half an hour from here, so if I need anything, it's pretty easy to get home to get it."

"I don't think my dorm room at Tennessee is going to be big enough," Sarah joked.

Maddie crossed one leg over the other. "She's practically taking everything she owns," she said as her phone dinged a new text message and she looked down, then added. "Oh, man. I forgot that I was supposed to pick up my little brother tonight, Sarah," Maddie said, standing and shoving her phone into the back pocket of her jeans. "I've got to run. I'm sorry, guys. Brady, can you get her home . . . she rode with me."

Brady narrowed his eyes at her as he adjusted his ball cap. *What are you doing, Maddie?*

She gave Brady a grin, waiting.

"Yeah," he finally said. "I'll get her home."

"Thanks. See you guys later," she said as she leaned over to hug Sarah, then straightened to hug Brady. "Go Flames," she said. Her joy was noticeable. She had always dreamed of going to Liberty and that dream had come true.

"So, are you finished shopping, or do you have more to do?" Brady asked after Maddie left.

"I think I'm done," Sarah replied, tucking her hair behind her ears and looking up at Brady. She wore her hair straight today; he liked it but appreciated her curls more. "I am hungry, though. Did you eat yet?"

"I can always eat," Brady responded, knowing he wasn't hungry but also knowing that he needed closure. A night with Sarah could be damaging but at least it would be memorable.

"Awesome. Where to?" Sarah asked, pausing before making a suggestion. "Blackjack's? We can walk there."

"Of course. Let me drop this bag into the truck and we can go."

The stroll only took a couple of minutes, but long enough for Brady to wrestle with a range of questions while Sarah walked beside him, talking nonstop about the University of Tennessee. Should he just eat a last meal with Sarah, then let her go . . . or was this the chance he needed to throw everything out there, hold nothing back, and see what the future held without holding on to what might have been?

When they reached the restaurant, they sat near the front, ordered burgers, then exchanged small talk while waiting on their food to arrive. Brady had always liked sitting at that particular table and he told her so.

"Why?" she asked.

He pointed to the plaques of Cal Ripken Jr. and Tom Glavine hanging beside them and smiled.

She laughed. "I should have known," she said. "Me? I like these high stools." She swiveled from side to side and grinned. He couldn't help himself; he smiled in return.

He caught their reflection in the mirror beside them, the one featuring the drink specials. With each glance, with each reflection of her in the mirror, his breath was taken away. She was so beautiful, probably more beautiful than she knew. He glanced over at the bar. Above it, mini-football helmets had been angled to show off each team's logo. Brady clenched his jaw, let his fingers play with the rim of his cap. Those helmets were nothing more than a reminder that Sarah was still with Aiden.

He looked away just as their server hurried over, bringing their platters of burgers and fries with a "Here you go."

"Best fries ever," Brady commented, popping a short one into his mouth.

"You know it," Sarah agreed before taking a bite of her burger, then added around it, "I would come here if only for them." She swallowed and laughed at the same time, nearly choking. "Actually, I have."

Brady took in the moment. The way she smiled. The sparkle of her eyes even behind the lens of her glasses, the slight upturn of her mouth, the arch in her brow and the little dimple in the middle of her chin. He wanted—no, he *needed*—to take in everything about her, because this was it. Tonight was it.

She talked. He absorbed. In between bites, she played with a necklace and he wondered where she'd gotten it. A gift from her parents? A gift to herself? Or had Aiden . . .

"Wanna grab a cup of coffee before we go home?" she asked, pointing across the street to Bohemia.

"What?" he asked, startled. Somewhere, in the middle of the food and her chatter, somewhere in the middle of his being completely immersed by her, they'd finished eating and their plates had been cleared.

She blinked. Smiled. "Coffee?" she said again. "Want to grab a cup?"

Heat rushed through him. "Sure." He reached for his wallet. "Just let me pay for this."

Sarah dipped into her purse. "I can pay for mine."

Brady reached toward her. "Not on my watch you won't."

Later, as they crossed the street and turned toward Bohemia, a sense of normality washed over Brady. This was what he wanted out of life. A night like this was how he wanted every day to end.

The coffeeshop was full for a Thursday; a local artist was playing live music, which helped to draw an even larger crowd. "Welcome to Bohemia," Luke said as they entered and walked toward the counter. His face was bent over the computer register; his greeting could have been for anyone. Brady braced himself for what would happen once he saw them. "What can I get you?"

"Let me get a caramel macchiato," Sarah said.

Luke froze when he looked up, his eyes going from Sarah to Brady, then back to Sarah again. "I'll get that right away," he said, wide-eyed as he looked back at the computer to type the order in. He called out her order to the barista standing near him. "And you, sir?" he asked, shaking his head in disbelief.

"Hot chocolate, Luke Bryan."

"It's like ninety degrees outside. Why are you getting a hot chocolate? And it's Luke . . . *just* Luke."

"I know, man. It's just my thing," Brady responded with a grin.

"The hot chocolate or that name thing you always do, *Bradley*?"

"Both."

Brady chuckled as Luke shook his head again. "Dude, you need new things. And I mean that in multiple ways," Luke said, jutting his head toward Sarah who had turned toward the front door. "Oh, Sarah," he sang, breaking her trance. "Yours is already at the other end of the counter."

She turned. Smiled. "Thank you, Lucas," she said, then laughed along with Brady at the look on Luke's face.

"I hate that . . . just so you know . . . I'm not Lucas."

Sarah moved to the end of the counter to get her drink and to talk with Sharon. When she was out of range, Luke glared at Brady. "What are you doing?" he muttered. "She's still with Aiden, you know?"

"Not my idea. Maddie bailed in the middle of a shopping trip. Got stuck."

"Get unstuck. Get unstuck fast. Brady, you're my boy but I'm telling you . . . take her home . . . drop her off . . . and then go home and forget about her." He punched the rest of the order into the computer. "You nor I cannot afford another beating."

Brady appreciated Luke's concern. Many a night, he had listened as Brady poured out his feelings for Sarah. "It's okay, Luke. I promise."

"Order for Brady," Sharon called out.

Brady grabbed his drink and looked for a place to sit. There was none.

"Let's just take it to go and walk downtown," Sarah said, turning toward the door.

Brady nodded, then said goodbye to Luke.

As they walked back toward downtown, Brady walked next to the street as his dad had taught him, while Sarah continued to talk. He took sips of his hot chocolate and allowed himself to ponder something that had just occurred to him. Sarah was stalling.

But why?

He readjusted his ball cap as they walked. He'd done this as long as he could remember. Ever since he was old enough to wear a ball cap, which had been just about forever ago. The motion took his mind to another place, even for a second, and allowed him to re-center his thinking.

Sarah stopped as they neared his truck, and he did the same. "You think you'll miss this place?" she asked, her voice whisper-soft.

"I will." He didn't even have to think about the question. "Will you?"

She looked around them then, almost as if she were seeing the town for the first time. Or the last. She took a sip of her coffee before answering. "I don't know."

Chapter 16

SARAH SAT ON THE BENCH.

The struggle of wanting to keep the time from dragging on but wanting to embrace the moment left Brady standing momentarily.

"My toes are killing me from these sandals," she said as she removed the shoe from her left foot and began to rub between her big toe and the one next to it. She set her coffee down to use both hands to find a momentary comfort. "You'd think I'd be used to it by now. I wear these things all the time."

Brady looked around them, trying to avoid the sight of her and where she sat. This wasn't a random bench. No. There were dozens of benches in downtown West Jefferson, places for people to take in the beauty and the serenity of the town as well as opportunities to take a load off their feet. A bench sat right down from the coffeeshop, but that wasn't the one she chose. This was *the* bench. The one beneath *that* streetlamp, the very place where it all began. A year and a half earlier, she'd sat crying there when Brady approached her on Christmas Eve night. Whether she noticed it or not, he didn't know, but he remembered the place. In fact, every time he walked past it, he remembered. The snow falling. The brokenness he felt for one he hardly knew.

Brady finally sat, guarded to some degree.

The summer breeze shifted enough that a hint of her perfume blew in his direction. The scent of the perfume brought flashes of the prom. The bench brought the images of the first night their worlds had come together. Luke was right; he needed to get away.

"Brady?"

He looked at her.

"Are you happy?" She slid her sandal back on and retrieved her coffee.

What kind of question was that?

"I—I don't know. At times, yes, I guess I am. At other times, no, I reckon I'm not. I guess I'm kind of content in life, but honestly, I don't know." He looked at her full-on. "What about you? Are you happy?"

Say it. Tell me you're not.

"I tell myself I am."

He scoffed internally at her words but tried to embrace what she said. He figured she had it all so why would she want more? "Come on. You're Prom Queen, Homecoming Queen, and you're dating the stud quarterback who's going to the same college as you. Isn't that what you wanted?"

Her expression changed from a look of happiness to sadness, to almost disgust at his answer. "Yeah . . . well . . . never mind," she said as she shifted on the bench, turning in toward Brady to shift the conversation. And just like that, the disgust was swept away as she gathered herself, a noticeable trait of hers Brady had come to recognize. When Sarah prepared to get to the point in a conversation, she tucked her hair behind her ears, rubbed her hands together, and sighed. She went through each of the motions before speaking again. "Well, since we probably won't see each other for a while, I say we make a deal tonight . . . right here."

His pulse rate increased. Something inside echoed Luke's words from earlier in the coffee shop. *Run, Brady. Get as far away from this girl as you can.* He wished he could, but he couldn't.

"What kind of deal?"

She looked him in the eyes. It didn't really matter what she said at that moment, he was going to do it. Her eyes had a way of drawing him in. She smiled slightly; the smile that made him feel like he was more than just her friend. "If neither one of us is married in five years, we meet back at this bench, on Christmas Eve, and we get married," she offered, waiting for his response before saying anything else.

On Christmas Eve? So she did remember. Sitting here had been no accident.

"Okay." Brady nodded in his best "trying to play it cool" motion. "Same place on the same night as when we first met. I mean, like, really first met." He raised his brow. "What time?"

"Midnight," she said without hesitation, her grin growing to a smile.

Was she kidding? Or had she thought this up long before now? If so, why five years? Why not tomorrow? Tonight?

Brady smiled with her. "All right."

Sarah tilted her head. "Kiss to seal it?"

Brady was tempted. God knew he was tempted. But . . . no. Not like this. "No, Sarah," he said firmly. "You're dating someone else."

"Then . . ." she said, frowning again. "How will I know you mean it?"

He placed his now-empty cup of hot chocolate between them. "You have my word," he said.

She placed her cup next to his, her lid lightly stained by strawberry lip gloss. "I can live with that."

And so the deal was forged. Nothing was signed. No handshake. As far as Brady was concerned, the words of the two individuals would suffice in this matter of the heart.

He pointed toward where he had left his truck. "We'd best get going."

Too soon, they pulled up to Sarah's house and Brady slid the gearshift into park.

Sarah slowly unbuckled her seat belt as though, again, she were hesitating, then leaned over to give him a hug. "I'll keep in touch," she whispered, then kissed his cheek. "Don't you dare forget me," she added before opening the door and walking toward her house.

Away from Brady.

She had his heart. Now, he had to wait.

It wasn't until he was on his way home that he realized they'd left their empty cups side by side on the bench downtown.

Chapter 17

THE TEXTS AND CALLS WERE sporadic. Somehow, he knew they would be. The frequency increased when Aiden was being a jerk, decreased when their relationship was going well. Truth be told, he learned more about how she was doing from Maddie than he did from Sarah.

According to Maddie, Sarah wanted to reach out to him more, but her relationship with Aiden had a strong pull, and his hatred of Brady dictated when she could reach out without fear of a fight.

And then, four years had passed. Life began to get a little more real for Brady as the final semester of college ended. A few dates presented themselves to him while he was at Appalachian State, but his heart was invested in a girl in Tennessee. He kept most everyone to a friendship. Regardless of where Sarah was or what she was doing, his heart was with her.

Graduation day came with all its pomp and celebrations, and then, when the last of the pictures had been snapped, the final goodbyes had been said, and the final moving box had been secured in the back of his truck, Brady went back home. He spent the first couple of days sleeping and unpacking. Taking care of some business that would shape his future. Business he hadn't talked to either of his parents about. The following day, his father roped him into helping on the farm. Not that he minded. The time would give him a chance to talk to his father man-to-man. After all, he was older now. A man himself. As his mother often told him, much to his chagrin, he had "filled out quite nice."

"So, what's the plan now, son?" his dad asked as he threw a bale of hay off the trailer at the barn.

"Woodworking," Brady replied as he bent to pick up another bale.

"So, you are really going to do it. Really going to own your own business. Laid out any plans yet?"

"Yes, sir." He took in a breath. Released it. "Dad, I've decided to rent the old Ferguson place for the time being, but I'm going to buy it as soon as I can."

His dad paused in his labor. Looked at Brady as though seeing him for the first time as the man he'd grown up to be. "So, you're moving out."

"Yes, sir. I know Mom probably wished I'd stick around all summer, but . . ."

His father nodded in understanding. "Well, the old Ferguson place is not that far away."

"No, sir. And I know it needs some work, but I've got plenty of time. In the meantime, while I try to build up the business, I'm going to help Mr. Johnson to bring in some income." Brady pulled a bandana from his back pocket and wiped the sweat off his brow. "I went by yesterday to see him, too. He needs some help on the tree farm and I need money to pay the bills."

His dad chuckled, then sneezed. He wiped his nose with a faded bandana from his pocket that had seen better days. At one time, Brady reckoned, it might have been navy blue. Now, between his mother's Tide and being exposed to the blistering hot sun, it looked more gray than anything else.

"This hay messes up my allergies," his dad quipped. He reached for another bale and said, "At least you're going to stay in West Jefferson."

Brady followed suit. "Yes, sir. I can't see living anywhere else." He paused long enough to grin at his father. "Plus, being here, maybe Mom will still cook for me and do my laundry."

His dad laughed. Nodded. "I'm sure she will. She worried about you eating the whole time you were in college. She wanted to go up there every week for four years." His father tossed another bale, straining as he continued, "So you can thank me for stopping her. You know she'll be glad you aren't moving away. She's been fretting over it. Praying about it."

Brady grinned as he looked down. Only a few bales to go. He rolled his shoulders—he'd nearly forgotten what it took to do this job—knowing that his mom wasn't the only one thankful for his decision to stay in West Jefferson. Just to be sure, he poked back by saying, "Oh, so only *Mom* is happy about that?"

His dad couldn't hide his smile. "Well, I reckon I am too. Now that you're out of college, I consider you cheap labor."

They threw the last of the hay bales off the trailer. The cloud of dust and particles brought another sneeze. After Brady drove the tractor under the covering, he and his father ambled toward the house. "Bet your mama's got supper ready." He slapped Brady on the back and Brady flinched.

"I'm gonna be sore tomorrow," he moaned, then smiled again at his father. "But it's good to be home, Dad."

❅ ❆ ❉ ❆ ❅

The following day Brady started the process of hauling stuff from his parents' over to his new house. By the end of the afternoon, he had thoroughly cleaned out his childhood bedroom. He had also stopped in town and purchased a cheap sofa and a couple of lamps—one he set up in the living room, the other he placed on his nightstand. There he also put up the two framed images he wanted to see before he went to bed each night. Then he hung his clothes in the closet.

Brady sat to make a list of what he needed for the house. He had no curtains, needed a dining table and chairs. He also needed a coffee table and a bed for his guest bedroom. His mother had given him two towels, a hand towel, and a washcloth from her linen closets but he needed a bathmat and, probably, some pots and pans for those days he didn't go back to his parents' for a homecooked meal. Maybe a toaster. After he made the list, he decided to buy at least one thing with each paycheck from the tree farm. Until then, he'd make do.

He walked around the house to see what needed to be fixed. They called it "the old Ferguson place" because it was, well, old. The house had been constructed in the 1930s, a fact that added to its value in Brady's eyes. He liked old things. He also liked taking things no one else saw any use for and breathing new life into them.

No one had lived in the house for five years, and that was just a renter who lasted only nine months. The previous long-term tenant was Mr. Ferguson himself, who had died nine years prior at the age of eighty-nine.

Mr. Ferguson was a simple man. His wife had died ten years before him and, without her around, he allowed some of the "female touch" she had put into the house to age. As Brady peered around and jotted notes, the list grew lengthy.

Luke had also returned to West Jefferson after graduating from Mars Hill College, so Brady knew he could enlist the help of his best friend to tackle the work.

Over the next week, Brady spent his days taking care of over a thousand Christmas trees and his nights in his shop, working on the next piece of woodwork for his up-and-coming business.

Friday night, he called Luke and asked him to help paint the living room.

"Am I getting paid for this?" Luke asked when he arrived, a box of pizza in one hand and a two-liter bottle of Coke in the other.

"Yes," Brady responded. "You get to hang out with me . . . that should be payment enough."

Luke dropped his head. "I'm getting ripped off."

Brady laughed, but agreed. "You probably are."

After pizza and small talk, they got to work painting the living room, with Luke in charge of the trim and Brady using a roller. "Hey," Brady said after a while, "how are things with you and Maddie now that y'all are both back home?"

"Really good, actually. Surprised we made it through college, you know, with all the distance and everything."

"It's a wonder y'all made it past the first date," Brady joked.

"Aren't you funny?" Luke shot back, threatening to fling his paintbrush across the room.

❄ ❅ ❄ ❅ ❄

For nearly the entire summer and almost every night, Luke and Brady worked on the house, often drawing Maddie in to help. They became more of a family throughout the process, the three of them, their friendship growing beyond what it had been in high school. They had been kids then; they were adults now.

Brady enjoyed his work at Johnson's Tree Farm. Douglas Johnson and his wife, Rickie, never had any children, but over that summer, Brady became less an employee and more like a son. He also finished enough woodworking items to set up a booth at the West Jefferson Christmas in July event. He mostly had cutting boards but had found time to build some small tables, and even a couple of wooden desks for children. The items gave him a chance to make a good first impression on those at the festival in hopes they'd take one of his business cards and call on him to do private work.

His booth sat near the church on Backstreet. Todd and his bride, Melanie, went out to see his work and support him, especially since Brady had been in their lives for so long. As they walked up to the booth, seven or eight others stood around looking at Brady's work.

"How's it going, Brady?" Melanie asked.

"Really well," Brady said, amazed himself by the results of the day. Though he hoped to be successful, he had set his expectations low. His greatest fear was only having sympathy sales for the day, the ones that went to the people who knew him and felt like they had to buy something.

Todd looked at the merchandise remaining on display at the booth. "Wow! This is all you've got left?"

"Yeah," Brady laughed. "I'm as shocked as anyone else."

"Well, hook us up with one of the cutting boards," Todd instructed as he pointed toward the table. "How much are they?"

Brady reached back to retrieve one of the cutting boards. He felt guilty taking money from his preacher and former youth pastor. Todd had been there for Brady throughout the years. Taking money from him for anything didn't feel right. "They're twenty-five dollars for everyone else, but for you, they're my gift."

"No way, Brady. We want to be a part of what you are doing," Todd said as he removed the money from his wallet.

"Buck Mountain Woodworks," Melanie said as she retrieved a business card from Brady's table. "I like it, Brady."

"I came up with that about a week ago," Brady responded with a grin. "I'm glad somebody thinks it sounds good. I was afraid it would be boring."

Todd watched Melanie as she looked over the card. "Well, I would say that people really like your work," he said.

Brady shied away from compliments. One of the greatest deficiencies he had in life was seeing any value in himself. Even the smallest hint of success led him back to his self-deprecating form of humor.

"Brady . . ." Todd said with a shake of his head.

"Yeah, I know." Then he smiled. "I thought it was just the free candy that brought them over at first, because, I mean, who doesn't like free candy? But I guess you're right." He looked over at the nearly empty tent that had been full only a day earlier. "If my calculations are right, I've made over seven hundred dollars today. Who would have thought that?"

"Well, I think you better get to work on making more stuff," Todd noted.

"I think you're right." Brady straightened up the last of the cutting boards.

Within a half hour, the rest of the cutting boards were gone and by three o'clock on Saturday afternoon, Brady had nothing left to sell. As he was closing up, his parents walked up and, seeing that he had sold out, suggested a celebration.

"Let's get something to eat," his dad said, his hands splayed on his hips. Brady couldn't help but note the pride in his father's voice and, in the deepest part of himself, he smiled.

After dinner, Brady shook his father's hand and kissed his mother goodbye, then drove home, returning to his shop to get an hour or so of work in before bedtime, tired though he was.

Because a dream within reach, he told himself, becomes a dream that cannot be set aside.

Chapter 18

SUMMER BROUGHT LONG DAYS AS Brady took to the fields of the tree farm for work, the fields at his house where he had planted a large garden, and the nights spent in the shop. He planted the garden to take care of himself and others in the community, but also because his father had done the same when Brady was growing up. Some things of the past, he decided, should be carried into the future.

His woodworking was growing in popularity, so an endless stream of projects kept his evenings busy. At twenty-two, he was achieving his dream by doing what he wanted to do. His drive served as his boss and he needed no one to force him to get the work done.

But every day, there was the question—come Christmas Eve, would she be there?

She and Aiden had been on-again, off-again throughout college. Aiden had signed with the Atlanta Falcons after college but during preseason his future was left undetermined due to a hip injury. As the days went by, Brady couldn't help but look for signs of her presence in town when he passed through. Perhaps he would see her, he told himself, during the Thanksgiving holidays, which provided a glimmer of hope to hold on to.

But not one sighting.

Surely, she'd come home to see her mom.

But from what he had been told, she had not.

❋ ❋ ❋ ❋ ❋

With the passing of Thanksgiving and throughout the month of December, West Jefferson became a wonderland, each storefront showing off displays of holiday delights. The weather began to bite, and the tree farm was more than a "little busy." As was Brady. Still, his every waking moment centered on not too much other than the night before Christmas. Midnight, to be exact. One question lingered: would she be there? She wasn't married—that much he knew for sure—but had she forgotten their promise?

Brady made it to the church early on Christmas Eve to help Todd set up for the Sunday night candlelight service. When he arrived, he found Todd setting a box of candles on the front pew beside the bulletins for the evening program.

"Thanks for the help, bud," Todd said. "I appreciate your coming in early."

"Not a problem."

Brady began to unpack the candles and disperse them in the pews.

"What're your big plans for tonight after the service?" Todd retrieved his Bible from where he'd left it on the altar's table, then placed it on the podium.

"Don't know," Brady responded.

"If you want, you can come by and hang out with me and Melanie."

"I can't. I have to be somewhere." Brady exited one row and entered another.

"Uh, Brady…"

Brady stopped, looked up to the front of the church. He'd given two opposing answers to essentially the same question and, knowing Todd, Todd caught it.

"You just said you didn't know what you were doing tonight. What gives?"

Brady hesitated. He hadn't wanted to discuss it with anyone. Not Todd and certainly not Luke. But now, he had to clean up the mess his words had just created. "I lied," he responded, wishing at that moment he was anywhere but in church, in front of the preacher.

Todd made his way off the platform toward Brady. "What for?"

"Because, man, it's kind of ridiculous and I want to keep it to myself."

Todd rested against the side of a pew. "No problem . . . just odd that you would lie about it."

Brady resumed placing the candles along the pews as the door opened and Luke entered.

"You're late," Todd chided him.

"You know me," Luke countered. "Even if I set my watch a half hour ahead, I'd still run behind." Then he looked from Todd to Brady and back again. "Did I interrupt something?"

"No," Todd answered as Brady said, "I've got somewhere to be at midnight."

"I thought Cinderella had to be home *by* midnight," Luke joked.

Brady stayed focused on dispensing the candles. "You are so funny, Luke Perry."

"Really . . . Luke Perry? That's what you've got tonight?" Luke asked as Todd handed him a stack of bulletins and asked him to place them on one of the tables near the back of the church.

"So, where *do* you have to be . . . at midnight?" Todd asked, nearing Brady now.

Luke stopped right in the middle of the aisle, bulletins firm in his hand. "Dude, tell me this is not what I think it is."

"Just let it be," Brady responded. If he had been up front with Todd to begin with, he could have avoided Luke hearing any of this. He would have told Todd and asked Todd to drop it, which he probably would have done. But not Luke. Luke meant well, but Luke, who'd had Maddie by his side all these years, could not understand where he was in life.

"She's not going to show, Brady. You have to know that," Luke said, dropping the bulletins to the highly polished mahogany table. His exasperation was evident. "When was the last time you even heard from her?"

Brady placed the last of the candles on the back pew. Sure, the dream of Sarah fulfilling a silly promise made nearly half a decade earlier was somewhat crazy, but he still held on to the hope. "It's been a while."

"Brady?" Todd asked as he returned to the front to arrange the communion trays. "Does this have anything to do with Sarah?"

"Of course it does," Luke said, coming up the aisle. "Todd, he's crazy. I mean, I love the guy, he's my best friend, but he is certifiably crazy. Five years ago, she made some ridiculous promise that if they weren't hitched to anyone by this point, they'd meet up in town and get married. Now, Brady-boy has put his life on hold for five years . . . *five years* . . . while she has been out living her life."

Todd held up a hand. "Take it easy, Luke. You never know what's going to happen."

Brady opened his mouth to excuse himself entirely, but the front door opened and Mary, the pianist, strolled in. She said hello to everyone, then continued to the piano.

Todd and Luke joined Brady at the back of the church.

"Look, Brady—"

"Don't say anything," Brady countered as Mary warmed up with "O Holy Night."

"Neither of you say anything," Todd interjected, looking at his watch. "People will be here shortly."

The congregation began to file in less than ten minutes later. During the service, Brady sat with his family and tried not to look at Luke, who sat with Maddie. His best friend had it all; Brady could only wonder if Luke knew it.

During the service, as the candles were lit and the congregation lifted up the lyrics of "Silent Night," Brady glanced over at Luke for a final time to discover him staring back. Luke lowered his eyes and nodded once—his way of apologizing—then turned to face the front. At the very word "Amen" to close the prayer concluding the service, Brady kissed his mother and hugged his sister and father, told them he'd see them early in the morning, hurried out of the door, then jumped in his truck to head home. He hadn't bothered to say anything more to Luke, but his words wrestled within him.

His heart said, "Go. Wait for Sarah."

His mind said, "Luke is right."

❄ ❄ ❋ ❄ ❄

He normally let his beard grow a bit in the winter—an extra layer of protection from the cold—but tonight he shaved so she would see the boy from high school. He donned a brown Carhartt coat and a Wake Forest beanie. Before leaving, he mixed up some hot chocolate. Inside his truck, the aroma of the drink, the joy of Christmas, and the hope of love offered a sense of magic to the night. Even if it seemed ridiculous to others. Even if it was a little ridiculous to Brady himself.

He drove into town. The streets were desolate but festive in the glow of colorful lights. Flurries had begun to fall but the roads were clear. With his pick of parking places, he chose the one in front of Town Hall across the street from the bench, the one place he hoped his future might unfold.

For a while, he remained in his truck, enjoying the heat. His mind flashed back to the night they met, prom, and the day the promise was made. The smell of her perfume and the way she looked at him, had hugged and kissed him, were as fresh and real to him as the moment they'd happened. He prayed silently, pleading with God for this one request to be fulfilled, even if it meant other requests were left unfulfilled. If God would give him this one thing—just this one—Brady would never ask for another thing, ever.

His phone showed the time as 11:45, so he climbed out and walked across the street, two insulated cups in hand, slowly making his way to the bench. He looked around, then lowered himself to the bench, the aroma of chocolate swirling as doubt crept in. But the lights of the season—strands wrapped around the pole of each streetlamp—told him *anything* was possible. In fact, he reminded himself, the season itself was a celebration of a night when impossible became reality.

He studied the wreaths hanging high on the streetlamps, each lighted and vibrant, their very shape a reminder of love eternal, unending. Brady remembered when Todd spoke about the wreaths at the Hanging of the Green service years prior. The words had stuck with him and now the wreaths hung as a reminder of God's love for him. Eternal love. Unending love.

Like the love he felt for Sarah.

Silent Night. The words to the carol they'd sung earlier played in his heart. His head. Lyrics so lovely, but now the silence seemed to make the wait even more agonizing. Snow continued to fall around him, the flakes growing larger. Louder. Sighing collisions of beauty meeting the lifeless tree branches and sidewalk cement. Grass that had grown brown over the season.

Over and over, he wondered . . . what would she look like? He tried to rehearse what he might say in case . . . in case she did come. He would stand, of course. She would say, "Hey, Brady . . ." and he would say, "You came," their words coming together. And then he would hand her the hot chocolate and she would smile and say, "You remembered."

"*You* remembered," he would say, meaning that she came at all.

He placed one cup beside him to look at his phone. Midnight.

A set of headlights traveling east on Highway 163 appeared, heading straight into town.

His heart pounded. His stomach knotted. *This was it. This was it.* He picked up the cup, feeling its warmth press into his skin. Brady knew cars. From a distance, the headlights and body looked like a Mustang. He had no clue what to expect her to drive up in, but he was fairly sure it was her.

Who else would be out at this time of night?

He stared at the car, which idled at the stop sign for what seemed forever. He waited, his breath caught in his throat until the left turn signal blinked, the light interrupting his trance. The car turned left, traveled down East 2nd, and continued out of town.

Who knew the panic that would come with the thought that it could be her, that his dream could be coming true? Brady released his breath, a white cloud into the dark night.

The moment was gone. Five years of hope, diminished. The sigh seemed to be the last of the energy he had left inside. He needed to leave, but for a moment, he remained seated.

After a while he looked again at his phone. Midnight had become 12:07.

Christmas had come. Sarah had not.

Chapter 19

THE NEXT MORNING, BRADY SHOWERED away his lack of sleep, loaded up the truck with packages, then drove to his parents' house. Not that he wanted to. He had to. Christmas morning meant he had to put himself in a different frame of mind.

"Good morning, Bubba," Chelsi said, hands planted playfully on her hips.

"Morning, Chelsi," he said to the baby sister who, in only a few short years, had grown into a lovely young woman. Cropped blond hair. Kind ice-blue eyes. A smile that could stop traffic. "Merry Christmas."

"Those all for me?" she asked, noting the gifts that weighed down his arms.

He grinned at her. "Not a chance."

He moved to the living room and laid the gifts underneath the tree. As he did, his eye caught one of his mother's favorite ornaments. Inscribed were the words "Faith, Hope, and Love." The irony hit him; he'd stepped out in faith, he held on to hope.

He was still searching for love.

As always, his mother was the Christmas decorating machine. Every year, the house was transformed the day after Thanksgiving and remained that way until the New Year. This year was no different. The tree she'd purchased from the tree farm nearly a month ago stood nearly seven feet tall. He smiled at a sudden realization—age and experience change perspective. What once would have seemed to be a towering tree to him was now a mere foot taller.

"Is Brady here yet?" his mom called from the kitchen.

"I'm here, Mom," Brady called back as he placed the last gift underneath the tree.

"Good. Biscuits just came out. Come in here and eat while it's hot," she instructed.

It didn't take much more than that to draw the family into the warmth of one of Brady's favorite rooms in the house. Once they'd gathered around the table, Chelsi volunteered to say the blessing over the food.

"So, Brady, anything new?" his mother asked as she reached for the tongs to put bacon on her plate.

"Well, Mother, I just saw you last night, so . . . no, not really," he replied with a grin, drawing a smile out of his dad as well.

Brady grabbed two biscuits, then scooped out some grits to put on his plate.

"Did Sarah show up last night?" Chelsi blurted.

All hands went still as Brady looked from his sister to his mother and father, who both looked horrified by the bluntness of their youngest child. Chelsi noticed it too and she looked at her mom, ready to defend herself. "What? It isn't like he didn't know what you were wanting to ask, Mom! I just got to the point a little faster."

"Ladies, Brady may not want to talk about it," their father remarked as he started passing the food again.

"No," Brady said, dreading the next line of questioning, wishing he had never said anything to his family about the promise made all those years ago. A moment of weakness—a response to their push for him to date someone from church—had led Brady to tell them about it. If only he could have that conversation back.

"No, she didn't show, or no you don't want to talk about it," Chelsi pressed for clarification.

His sigh became his answer. "She didn't show."

"Oh, Brady, I'm so sorry," his mom said. Tears pooled in her eyes. It was Christmas and her son was hurting.

Brady focused on the meal in front of him, not that he felt much like eating now. "It's not a big deal," he said. "Let's just eat and—"

"—Umm . . . *yeah*. It *is* a big deal. You've been waiting five years for this," Chelsi said.

"Chelsi," their father now said, bringing the table's attention to him. "Hush."

Brady waited a moment before saying, "Just means I need to get on with my life, right?" He took a bite of bacon so perfectly crispy, it crumbled in his mouth, then swallowed. "It was a long shot anyways."

Awkward silence fell, broken only by the sound of clanging forks on plates and a turn in the conversation: Chelsi's next semester's classes.

After breakfast, they moved to the living room to open gifts. Enjoying the surprise of what was inside the boxes readjusted the atmosphere. Later, when Brady gave goodbyes as jovially as he could, his dad followed him to his truck, supposedly to help him carry his gifts. "You okay, son?" he asked after handing him the last of them.

"It's all good, Dad," Brady said, closing the passenger door to his truck. "Sometimes, life just doesn't go as planned."

His father nodded, then studied the landscape. "Be careful driving home. Roads are slick with this fresh snow."

"I will."

On the way home, he tried to convince himself that it wasn't ridiculous to feel so broken. In his heart, he'd known she probably wouldn't show, but he'd failed to prepare himself fully for what life would be like when she didn't.

Like it or not, a tear trickled down his cheek.

Chapter 20

BEFORE LONG, SPRING ARRIVED, SENDING Brady out to the side field to plow and plant his garden. Behind him, dust flew with every turn of the tractor's wheels while the sun beat down on his shoulders. As he worked, he focused on how to keep the deer from eating his crop, proud that at least he wasn't thinking about her. About Sarah. Something about plowing a field took his mind off everything else, as if the garden was his therapy. But as is the case with therapy, time runs out, the session ends, and there are issues still to be dealt with. At least the garden didn't cost him $150 an hour.

He circled back toward the house as a car pulled up in the driveway, a car he didn't recognize. The car parked and a figure exited. Brady squinted to make out who now stood at the fence. As he drove closer, with each turn of the giant wheels the image became clearer.

Sarah?

Her straight, dark-brown hair was pulled through the back of a Tennessee Volunteers hat. She wore a gray tee with an orange University of Tennessee "T" above her heart and a pair of skinny jeans.

Brady killed the engine on the tractor and jumped down, then made his way over to the fence. He couldn't believe she was here. Just as he had nearly gotten over the disappointment of her not showing up on Christmas Eve, she stood before him.

"Hey, buddy," she called out.

Buddy. Okay. He could deal with that. A starting point. "Hey, yourself." He adjusted the ball cap on his head. Once. Then twice.

"It's kind of hot to be out on the tractor today, ain't it?"

He reached the fence, the wood separating them. "Sarah."

She climbed up on the bottom board of the fence to reach over and give him a hug.

"Sorry, I'm all sweaty," Brady remarked.

"It's all good," she said, but she wiped the sweat off her neck with her hand.

He studied her carefully; nothing, not even his wet grime, could wipe the smile off her face.

"Hang on a minute," Brady said as he walked to the gate to get to her side of the fence. He couldn't decide if he should be happy or if this interaction was going to make the hurt come back in full force. There was so much to say. To ask. Why was she here? Why hadn't she shown up at Christmas? Why hadn't he heard from her in forever? But instead he asked, "What are you doing here?"

"I'm in town to visit Mom. I went by your parents' house and they told me where you are living now. So . . ." She shoved her hands into the front pockets of her jeans. "I thought I'd stop by and say hi. To see how you are doing."

He leaned against the fence. "I'm doing okay. Just getting adjusted to reality, I guess. What about you? How are you? Where are you living now?" But before she could answer, he pointed toward the shade of a large oak. "Let's get out of this heat," he said.

They turned and walked toward the tree. "Good, everything's good," Sarah said a little too quickly, although she never looked at Brady while answering.

Which meant she was lying. Brady could always see through her lies.

"So . . ." Brady poked. "What's new since we last talked?"

She reached for her ponytail and twirled it, as if she hadn't thought of how to answer the most basic of questions. "Oh, yeah. Well, I was in Atlanta with Aiden. I moved there after he got drafted last year. After he got hurt . . . well, things just got worse. I hung in there until February, but I couldn't take it anymore. So . . ." She took a deep breath. Exhaled. "So, now I'm in Asheville doing graphic design work for a company downtown." She looked up at him. Smiled. "I love the city. I have an apartment downtown, near the Thomas Wolfe museum. Everything is real artsy there."

"Yeah, I've been down to Asheville a few times." He paused to gather his thoughts. "Do you—do you want to come inside? Get something to drink?"

She smiled again. Looked almost as if she were relaxing now. "Sure," she said.

They walked in silence until Brady opened the door and held it as Sarah walked into the house. "Excuse the mess," he said. "I definitely wasn't expecting company today. I don't have too many visitors, other than, you know, the family. And Luke and Maddie from time to time."

"How's Chelsi?"

"She's good," he said, guiding her further into the living room. "She moved across the state to go to Mount Olive, studying business. She was home for Christmas and for spring break. Dating a baseball player from Virginia. Already talking about marrying him," Brady said with a smirk. "But you know Chelsi. She thinks she's going to marry nearly every boy she's ever dated."

Sarah chuckled. "Say, do you have plans for tonight?"

Brady wasn't sure how to answer. "I thought you came home to see your mom."

She smiled. "I was with her all night last night and I still have a couple of days before I go back to Asheville, so . . ."

Sarah took a seat on the couch. She sat back and adjusted her hair so it would fall over her shoulder, then scanned the living room as she waited for his answer. He wanted to say no as a means of protection but every minute with her brought a sense of fulfillment. A breadcrumb of hope. "What do you have in mind?"

She looked up at him with a grin. "Well, let's go get something to eat and go see a movie. Come on, Brady, it'll be fun. We can catch up."

Brady had no way out. Part of him wanted to go, to spend precious moments making another memory. However, he knew it could prove costly. Once again, his heart and his head were at war and they, like

Sarah, waited for an answer.

He erred on the side of his heart, finally breaking through with a grin. "Well, I will have to take a shower first. I'm not going anywhere with you if I'm this nasty."

She smiled. Perhaps his words assured her of the special place she had in his heart. Maybe they told her that everything was okay between them, even though she hadn't shown months earlier.

"That's fine." She pulled her phone from a back pocket. "I'll return some phone calls while you get ready."

Brady walked down the hall, retrieved some clothes and a towel, then headed to the shower to wash away the dust and grime from a day on the tractor. For months, even years, she'd been like a ghost. Now, she was there, sitting on his couch, wanting to spend time with him. He shook his head at the irony. She'd ripped out his heart more than once, now *she* wanted *him* to go out with her.

The workings of the mind can be dangerous. He tried to shut off the voices as the water ran over his shoulders.

Keep your distance. Don't get attached.

Even under the spray of water, which was barely a spray at all, he heard her walking past the bathroom. He turned his head in the direction of the door. It was okay. Let her see whatever she wanted to see.

The creaking of his bedroom floor told him she had gone into his room. What was she looking for? Some sign of a female's presence in his life? A photo perhaps?

Brady imagined what she might be seeing. The dark-blue comforter covering the bed he'd, remarkably, made that morning. The two framed pictures on the nightstand. The creaking continued, tiny steps toward them. He imagined her then, picking up one, then the other. Studying them. The first was Brady and Chelsi as kids at Christmas. The second was a picture she probably didn't know existed—a photo of her and Brady. Prom night. Them, dancing together. A couple of weeks after prom, a classmate had given it to Brady. Said she'd taken several snapshots for the annual and thought he'd want this one. He surely had. Since then, every night, when he closed his eyes, that image was the last thing he saw.

And now . . . now she would know.

Brady turned the shower off. Waited as she tiptoed back to the living room. Only then did he emerge from behind the curtain to wrap himself in the towel. Ten minutes later, Brady walked into the living room, his hair still damp and spiked. She sat on the sofa, legs crossed, her attention on her phone.

"You ready?" he asked. He grabbed his keys off the entertainment center, pretending to be none the wiser.

"Yeah," she said, now looking up as if she'd only just realized he was out of the shower. She smiled at him, but the blush across her cheeks told another story. "Um . . . yeah," she said again, standing. "Let's go."

Chapter 21

HOW MUCH DAMAGE COULD HAPPEN in one night?

Depends.

Brady opened the passenger door of his truck for Sarah, then walked around to the driver's side whispering, "Stupid, stupid, stupid."

The plan had to be to guard himself.

He hoisted himself into the truck, bit the inside of his lip, and turned the key in the ignition. Outside the world—familiar and yet, somehow, at this moment with Sarah sitting so close beside him, her perfume swirling inside the cab, unfamiliar—blurred past them as he increased his speed toward town. Inside, Sarah rambled on as if he were holding on to her every word. But he was not. His thoughts were elsewhere, wondering . . . *was he dreaming this?* He'd wanted it for so long. Waited for so long. There was always the possibility that, right now, instead of heading toward a bite to eat, he was asleep in his own be—

"So, what do you think?" she asked.

Horror slipped in and rushed over. Whatever story she'd been telling, whatever tale she'd woven, had ended in a question that needed an answer. One he was required to give.

Something about Asheville. She had been talking about Asheville. And, if he could put this together quickly enough—he thought she had asked for his approval of a place that he neither knew, nor cared, anything about—he could come up with an answer to satisfy her.

"Sounds cool," he said.

"*Really?*" she asked. Her excitement had her nearly bouncing in the truck. "So, when do you want to come down?"

He looked from the road to her and back to the road again. What had he done? A simple affirmation now meant a trip to Asheville? To visit her? See where she lived? Where she worked? *What had he done?* "Um—soon—uh—I'll have to see how things are looking."

Evasive. Good enough. Because he needed excuses and he needed to think of them fast. Going out to dinner was one thing, but what would a trip to Asheville mean? For him? For them? At least he bought himself some time to work his way out of the corner his lack of focus had boxed him into.

They turned down Jefferson Avenue.

"Not too busy tonight," he mentioned. "Where would you—"

"How about Boondocks?" she asked, taking the question from him. "We could sit outside. Evenings in April were always nice here."

"Sounds good," he said as casually as he knew how. But he wondered. Did she remember? They'd eaten at Boondocks years before. Gone to get a coffee. Sat on the bench. Made a promise. Did she remember? Because he certainly had. He'd been there, at midnight, on that bench.

Brady pulled the truck into a parking space across from Boondocks. He helped her from the truck, they walked across the street, Sarah still talking. He opened the door that stood under a green awning flapping gently in the cool breeze coming off the mountains. She walked through, he followed.

They sat outside under the shelter of the Boon Deck. Tiny white lights twinkled brighter as the sunlight dimmed. They placed their orders—the same as before—and chatted lightly about this and that. He tried to play along, laughing at some of the old stories, answering questions about those who had lost touch, and added in memories he had never forgotten. As their food came, Luke and Maddie walked by.

"*Sarah?*" Maddie cried out, obviously surprised to see her best friend.

Sarah leapt up. "Maddie," she squealed as the two hugged.

Luke gave Brady his best "what's this?" look.

"How long are you in town for?" Maddie asked.

"A few days," Sarah responded. "Hey." She pointed toward the table where their food grew cold. "Do y'all want to eat with us?"

Maddie looked at Brady, to gauge his response, he knew. He nodded with an emphatic "Yes."

"Is that okay, Luke?" she asked her date.

"Come on, Luke Duke. Eat supper with us," Brady teased.

"You've used that one before," Luke responded as the four sat.

"Don't care," Brady replied, surprised at his relief that Maddie and Luke had joined them. He would not be alone with Sarah now, which was for the best.

Sarah and Maddie talked as if they were around each other every day, not missing a beat. Luke and Brady carried on, joining in the conversation with the ladies at the right moments.

But Brady couldn't stop the voices in his head reminding him that Sarah had left this place. This was her past. Yet, on this night, she talked as if she missed what she had left behind.

"You know what," she said at one point, almost as if in passing, "so precious are the moments we have that we fail to see their worth until after they have passed."

The rest nodded in agreement.

After supper, Luke and Maddie said their goodbyes as they had plans to visit Maddie's grandfather who had been in the hospital after back surgery. Brady paid the bill, then he and Sarah walked down Jefferson Street and turned to go to the theater.

"I wish a new Nicholas Sparks movie would hurry up and release," Sarah said. Sarah adored all of Sparks' movies, falling in love with *A Walk to Remember* and watching every film that followed. She cried at each one, she told him. She owned every DVD. "Did you see *Safe Haven* last year?" she asked, but before he could answer, she added, "Ohmygosh. So good."

They stopped long enough to look to see what was playing. "Chelsi said *God's Not Dead* is pretty good," Brady said, pointing toward the poster. "Want to see that one?"

Sarah smiled. "Works for me."

The old Parkway Theatre sat nearly dormant on a Thursday night in April—a school night—so they had their choice of seats. Brady let her choose; she picked seats near the back, dead center. She sat so near, leaning in to be even closer to Brady. In high school, this would have been considered a date. In one's early twenties, who knew how to classify it?

Brady tried to concentrate on the movie but found it difficult. The film was good, but things had changed. Sarah looked different. Not in a bad way. More grown up. The way she walked, the way she talked, how she held herself spoke volumes about her years since living in West Jefferson. She was no longer that young girl from the prom but was now a woman, charting her course in life and, from everything she had said, doing so quite successfully. But one thing that hadn't changed was the perfume. Every time she shifted another hint of the scent blew toward Brady.

If she only knew what that does to me.

After the movie, they walked to Bohemia for coffee to go, then decided to head back to Brady's house. On the walk back to the truck, they passed the bench. Nothing was said. She passed it as if it were a random bench on any given night in an ordinary town.

❄ ❋ ❄ ❋ ❄

Night had fallen and all the stars were on display. "Sometimes, you forget the beauty of looking up," Sarah commented.

"Yeah, I think we all take things for granted in life." But Brady wasn't looking at the stars; he was looking at her as she gazed upward.

Back at Brady's, he turned on the television, but it only served as background noise to their continued conversation. They spoke of the trappings of life and of times simpler, but never spoke of the promise, never referenced the bench.

Midnight came and Cinderella needed to get home. She picked up her purse and made her way toward the door, Brady behind her. "Be careful driving home. You need me to follow you to make sure you get there all right?"

"I'm good, Brady. I'm a big girl," she said as she cracked a grin. Then she blinked. Once. Slowly. "I had a great time tonight." She leaned over and gave Brady a hug in the doorway. He held on, inhaling the scent of her, not wanting to forget a second of the moment, then eased back, not wanting their time together to end in the epitome of awkward.

"I did, too," he assured her.

"I'll text you tomorrow. Whatcha got going on?"

"Finishing a toy chest and the plowing."

She tilted her face toward his. Smiled. "Always working, huh?"

"It's the life of a business owner . . . I'm livin' the dream," he smiled back.

She opened the door and together they stepped outside. Again, she looked up at the display of stars. Again, he watched her, continuing to do so from the front porch as she walked to her car, stopped to wave once more, then slipped inside. Maybe this was the last time, he told himself. The last time he'd watch her walk away.

He started to call out to her, then stopped himself. More than anything, he wanted to tell her she was walking in the wrong direction.

Chapter 22

BEFORE THE SUN COULD WAKE up and yawn, Brady was in the shop working on the toy chest. Unable to sleep, he decided to occupy his mind with stripping and cutting grooves into some wood.

Simple boards, when placed into the hands of a woodworker, become beautifully designed tables, jewelry boxes, and toy chests, just as, Brady believed, the lives of those placed in the hands of the Creator are shaped and fashioned into something beautiful. Sometimes it can be a painful process. Brady was learning such a lesson with Sarah. In fact, he surmised, he had been learning it for a long, long time.

A touchup sanding was finished by ten o'clock. The next day, he would begin the staining process. While the sun was out, he determined to finish the plowing interrupted a day earlier.

Back and forth, the smell of dust flying in the air, Brady tore the soil, thinking how much this was like Sarah tearing at his soul. He was guarded but all his defenses couldn't stop the penetration of his heart by the one who held it.

As lunchtime came, he stopped to get a sandwich. Not just any sandwich; his signature sandwich—a bacon and lettuce sandwich. That along with a nice cold Coke had been on his mind for the last several passes on the tractor, but he was trying to finish before stopping.

His hunger won out. As he walked into the house, a text came through.

Plans tonight?

He smiled when he saw the name on the screen. He knew he shouldn't, but he did. He also knew he should make up an excuse for the night. But he didn't.

Thinking about cooking out. Want to come over?

He hadn't been thinking about cooking out. In fact, he had planned on a frozen pizza, but he had to come up with something.

Sure.

He smiled again. Her text had come so quickly, he figured she hadn't even thought about it.

Come by around 6. He placed his phone on the countertop and opened the fridge.

What R U grillin'?

Steaks ok with U?

She returned his text with a smiling emoji.

His heart began to race. Where was this going? To keep it from getting awkward, he pulled the Luke and Maddie card. *I'll text Luke and see if they R free tonight.*

She returned with another smiling emoji and: *Deal. See you later.*

Luke and Maddie were free; Friday's frozen pizza became a cookout. He texted Todd and Melanie, who also agreed to come, stating that they wanted to see Sarah while she was in town. Brady also invited his parents.

He wolfed down lunch, finished his plowing, and put the tractor back in the barn before hurrying through the rest of the things he needed to do. He took a shower, then made a quick trip to the grocery store. By the time he returned home, it was already 4:30. He fired up the grill, then let it warm up while he went inside to prepare the food.

He wrapped potatoes in tinfoil after brushing them with butter and adding a hint of sea salt to their skin. He rolled ears of corn in foil as well, the same combination of butter and sea salt added to each ear. Outside, Brady let the sides cook for about fifteen minutes before putting the steaks on.

By quarter 'til six, the food was cooking, friends and family were arriving, and the aroma was intoxicating, but none of it more so than Sarah, who wore a pair of distressed jeans and a black button-down top, cropped at her hips. She had pulled her hair back in a loose ponytail, caught by a fat black "scrunchie," as Chelsi called them. Whatever they were, she looked stunning and his heart beat fast for a few measures before settling back to its regular tempo.

They fixed their plates and sat around the large kitchen table Brady handcrafted himself from the wood of an old oak tree that had fallen in his grandparents' yard.

"Larry, you must be so proud of Brady," Melanie commented, running her hand across the table in admiration. "He is so talented working with wood."

"Yeah, I guess he does pretty good," his dad answered with a smirk.

"We're going to get him to build us a table, too," Todd commented.

"Now that you are the senior pastor, are you expecting a discount?" Brady replied with a wink toward his father.

Todd didn't hesitate. "Of course I expect a discount."

Everyone laughed.

"You're the senior pastor now, Todd?" Sarah asked without waiting for an answer. "Congratulations. They're lucky to have a guy with a heart like you have for those people."

"Yeah, well, evidently, they were desperate," Todd joked.

Again, laughter broke out amongst them. This was what Brady loved about being back home. These moments. These laughs. And deep down, he hoped Sarah would see that she had the inner track to be a part of such moments.

"So, Sarah, how's life treating you?" Brady's mother asked.

"It's pretty good," she answered with a slight toss of her hair. "I'm living in Asheville now and doing graphic design work. I came home for a few days to see my mom while I had some time off."

"Oh, honey," Brady's mom said, "You should have asked her to join us."

Brady felt heat rush over him. No, *he* should have asked. He just hadn't thought . . .

"Sarah, Luke and Brady and I are going to come to Asheville to see you," Maddie announced, ending the uncomfortable line of conversation. "Soon."

"Anytime," Sarah asserted.

Brady shifted in his seat. The previous day had him on the hook, but he hoped to get out of it. If this conversation caught any traction, the dates would be set.

"Hey, Brady, weren't you invited to attend a festival or something in Asheville?" his mother asked.

Brady stabbed a piece of potato with his fork. "Yeah, they have a festival called Wood Day in Asheville." He popped the potato in his mouth, chewed, and swallowed. "In August. The organizers asked me to come down and do a demonstration at the Folk Art Center." Brady forced a grin with a dart of his eyes toward his well-meaning mother. Oh, how he wished she had said nothing, and that he hadn't accepted the invitation. Now he would have to go.

"Luke," Maddie said, nearly jumping in her seat, "we need to go with Brady to the festival, and Sarah, why don't you meet us there. It's a few months away, but—"

"I'll have to check my calendar," Luke responded.

Maddie reached over and pinched Luke's side, making him jump. "I'm free! We're good to go."

Again, laughter erupted as Luke rubbed his side.

But Brady understood Luke's fears about Brady and Sarah.

After supper was finished, Melanie and Brady's mom cleared the plates and began to clean up. "Y'all don't have to do that," Brady commented, perfectly willing to clean up the mess himself.

"You made supper tonight, which means I didn't have to," Melanie assured him as she washed a plate and handed it over to Brady's mom. "Here, Miss Lauri." She turned back to Brady. "The least I can do is clean the dishes."

"And I get to spend time with the preacher's wife, which I enjoy, so I am happy," his mother added as she dried the plate.

"Hey, Brady, I need a favor," Melanie chimed in again, which brought Brady a few steps closer to the duo. "I need you to teach Todd how to grill. The potatoes and corn were amazing, and I don't know what you did to that steak but it was better than a restaurant."

"I'll see what I can do," Brady replied with a grin. "Hey, Todd," he called out as he returned to where the others had gathered in the living room.

"Hey, Brady," Todd mimicked.

"I'm supposed to teach you how to grill. Melanie said your steak tastes like a Michelin tire," Brady said, then started laughing.

"She did not say that, Todd," Brady's mom hollered over her shoulder.

Brady and Todd continued on to the living room. Melanie and his mom joined everyone a few moments later and within an hour, the older adults made their exits, leaving the four younger people alone.

A fire in the fire pit meant there was more to the night. Brady and his guests—his family, his friends—continued the small talk until the conversation began to dwindle.

Like the fire.

Chapter 23

Summer means long days, as does a relationship that has no definition and no known destination. For the first week or so after Sarah returned to Asheville, the texts between her and Brady were fairly regular. But as weeks turned to months, they became more sporadic, even as they neared the August date of the trip to Asheville—his and Luke's and Maddie's.

When his phone rang that humid morning in early August, Brady placed his coffee mug on the counter and answered on the second ring.

"Hey Brady," Maddie began. "What time are you wanting to leave tomorrow?"

Her call was expected. Maddie had to go over every detail at least once weekly. As the day neared, sometimes twice.

"The festival starts at ten o'clock. I'll need a little time to set up and it's about two and a half hours to Asheville," he responded.

"So, what about six?" she asked. She had suggested the same a week earlier but perhaps, Brady reckoned, this was her way of ensuring no plans had changed.

"Six is fine with me. Can you get Luke to wake up that early in the morning?"

"I'll keep calling him until he does. That boy can sleep through alarms like nobody else, but phone calls drive him crazy early in the morning," Maddie assured.

"Sounds good. I'll drive so y'all just meet me here at the house and we'll roll."

"We'll be there, buddy."

Brady was about to hit the button to end the call but stopped. Hesitantly, he asked, "Hey, before you go, have you heard anything from Sarah?"

"Yeah, I talked to her Tuesday."

Brady sighed. He forced a smile, which at the time made no sense because he was on the phone and no one was around. "Okay, just checking. I haven't heard anything from her in a week or so . . . and I was just wondering if she was still going to come."

"I'm pretty sure she's just been busy, Brady. She only had a few minutes to talk the other day. But she said she's coming."

"Cool. I guess I'll see you and Luke in the morning."

"See ya then."

Brady laid the phone down on the counter and, ignoring the half-consumed coffee, went to his room to pack. They had decided to stay in Asheville for a night to spend more time with Sarah. The original plan was that everyone would stay at Sarah's apartment, but Brady had checked out local hotels in case the plan changed, which he had begun to fear it would.

❄ ❄ ❄ ❄ ❄

Brady's alarm sounded at five o'clock the next morning, giving him enough time to take a shower and wake up before winding his way to Asheville. He had decided to take Highway 221, coming out of Boone, a beautiful drive.

Shortly before six, Luke and Maddie strolled through the back door. "Brady," Luke said, looking like he had just rolled out of bed, "do you have any coffee?"

"Yeah. Get you a cup if you want," he said as he shook his head and grinned. His best friend was great in nearly every way, one of those people who could excel at most things, but one thing Luke was *not*, was a morning person.

"Thanks," Luke said before letting out a huge yawn. "I don't know how you people like mornings."

Luke threw a K-cup into the Keurig and, after his coffee finished brewing, they headed out the door. Brady chuckled as Luke sipped the coffee and tried to open eyes shadowed by a ball cap.

As they drove, Maddie asked, "Brady, when are you scheduled to do your demonstration?"

"Starts around ten."

"She wants us to go to the Thomas Wolfe house in Asheville at some point," Luke commented from the back.

"Cool. That sounds good to me. I read one of his books in college," Brady commented.

"Really?" Maddie asked, surprised Brady had read one of Wolfe's novels.

"Yeah. Now before you get too excited, it was an assigned reading, so I basically had to do it. *Look Homeward, Angel*," Brady explained.

"That's awesome. I've tried to get Luke to read it but, well, you know Luke and you know how that has gone."

Luke's sigh could be heard in the front of the truck.

"I still find it amazing that God put the two of you together," Brady said. "You're a librarian and aspiring writer and Luke can't read anything that isn't written in crayon."

"You are so funny, Brady Bunch," Luke said from underneath the cap he'd pulled over his eyes.

"I'm working on him, Brady," Maddie explained as she glanced back at her boyfriend. "He did read a Mark Twain book I gave him."

"Impressive," Brady replied, again looking back at Luke in the rearview mirror. "I didn't know you had it in you."

"I am a man of many surprises."

As they pulled up to the Folk Art Center, a bustling of people could not draw Brady's attention off the one he spied standing behind her parked car.

"Maddie," Sarah screamed as she ran up to the truck once Brady parked it.

Maddie jumped out. "Sarah!"

Brady hopped out of the truck and Luke rolled out behind him.

"Hey, Brady," Sarah said as she leaned over to give him a hug and, in doing so, sent a whiff of her perfume to the air around them.

"Hey, girl. Glad you came. What time did you get here?"

"I was only about fifteen minutes ahead of you guys. I had a much shorter drive to get here."

"Well, we would have been here about the same time but your best friend here, Maddie, forgot to put Luke's diaper on. One large mug of coffee, two toilet breaks."

Three people laughed.

"I can't help it. Coffee runs right through me. Speaking of which, where is the—?" Luke stretched his neck, looking beyond the parked cars and the entrance to the event.

Sarah pointed toward the building, then instructed, "It's inside, Lucas."

"Thanks, Sarah . . . but, as I'm sure Brady has told you, it's just Luke." He took several steps, then began to trot toward the building with a, "Okay, I gotta run . . . I'll be back in a minute."

Brady began to unload his equipment for the demonstration while Maddie and Sarah stood talking. Once Luke reemerged from the bathroom, he helped Brady finish unloading and then setting up. Brady's demonstration centered around how he made cutting boards, like the ones he'd sold in the Bohemia coffee shop in West Jefferson.

Crowds of people flocked to the festival on the cooler-than-normal Saturday in August. Brady and Luke drew in a crowd themselves as they made sure their demonstration was as humorous as it was informative. Brady fielded questions and passed out business cards to those who wanted to know more while Sarah and Maddie handed out some free coasters Brady had made and engraved with his Buck Mountain Woodworks logo.

By one o'clock, Brady had finished and the group had taken a walk around to see what others had to show and had spoken with the director of the festival about a demonstration for the following year. Luke and Brady packed up the truck, then Sarah led the way with Maddie riding shotgun as they made the short trip to the Thomas Wolfe House.

"How cool is this?" Maddie asked as soon as they arrived, joy painted on her face.

"I'll have to admit, it looks better than I thought it would," Luke said with a smile.

The tour took them throughout the home named "Old Kentucky House," revealing the history of the old Victorian and the stories of the author's life. The tour guide knew Wolfe inside out and, from Brady's viewpoint, Maddie held on to every word. Asheville held her Graceland, a yellow-painted house full of memories of the way life used to be.

Maddie pointed to a simple desk that held such importance. "Hey, Brady, check out this writing desk," she said.

"That's pretty awesome," Brady noted, fascinated himself by its patina and the various items displayed on top.

"You could most definitely build one of those," Sarah affirmed.

"Brady, how about you get some practice by building me one like that," Maddie instructed with a wink toward him.

"I'll try," Brady responded. "Snap a few pictures to help me remember what it looks like."

Maddie took pictures from nearly every angle imaginable. The tour concluded, and as Maddie stood talking to the tour guide, asking even more questions, Luke, Sarah, and Brady made their way outside to the porch.

Luke had been fidgety all day. Brady had noticed it fairly early on, and it wasn't just the cups of coffee and the constant bathroom breaks. Luke was nearly always laid-back, but something had him rattled. "What's up with you?" Brady asked.

Luke paid him no mind. Instead, he looked at Sarah and said, "Hey—um—can you get your camera ready, please? And, Brady, can you start a video on your phone and record Maddie as she comes out?"

"Okaaaaaay," Sarah agreed, but she looked baffled.

Brady, however, had a feeling . . .

Within a minute, Maddie appeared around the corner. "This is one of the greatest days of my life," she remarked, her hands raised and her eyes sparkling.

"Maybe this will make it *the* best," Luke said as he reached in his pocket, dropped down to one knee and both Maddie and Sarah gasped. "Madalyn, from the time we went on our first date, I never wanted anyone else. I can say that the woman you are is the woman I have fallen in love with and I want to spend every minute of forever with you." He grinned at her. "Will you marry me?"

Her eyes filled with tears as her hands covered her mouth. She hopped up and down with excitement. She finally dropped her hands to allow Luke to slip the solitaire onto her left ring finger.

"Yes! I love you, Luke," she exclaimed, throwing her arms around his neck. They held each other for a few moments and then, when Luke set her back on her feet, she hurried over to Sarah to show off the ring.

Brady shook Luke's hand, then held up his phone to show that he had gotten the video. "Thought it would be a great memory to do it here with Sarah's best friend taking pictures and my best man filming."

"Really, man? You want me to be the best man?" Brady asked.

"Yes, sir. Who else would I ask, Bradford?"

Maddie looked at Sarah. "Are you going to be my maid of honor?"

"Absolutely," she responded before a shriek projected from her and Maddie pierced the air around them. Luckily, Luke and Brady had covered their ears in anticipation.

"By the way," Sarah said as she looked at Maddie's ring again, "Luke, you have great taste in women and in rings. Did you pick that out?"

"Yes, I did," Luke said, proud of her approval of his choice.

"Maddie, it's beautiful," Brady agreed. "But I have to admit, I didn't realize Luke had become a drug dealer!"

Sarah squinted as she looked up at him. "A drug dealer?"

"He must be selling something illegal to afford that rock," Brady joked.

Sarah laughed. "Oh, I get it ... I get it."

"Do you like it, honey?" Luke asked Maddie, his arm now protective around her shoulders.

"Luke, it's perfect," she assured him as she stared down at her hand.

Brady rested his hands on his hips. "Well, now it's time to celebrate. Sarah, any suggestions?"

"I can think of a couple of options."

"Can we go to your apartment first and drop off our stuff, then we could just all ride together?" Maddie asked.

"Sounds like a plan," Sarah agreed, instructing them to follow her.

They made their way to Sarah's apartment, took their bags in, and got the two-dollar tour. With Sarah's apartment so close to downtown, they walked to a nearby restaurant and ate supper, celebrating the joy of the day. Afterward, they returned to the apartment for a movie before heading to bed.

On Sunday, the group visited Sarah's church with her. She had been attending Biltmore Baptist since she'd settled in, she told them, and she hoped they liked it as much as she. Luke and Brady were blown away by the size of the church, but they were equally impressed by the worship service.

After lunch, they said their goodbyes and headed back home with Maddie in full planning mode on the way home; a wedding awaited. She asked Luke if he was okay with a spring wedding and he agreed. She asked about flowers and china patterns and all the other things Brady imagined young girls dreamed of from the time they knew to.

Brady listened as the miles stretched behind them, nodding occasionally, and smiling at his two best friends who sat together in the back seat, leaving him alone with his thoughts and feelings in the front. He'd managed to keep Sarah at arm's length during the weekend. He'd been successful at pushing his feelings beneath the surface. But now, with only the road before and behind him, and Luke and Maddie in their own world in his backseat, he could only wonder—as Luke and Maddie planned the first day of the rest of their lives, who would be there for him? Who would love him—cherish him—the rest of *their* lives? Would it be—could it be—Sarah?

Only the One who planned his existence could answer such a question.

Chapter 24

AUTUMN HELD ENDLESS PLANNING FOR Luke and Maddie, work for Sarah (according to her texts, which were more frequent in the beginning, but had become less regular), and wonderings for Brady. Now, Christmas Eve returned. Sarah hadn't come home for Thanksgiving, which brought a load of disappointment. He wasn't even sure if she was coming for Christmas. Which may have been why, over the past few weeks, Brady had conceded to go out with a lovely young woman named Maria, who was everything most men could ask for . . . except that she *wasn't* Sarah. She and Brady were also "just friends," but he didn't expect Luke, who was helping him load the Christmas trees that hadn't sold at the downtown tree stand where they'd volunteered throughout the season, to understand.

"So, Brady . . . got plans for Christmas? You and Maria?"

Brady looked up through the fringe of hair that had fallen over his eyes. "No. Nothing with Maria. But, you know, the usual with the family."

Luke slid another tree into the trailer hitched to Brady's truck. "What about tonight?"

Brady added another tree, the scent of evergreen wafting in the air. He paused, not sure how to answer. Avoidance? The truth? He opted for the second. "Christmas Eve services and then . . ." He turned to hoist another tree into the trailer, then mumbled, ". . . and then I'm going to the bench."

Silence permeated the distance between them until Luke commented with, "I thought we were beyond all of that, Brady." The exasperation in his tone was noticeable.

"Still not married," Brady reminded him. "That was the baseline for the promise. Besides, maybe she thought *this* year was the fifth year. Maybe I got it wrong."

"Dude, she's in a relationship, okay? Maddie told me. Some guy named Peter she met at that woodworking festival we went to got her number and called her. They have been dating exclusively for at least two months now."

The news kicked Brady square in the chest, but he managed not to show it. "Not married," he responded, never looking up.

Luke shook his head. "Brady, you're my friend. You're my *best* friend. Please don't set yourself up for this. You're going to get your guts ripped out again."

"I'm not expecting her to show. I don't even think she's in town."

"So, why go?" Luke said, his hands on his head, his tone rising.

"Just have to for some reason." Brady turned to leave. The time to shut down the stand had come.

"What about Maria?" Luke exclaimed. "You guys have been hanging out. Go after her. She's perfect for you and every man other than me in West Jefferson would love to be in your shoes."

"Just friends. Neither of us want to *be* with each other. I think that's why it's easy for us to hang out without it getting complicated."

Luke dropped his head. He slowly looked up at Brady, his voice nearly begging his best friend to go forward in his life by not looking back. "Look. Just drop the trees off the trees at Mr. Johnson's like he asked you to and go home. Hang out with Chelsi tonight. I'm sure she wants to spend some time with her older brother now that she's home."

Brady wanted the conversation to end, so he muttered, "Maybe you're right," trying to reach the finish line to the awkwardness the situation had presented. Because Brady knew . . . he was going to the bench, even if everyone thought he shouldn't. Even if they thought he was crazy and talked about him in their own circles. He knew Luke would never approve, but at that point he had no desire to try to win an endorsement.

Brady muttered a "thank you" to Luke for his help, then drove the five miles to Mr. Johnson's tree farm to unload and give Mr. Johnson his money.

Brady pulled up to the house, hoping to catch Mr. Johnson before he went to bed. Mrs. Johnson had teased Brady that her husband, once the night owl, was now known to retire early, sometimes as early as seven o'clock. He could see the living room light on, smoke billowing out of the chimney, assuring him that Mr. Johnson was still awake.

"Brady, I don't know what I would do without you," Mr. Johnson said before pointing the way for Brady to unload the remaining trees. "If you don't mind, you can throw those trees on the brush pile down in the field, near the southeast corner. But if you can use 'em for anything, you are more than welcome to take 'em with you."

Brady looked back at the trailer, then nodded in agreement. "Actually, I might be able to use them, if you don't mind me taking them."

"Well, then, they're yours."

"Thank you, Mr. Johnson," he said as he shook the older man's hand and turned to go back to the truck, before stopping. "Oh, I almost forgot. Here is the money you made today and the receipt book. We sold five today."

Mr. Johnson let out a chuckle and shook his head. "That's hard to believe, to be honest. We rarely sell any trees on Christmas Eve. Guess folks are so busy nowadays that even gettin' a tree is becoming last-minute shopping."

"You're probably right about that. You know, my mom gets hers up as soon as Thanksgiving is over." Brady opened the driver's door.

"Wait up, Brady. How much do I owe you and Luke?"

"Not a dime. We didn't have anything to do today anyway. I was caught up on my work and Luke needed something to keep himself occupied, so it worked out perfectly."

"Well, I appreciate it."

"Merry Christmas, Mr. Johnson," Brady said as he stepped into the truck. "If you ever need me, give me a call."

"I sure will. Merry Christmas, Brady."

Mr. Johnson stepped back into his house while Brady shut his truck door. A thought crossed his mind to make jewelry boxes out of the trees that hadn't sold. If he stripped the wood, he could make some small boards long enough to piece together. He hated for things to be wasted. The church had been blessed after an ice storm the previous year when Brady took the wood from the fallen trees to build a podium. Rather than throw the wood away or burn it up, Brady wanted to bring life to it.

He pulled around to his barn and unloaded the trees, the smallest of which was six feet tall and the tallest measuring ten. He scanned them to estimate again if there would be enough wood to do what he wanted, then grabbed a retractable tape measure to get more precise figures.

Just stay home.

He unhooked the trailer while trying to convince himself to give up and stay home, the same internal pep talk he had given himself all day. The mind, as he well knew, rarely defeats the heart. The mind also had put up a better fight this year, but at 11:40, he conceded, crawled into the truck and drove into town. The downtown clock showed ten minutes until midnight when he pulled up to that familiar parking spot in front of the town hall. By the time he got out of the truck and made his way to the bench, the clock allowed only five minutes until midnight.

The night was unseasonably warmer than the year before. The mild December had taken everyone by surprise. What was also unexpected was the number of people who were out at this time of night on Christmas Eve. Four teenagers were laughing and cutting up as they walked across the street, reminding Brady of the way of things in high school. He could almost see himself and Sarah, Luke and Maddie in their energy.

The manager of Boondocks startled Brady when he locked up and walked down the street, then on past Brady's truck as he made his way to his downtown apartment. From Brady's place on the bench, he turned to see someone walking past the *Ashe Post and Times* office and, to his left, someone else walked toward the lights display behind the Old Hotel Pub. Still, out of all those walking around, he never saw Sarah, the one person he wanted to see, the one he came to see.

Midnight passed. Last year had nearly killed him. This year, though, the hurt was less intense. He told himself ahead of time she wouldn't show and, this time, he had almost convinced himself not to come.

Almost.

Chapter 25

A WEDDING LOOMED SO EVERYONE involved hurried to finish what needed to be finished before Luke and Maddie exchanged their vows.

Brady was consumed with the arbor, his gift to the bride and groom. Everything had to be perfect, so Brady spent time ensuring that the flowers hanging from its top wouldn't be an issue for Todd, who was to preside over the ceremony.

On the front, Brady engraved "Madalyn and Luke—Love Never Fails" with "1 Corinthians 13" just below their names. He kept it all a secret until the wedding rehearsal, only showing it to Todd when he came by to check the arbor's height and width, and the florist, so they could design the arrangements.

The evening of the rehearsal arrived. The night air was clear and sweet with promise. Maddie wanted the wedding to be held outside next to the pond near Brady's house. Brady had covered the arbor with a carpenter's sheet. As Maddie, Luke, Sarah, and the others arrived, Brady and Todd pulled the covering off, Brady beaming as both Maddie and Luke gasped their approval.

"Not bad, Brady," Sarah quipped, and Brady smiled. "Okay, in all seriousness . . ." She pointed up to the names and scripture and said, "That's gorgeous."

"Thanks," he said as he stared at it for a final inspection. "I was hoping they would like it." Almost as much as he hoped *she* would like it. Or, at the very least, approve of it. And she had.

"Like it?" Maddie said as she hugged him. "Brady, this is more incredible than anything I could have dreamed of."

Chelsi walked up, having just arrived, and tapped Brady on the shoulder. "Good job, big brother."

"Thanks, Chels. Luke, is it okay?"

Luke clapped him on the shoulder. "I thank God for you man, even when you call me crazy names."

"Glad you like it," Brady said with a nod. "You should be proud of me that it doesn't say one of those names I've been known to give you."

Luke laughed lightly. "How much do I owe you for this, man? It must have cost you a fortune and, if not, it surely took up a lot of your time."

Brady turned toward his best friend. "Luke, it's a gift. You've always been there for me and now I had a chance to do something for you."

Before Luke could respond, the wedding director walked up and clapped her hands. "All right, people. Let's get this in motion. We want a beautiful wedding tomorrow and the only way that will happen is if everyone is in their places. So . . ." She looked around until she spotted Todd. "Pastor, you get underneath the arbor. Everyone else, please get up to the top of the walkway."

When they approached the top of the walkway, Brady spotted a few people standing off to the side he didn't recognize. "Who's that?" he asked, not pointing but his gaze serving as the direction of his inquisition.

"Who's who?"

"That guy. The one in the green shirt staring at his phone."

Luke blew out a breath that Brady suspected he'd been holding inside. "I was really hoping you didn't see him. Of course, wearing such a shade of green makes him hard to miss."

"Why?"

"Well, because the green is so bright. The shirt makes him stick out in a crowd. I mean, how could you not see that guy coming," Luke answered, avoiding the other possible reason for Brady's question.

"No. Luke. Why did you hope I didn't see him?"

"Because that's Peter. I was supposed to tell you that Sarah was bringing him, but I kept hoping the relationship would be over before this weekend." Luke's eyes found Brady's. "Please be cool, Brady."

Brady bit the inside of his lip. He shook his head but knew there was nothing else he could do. This weekend was about something more than him or Sarah. "It's all good, Luke. You have nothing to worry about."

The wedding planner called out the marching order like a good drill sergeant and everyone followed. All the while, Brady tried to focus on Luke and Maddie, but the presence of Peter had him distracted. Soon enough, the rehearsal concluded, and everyone left to go to the church for the rehearsal dinner.

Brady stared as Peter and Sarah walked to the car together, their fingers laced together. But Peter never looked up from his phone, seemingly tied to it.

Todd approached Brady. "You okay?"

"I'm great," Brady assured, finally breaking his stare and forcing a smile. "My best friend is getting married. This is going to be great."

He started for his truck, Chelsi running up next to him. "Can I hitch a ride?" she asked.

He smiled at the young woman she'd become. "Of course you can." He only hoped she wouldn't bring up Sarah . . . or Sarah's date.

But, as soon as they started down the drive, she started with, "Boy, that was a surprise, huh?"

"She's not mine, Chelsi," he remarked, his eyes trained on the road, his knuckles white from his grip on the steering wheel.

"I know, but I also know that you were not expecting him to be here."

"It's all good, Chelsi. I shouldn't have expectations for her. She owes me nothing. I mean, I wish it was different, but it's not, and honestly . . ."

"Honestly?"

"I have to accept it."

Chelsi looked away, staring out her window at the landscape that slid past them. For that, Brady was grateful; it gave him a chance to swipe the tear that threatened to escape his left eye.

He loved her. She had stolen his heart a long time ago. He wanted to be with her so badly it felt raw, yet more real than anything he'd ever experienced before. He couldn't hide his feelings and he knew it. He also knew that it would take everything tonight to keep his emotions inside.

"It's okay to be hurt, Brady," Chelsi said from beside him, her voice whispery and kind.

"Hurt was a long time ago, Chelsi. I'm pretty much numb to it now."

"If that were true, Brady, you wouldn't be sitting there pretending not to cry." Brady looked over at her, saw the compassion she felt for him. "She's special to you."

Brady smiled briefly before returning his attention to the road. "I can't think about this right now. Everyone needs to focus on Luke and Maddie, including me."

As they pulled up to the church, he tried to mentally prepare himself for what promised to be long hours ahead. He walked into the fellowship hall and found his seat at the front table for the wedding party.

"You good, man?" Luke asked quietly, looking out at the crowd as he took his seat beside Brady.

"I am great. You good? You ready to get married?" Brady shifted, getting the focus off where Luke was leaning and putting the spotlight back onto the couple who deserved the attention.

"I'm ready. I love her. I mean, honestly, I love her in ways I can't even explain."

Brady smiled sincerely. "I know you do."

The sweet, Southern aroma of barbecued pork and chicken filled the air. In true Luke and Maddie fashion, sweet iced tea was served in Mason jars. The bridal party stood in line to fill their plates with the perfect meal for the perfect night. The meat was complemented by green beans, baked beans, roasted red potatoes, and baskets full of buttered rolls. In short order, the room filled with laughter and joy along with a spirit of love and unity.

Todd sat beside Luke and Brady. Though it was an unusual spot for the minister, the three had such a bond it was only fitting they sit together.

"Hey Todd," Luke called out while they were eating, "do you think you can get this thing done in about ten minutes tomorrow?"

Brady chuckled as Maddie leaned over from her place to glare first at Luke, then at Todd. She shook her head, disagreeing.

"I think I'd better do what Maddie wants me to do tomorrow," Todd responded.

"Good choice, Todd," Maddie chimed in, letting a smile sneak through. Sarah, who sat next to Maddie, leaned over and laughed, and for a moment, it seemed to Brady that the four of them were a team again, and that Peter, who had been relegated to another table, wasn't there at all.

"Hey Todd, do you remember that white water rafting trip we took?" Luke asked.

"I can't forget it," Todd said, shaking his head.

"Nantahala," Sarah said.

"It was drizzling, and that water was so cold. I remember when we put the rafts in the water, I thought I was going to freeze. When we all fell out, it was like falling in ice water," Brady recalled.

"Yep. Remember the last rapid?" Luke asked.

"Bodies everywhere. I still haven't figured out how we got everybody out of that river," Sarah commented, laughing at the recollection.

"I remember feeling frozen from the waist down," Maddie recalled. "Then, I lost my left shoe and Luke lost his right shoe."

"My toes still hurt when I think about that trip," Luke added. "In fact, my feet are freezing right now just talking about it."

"The heat in the van still sticks out in my mind," Todd pointed out. "We kept it on high the whole way home trying to thaw out."

Brady leaned back, relaxing in the conversation. The banter. After tonight, he knew, life would change. After tomorrow, Luke and Maddie would be a married couple. They'd have children and, in time, moments like these would be nearly extinct.

But they'd always have their stories. And they'd always have their memories.

Chapter 26

BRADY STOOD AT THE ALTAR that beautiful spring day to hear vows of love and an unending commitment of two souls. Though he wished it could have been *his* day, he settled for the moment Sarah walked down the aisle in a purple dress, and a smile stretched across his face. She looked at Brady and the scene was nearly what he had envisioned for years. Only in his mind, she was wearing white.

For a moment, their eyes locked. Who knew what was running through her mind? But he imagined her coming to meet him, there . . . at the altar and before God. Before he could focus too hard on the moment, he looked toward the ground and stared at the grass beneath his feet. He couldn't go there. It would only make the hurt worse.

Sarah took her place; she remained in his peripheral vision, but a single blade of grass became his focus.

The music played and Todd called everyone to rise. Now Brady refocused to watch Maddie, then glanced casually to see Luke's reaction to his bride.

"What do you think?" Brady whispered.

"I'm about to have a smokin' hot wife," Luke said.

Brady and Todd fought back laughter.

"She's yours forever, Luke. You take care of her," Todd reminded him as Maddie drew ever closer to the arbor.

She walked down that aisle as Pachelbel's "Canon in D" played in the background. Her father attempted to wipe away the tears as they walked, each step drawing closer to giving away his little girl.

Almost at the altar, she looked at Luke and mouthed the words, "I love you."

He beamed as bright as the abundance of sunshine provided by the Almighty that day. She was radiant, her joy shining with each step closer to her dream. After her father handed her off to Luke, he took his seat and the ceremony continued.

"Luke, will you promise to love her, honor her, promise to be there for her in sickness and in health, forsaking all others, until death do you part?" Todd asked.

"I do," he said.

"Maddie, will you promise to love him, honor him, promise to be there for him in sickness and in health, forsaking all others, until death do you part?"

Brady had a clear view of the bride whose face now streaked with tears, and he knew . . . what and whom she had dreamed of as a little girl stood before her in the man who was his best friend.

"I do," she said.

"I now pronounce you husband and wife. Luke, you may kiss your bride."

They shared a sweet, simple kiss in front of their family and friends, then walked up the aisle to the applause of those who loved them. As the best man, Brady escorted Sarah, the maid of honor, up the aisle, passing her boyfriend Peter who had chosen a seat alongside the aisle. As they passed, Brady looked his way, surprised to see that, even in this most solemn of occasions, his phone remained the captor of his attention. Brady glanced at Sarah and offered a smile he knew didn't reach his eyes.

"I'm sorry, Brady," Sarah whispered after they were clear of Peter. "I thought they told you he was coming."

"Nothing to be sorry for," Brady replied, never wiping the fake smile off his face. His hand slid over hers, cupping it. "Sarah, you don't owe me anything."

"I know, but I feel like it bothers you that he is here," she replied.

"I promise you, Sarah. I'm fine. If you're happy, then I am happy for you." His words were a lie, but hopefully, this one time, she wasn't so good at reading him.

"Can we have a dance later?" she asked.

Not this again. He still hadn't recovered from a dance on prom night nearly a decade ago.

"Sure."

At the top of the aisle, they were pointed to a place where the pictures would be taken. Forty minutes of various poses felt like forever but once that concluded, they went to the reception, which had been set up in the open barn Brady had repurposed for events such as this.

As the introductions were made by the DJ, once again, Brady was joined to Sarah. Luke and Maddie were introduced, the food was blessed, and the newlyweds began their first dance. Seeing Peter standing alone near one of the farthest tables, Brady decided that the best thing to do, at the very least, was to get to know the guy. Give him a chance. Because if Sarah liked him . . .

"It's Peter, right?" Brady asked as he approached.

"Yeah, I'm Peter," Peter responded, extending his hand. "You're Brady, right?"

Brady shook his hand. "Yeah. So, I heard you met Sarah at the woodworker's festival. What type of woodworking do you do?" Brady asked.

"Not really a woodworker per se. I'm an artist. I primarily paint but I also do some sculpture pieces. I went to the festival to learn some tricks for working with wood and perhaps to find some inspiration." He attempted a smile that Brady didn't buy for a minute. "Always trying to get inspired for new pieces."

"Well, that sounds pretty cool. I work with wood, so we went down to do a demonstration."

"Yeah, I watched your presentation with Luke. That was a nice cutting board you made."

"So, what type of paintings do you—uh—paint?"

"I like abstract," Peter answered. "I want someone to figure out a painting on their own, to interpret it from their own worldview and mindset rather than painting something that leaves no room for interpretation. My work is featured in galleries in downtown Asheville. If you are ever in the area, stop by and see them. I'd like to hear what you think about the pieces."

"I'll have to do that. If you look as you drive through town, we have murals painted on the sides of some of the buildings," Brady noted, trying to connect with someone he obviously had little in common with.

Peter's phone, his lifeline, rang in vibration from his front pocket. He retrieved it, declined the call but responded to two texts before answering. "Yeah," he said, finishing the second text with a push to the SEND button. "I saw those murals. They were nice."

"So, what type of sculpture are you looking to make?"

Peter looked back to his phone, which had lit up in reply. "Uh— don't know yet." He gave Brady a half smile. "Sorry, man."

Brady turned to go only to see Sarah walking toward them.

"What are you guys talking about over here?" she asked, smiling.

"Just asking Peter about his artwork," Brady answered, his voice laced with disapproval at the disrespect of Sarah's date. Again, Peter never looked up. His work on his phone seemed to be more important than anything else.

"He is an amazing artist," Sarah slid her arm around Peter, who didn't acknowledge what was said or her presence at all.

"Yeah, he told me they feature his work in the galleries in downtown Asheville. I told him to check out the murals in town."

"I showed him the murals. My favorites are the ones Stephen Shoemaker painted, especially the winter scene with the church."

"I have always loved that one as well. Stephen said it took him about four months to finish it."

Sarah tried to engage Peter in the conversation. "You know, Peter, Brady's cutting boards are sold in the coffee shop and he made the arbor for the wedding today."

"Uh-huh," Peter commented as he slid the phone into his front pocket.

"He also makes furniture for many of the people in the town. They commission him to make all kinds of things," Sarah pointed out.

"Uh-huh."

"Yeah," Brady responded, mocking Peter's lack of interest in the conversation, "I guess it's not as exhilarating as your paintings are."

Peter's phone vibrated again and, again, he pulled it from his pants pocket and looked at it. "If you will excuse me, I need to return this call." Peter turned away, never waiting for any response.

Sarah looked perturbed, but rather than pounce on the opportunistic moment that had presented itself, Brady simply redirected her. "Looks like Luke and Maddie's first dance is about over." He pointed to the buffet. "We need to get our food and get to our places. It won't be long before we have to give the toasts."

Sarah smiled in gratitude, linked her arm again in Brady's, and said, "Let's do it."

When the time came for the speeches to be delivered, Sarah stood first and straightened her dress before addressing the crowd. She tapped her knife against her glass to get everyone's attention, then raised the glass.

"Maddie and Luke," she began, "the honor of being maid of honor is truly an honor that a more honorable person should be given." Sarah grinned and the crowd laughed.

Sarah turned more fully to her best friend. "Maddie, it was in my room on a Saturday night in high school that you told me that you liked Luke. I remember asking, 'Luke Perry?' and you smiled and said, 'No . . . Luke McMasters.' I clearly remember my response." She paused for effect. "'Are you crazy?'" The crowd laughed again, and Brady bit his lip against the urge to poke Luke in the back. "That night, you talked about the qualities I had not seen in him before and did so in a way that told me that your *like*—and eventual *love*—for him was sincere." Sarah took a breath and smiled again. "Maddie, we have shared almost everything—lipstick, deodorant, hair spray, gum, and once, you even—ahem—borrowed my underwear." Sarah waited until the laughter subsided, then said, "But all joking aside, I am so glad that you asked me to share in this moment today. I am so happy for you that you have found your soulmate . . . even if it isn't Luke Perry." She giggled. "Just kidding, buddy," she directed to Luke as Brady reached for his water glass to take a quick sip before his turn came to give the best man's toast. "You are two blessings in my life, and I wish nothing but blessings upon your lives together . . . Madalyn . . . and *Lucas*."

Brady nearly spit water across the table but swallowed quickly and laughed with the others. He then took a second to prepare himself as Sarah hugged Maddie and Luke before returning to her seat.

Brady rose and began to speak. "For those of you who don't know me, my name is Brady and I have never worn Luke's underwear." Again, the crowd laughed. "I've known Luke my whole life and, as the best man, I am supposed to get up and say nice things about him. That being said, no one go to the bathroom cause this won't take long."

The laughter continued.

"Luke," he continued, "from the time we were little boys, you were the brother I never had but always hoped for. You gave me someone I could annoy, which I believe I have excelled at." Luke nodded in agreement; his smile as broad as Brady had ever seen it. "I remember when you decided to ask Maddie out on a first date." Brady turned to the crowd. "He told me what he was going to do and said, 'Dude, she is so hot. If she says yes, I am going to marry her.' I truly thought he would get shot down, but in an act of mercy, Maddie said yes to a date. As their relationship grew, I stood stupefied as he asked her to marry him and she actually said yes again. I thought he was crazy all those years ago but turns out he was right. Luke, you are a good man. You are a brother, a friend, and someone I will always respect. Life presents us with moments. Some are just fleeting but others begin a series of moments that last forever. I thank God that your moment with Maddie was a forever moment. May God bless you, Madalyn and *Lucas*, each day of your lives."

Brady hugged both and sat again at his place at the table. When the dancing began, the DJ called for the wedding party to share a dance together. The bridesmaids found their groomsmen for the special dance, which meant Sarah and Brady would share another moment together.

As the music began, Sarah pulled closer to Brady. The choice of song could not have been worse for Brady. DHT's "Listen to Your Heart" played, the same song they had danced to at the prom all those years ago.

"Where's Peter?" Brady asked.

Sarah shrugged. "He's still on that call, I guess. Or maybe another one."

"Oh."

"Peter is a big deal in his career, you know? He's important." Sarah's words came across as more excuse than reason for Peter's behavior.

"You are important, too," Brady noted. "I hope you see that one day."

Nothing else had to be said. He was absolutely going no further, leaving her the opportunity to pore over the words. Brady prayed the song would end soon. He wanted to dance with her, sure. And he wanted to be with her, of course. But they weren't together. He had to leave the moment behind; carrying it forward would only make things worse on him.

As the night wound down, Maddie and Luke left to go on their honeymoon. They'd stay a night in Charlotte, then fly to Miami where they'd board a ship for a cruise. Brady and a few others began the cleaning up process, loading up tables to return to the church and filling up trash bags with garbage left behind.

Around eight o'clock, Sarah came up, Peter in tow, to say goodbye.

"Y'all heading out?" Brady asked.

"Yeah. We're going to try to get home before midnight," Sarah responded.

Brady finished tying up the trash bag, then extended his hand to shake Peter's, smiling graciously, even if forcibly. "Peter, it was nice meeting you."

"You too, Brady," Peter acknowledged as he shook Brady's hand.

"Guess I'll see you the next time you're home," Brady said to Sarah, not opening the door to calls or texts he doubted would come, and if they did, would only last long enough to leave him shattered in their absence a week later.

"Guess so," she said as she hugged him.

Peter and Sarah turned to walk to their car, leaving Brady behind, a cinched trash bag gripped in his hand. He watched as they got in— Peter not opening the door for Sarah—and continued to stare as the car started, backed away, and then headed down the drive.

Chapter 27

Sarah texted a couple of times over the summer, the conversation reflecting the distance that had developed, both physically and emotionally. Both were no more than check-ins to see if he was still alive.

Brady understood, even if he didn't like it. Time has a way of creating separation. The hands on a clock continue moving. Life happens and that which isn't front and center fades a little more with the passing of each day.

"Hey, Brady," Maddie called one day as she entered his workshop.

He lifted his safety glasses. "Maddie, how's it going?"

"Need a favor," she responded, pulling a slip of paper from her pocket as she drew closer.

"Sure. I'll help in any way possible," Brady said, brushing the sawdust off his arms.

Maddie unfolded the paper, then handed it to Brady. "Do you think you can make one of these for Luke's birthday?"

Brady took a minute to study the craftsmanship of the work on the paper. He was a perfectionist and to mimic something, he had to ensure he had the ability before he made any promise to replicate. "I think so."

"Luke has wanted a new rocking chair for our front porch, and he commented on how he liked this one."

"Luke wants a rocking chair?"

"Yes, he does."

"That man is getting old. Look at what marriage has done to him already," Brady joked.

"Sometimes, I think he's an old man myself," Maddie agreed, laughing.

"Hey, Luke can rock in the chair and yell at kids to get off his lawn," Brady said, imagining such a scene unfolding.

"That's too funny. Hey, look . . . his birthday is only a month away. Do you think you'll have enough time to get it ready by then?"

"I think so. I have a lot of orders, but I am pretty sure I can get it done before then."

"Thanks, Brady. I owe you one." She turned to leave.

Brady paused a minute, then called out, "Hey, Maddie."

"Yeah?"

"Have you heard from Sarah?"

"Yeah, I've heard from her here and there." Her words sounded guarded, concealing, anything but the normal Maddie.

"How is she?"

"You know . . . busy as always. Started her own graphic design business and you know what that's like, being a business owner and everything."

"Don't I?" he agreed. "Is she still with Peter?"

"Yeah." Maddie crossed her arms and sighed. "Look, Brady, she is engaged to Peter now. I told her that she needed to tell you herself. I can only assume that she hasn't done it."

The words slapped Brady across the face, but he blinked to keep his emotions from showing. "No, she hasn't said anything. To be honest, I've barely heard from her since your wedding."

Maddie took the steps necessary to return to Brady. "I'm really sorry, Brady. You know that Luke and I, we—we love you more than anything in this world. We really, really do. But Sarah, well, she's gone on with her life. Maybe it's time you move on with your life, too, buddy."

Maddie's tone broke Brady's façade. The news wasn't upsetting; it was devastating. The heart of him hurt. He had heard from others that he needed to move on. Now, Maddie of all people was saying it and she had a reason to say it.

He leaned against the workbench and stared at the floor. He wasn't mad at Maddie. She was probably right. "I know, Maddie, but I *truly* care about her. I really do."

"I know you do."

A tear streamed down his cheek. "I've known for a while that it wasn't going to happen between us. I've—I've pretty much given up already. I guess I was just . . . wondering."

"You okay?"

Brady sighed. "Yeah, I'm good," he said, turning toward the bench, not wanting Maddie to see his hurt any longer. "I'll get the rocking chair done before his birthday."

"I appreciate it," she said as she turned again to walk away. She stopped as she got to the door, "Hey, Brady?"

He looked over his shoulder at her.

"You know you are a special guy. Can I just tell you that, as far as Luke and I are concerned, Sarah is missing out? And Brady, believe me when I say I have told her that more than once." She paused to allow her words to sink in. "If you need me for anything, Brady, anything . . . you call me."

Brady nodded, unable to respond. Maddie left the shop to go home and Brady went back to work on a bench he was making for the town of Sparta. Benches had become his specialty, because, as he said, "Every bench has a story."

Go on with your life. There is something greater out there for you.

But with each cut, with each nail being driven in, and with each step completed, before his eyes was another reminder of a place, of a person, of a moment in time, and of a hurt that wasn't going away anytime soon.

Chapter 28

As Christmas approached, Brady chose to ask no one about Sarah. He thought about her. Even when he didn't want to, there she was . . . in his thoughts. But he never spoke her name, giving the appearance that he had finally "gone on with his life."

The streets bustled throughout the season, as was the case every Christmas in the town that, to Brady, seemed the doorway to heaven. And, as the weather chilled and the lights twinkled, Brady continued with his charade while continuously looking to see if she made any appearances.

"What's your plans for tonight?" Luke asked Brady. Once again, the two friends helped Mr. Johnson by volunteering at his tree stand and, once again, Christmas Eve had arrived, which meant returning the unsold trees to their owner.

Brady carried another tree to the trailer and heaved it on top of the others.

"The usual . . . but I'm going to eat supper with Todd and Melanie. After that, I am going to bed . . . as early as possible."

"Really?" Luke asked, a hint of skepticism in his tone, a tone not lost on Brady.

"Yeah, *really*. Mom wanted an end table for the house. With all the other things I've had to work on, I haven't had time to do it. I was up until five this morning finishing it so she would have it for Christmas, and I am flat-out whooped."

Luke threw a tree on top of the pile on the trailer. "You do look rough today."

"All-nighters used to be easier than they are now."

Luke smiled, not able to resist. "I guess you're an old man now."

Brady grinned, but was more than ready to fire back at his best friend. "Hey. You're the one I had to build a rocking chair for this year. You've got no room to talk, Luke Donald."

"Who is Luke Donald?"

"Pro golfer. Don't you love how I have some names you have never ever heard of in your life?"

"To be my best friend," Luke replied, pulling off his glove and leaning against the gate of the trailer, "I sure do find you awfully annoying."

"And yet you keep coming back for more," Brady said, throwing the last of the trees on the trailer, clearing the lot just in time as the snow began to fall in large, magical flakes.

Brady climbed into his truck and pulled the seatbelt across his shoulder. He rolled down the window to speak one last time to Luke, but Luke spoke first.

"Be careful driving. It's only going to get worse, they say."

"Will do, Mom," Brady joked. "Seriously, Merry Christmas, buddy. I appreciate you."

Brady pulled away and headed home, six trees on the trailer attached to the truck. He dropped the trees and the trailer, then took the money to Mr. Johnson. His running around brought him to Todd and Melanie's at six o'clock, precisely when he was supposed to be there.

They enjoyed the evening. Melanie prepared a feast and Brady ate enough for the town. He watched Todd and Melanie, the way they moved around each other, the way they looked at the other. And he couldn't help himself; he wished he had something like what they had. But he would have to wait until someone came along.

Brady made it home by nine o'clock. The snow had begun to pile up and his eyes grew heavier with each tick of the clock. He turned the television on, hoping to catch a weather report.

"If you don't have to travel tonight, don't," the meteorologist said.

"Stay home. Stay warm. Stay safe. The snow is not going to let up anytime soon, which means that road conditions will only further deteriorate."

Brady watched as the totals projected grew by the hour. The first call was a projection of around five to eight inches; the last report said no less than ten inches would fall overnight.

Christmas Eve.

One of the worst nights of the year to be alone.

Just go to bed.

The grandfather clock chimed the tenth hour. Brady made his way down the hall, threw on some pajamas, and lay down in bed, then turned on the television in time to see the last few minutes of *It's a Wonderful Life.*

Didn't seem so wonderful.

Brady turned off the television, rolled over to turn the lamp off, and saw the picture.

There was something there. There had to be. Why would she make such a promise and have him agree to it if nothing was there?

The chimes at eleven o'clock told him only that his mind was stronger than his body. His eyes burned with exhaustion. His arms were sore, as was his back, and normally, he would fall asleep without hesitation.

He lay still fifteen more minutes knowing . . . he was going. But why? He couldn't tell.

By eleven forty-five, he sat on the bench, huddled in his coat under the shower of snowflakes, and stared off in the distance. She wasn't coming. What was he even trying to prove at this point? No one knew he was there. But he sat there, hoping for a Hollywood ending.

No cars.

No people.

The silence was so great, it was almost haunting.

In the distance, a horse-drawn sleigh rode by, someone cashing in on all the snow that fell. He could see lanterns on the sides of the sleigh, casting a shadow on what appeared to be a lone figure under a blanket. He sighed; at least he wasn't the only one alone.

"It's not going to happen," Brady said aloud to himself.

Midnight came but no one else appeared.

He made his way home, cold and soaked from the twenty-minute snow bath he'd endured. He took a hot shower and dressed again for bed. As he prepared to crawl in, the picture caught his eyes. Brady grabbed the frame and threw it against the wall. For Christmas that year, he decided, he would give himself the freedom to forget by removing the nightly reminder.

It was his first step toward freedom.

Chapter 29

Staying in bed would be the celebration he'd enjoy most. But today was Christmas. The season of joy and peace meant Brady had to give up the hope of staying home, fake joy for the day, and all while hiding the unrest inside him.

He felt like death. He *looked* like death. And he was certain his mother and father would be the first to notice. Still, at the appointed time, he pulled up to his parents' house, lucky to have even gotten there, considering the weather and the way he felt. This was more than disappointment. Brady was old enough to know the beginnings of the flu.

He forced himself out of the truck, picked up the gifts as if he were lugging sacks of concrete, and struggled with each step. He had aged overnight, and sickness did not benefit him in the least. And he had also aged because the innocence and hope of what could have been was now lost.

"Son, you look horrible," his mother, as if on cue, noted as he walked in.

"Merry Christmas to you, too, Mother," he said, forcing a smile in an effort against ruining the day.

His dad walked in then, arms outstretched to take the gifts and put them under the tree. But he stopped. "Brady? You okay?"

"Never better." Brady handed the gifts over, then sneezed. His head ached now; the last thing he should have done the night before was sit on a bench in the middle of town during a snowstorm.

Brady plopped down on the couch, reached into his back pocket for a handkerchief, and silently wished for the day to draw to a close. Maybe, if he got home in time, and could get to bed soon enough, he'd sleep until January.

"Honey," his mom said, her cool hand now on his forehead, "you need some hot tea."

He sneezed again. Nodded. Sneezed again, then fell over on the sofa, his head cushioned by a throw pillow. "Ugh," he said, and eyed his father, who studied him from across the room.

Chelsi bounced down the stairs, chipper as always on Christmas morning. She took one look at Brady, turned, and headed for the kitchen.

"When did this start?" his father asked him.

"Felt a little run down for the past few days but I got wet and cold last night and woke up this morning wishing I was dead."

"Well, you've come to the right place. Your mother will have you fixed up in no time."

Chelsi peeked around the door. "Mom says to come to the kitchen. Tea's ready."

Brady struggled to walk to the kitchen. The scent of hot tea mingled with the aroma of his mother's home-cooked breakfast, but he was in no mood for the latter. He all but collapsed at the table. His mom placed the mug of tea in front of him as his dad took his usual place. Brady glanced over at him as his fingers looped around the handle, knowing instinctively that his father had caught the words that would give him away.

"Why did you get cold and wet last night? Mr. Johnson has a shelter for you guys to sit in."

Brady didn't say anything but blew tiny waves across the top of his tea. Even he felt like a fool for what he had done the night before.

"You went to the bench again, didn't you?" Chelsi asked. She slid into her chair, one foot tucked under her.

Brady dropped his head and remained quiet.

"He went. I can tell because he isn't saying anything," Chelsi answered for him. "*Brady.*"

But his mother slid her hand along his shoulders, the light touch of her nails bringing gooseflesh to his skin. "Brady, hon, why did you go out there?"

He sat silent. He couldn't make sense of it and didn't have any strength left to defend his choices. Chelsi reached for her juice, then returned it without taking a sip. She stared at her brother who made momentary eye contact with her. "She's engaged, Brady. You know that, buddy."

"I know that," he finally spoke. He was embarrassed and even a little ashamed. There were no words. He felt like someone who had lost touch with reality. He took a sip of tea, felt it scald the tenderness of his throat.

His mother walked to the stove and returned with a plate of biscuits she placed in the center of the table. "Son, look, I know you truly care about Sarah. I love Sarah, too. But it's not happening. Seriously. I'm afraid you're going to look back one day, see the years wasted, and wish you had them back."

Brady couldn't help but smile, mostly at Chelsi. Mom had spoken in the tone Brady and Chelsi called "the mama tone." The voice that said, "I love you, but I also know what's best for you." Her deep Southern accent could get your attention on its own and when she spoke on matters of the heart, she had a special gift to get attention.

Brady sipped at the tea again.

"Do you know how many young women around here want to be with you, Brady? Nearly all of them," Chelsi noted. "Sarah's great but . . ."

"A bird in the hand . . ." his father noted.

But they weren't talking about birds. And he couldn't *make* himself fall in love with anyone else.

His mother kissed the top of his head. "Think about it, son. She's moved on in her life and now you have to do the same."

Brady picked up a biscuit off the plate, hoping a move toward the food would lead to mouths full of food around the table with no room left for lectures or opinions. Wasn't his father ready to say grace before the food grew cold instead of grunting every time someone said something?

"I'm moving on. I am."

"Doesn't look like it," Chelsi said as she rose from the table to pour herself a cup of coffee. "Doing the same thing you have done before isn't a sign of somebody who is moving on or going forward in life."

His mother sat now, a sigh slipping from her lungs. "And Brady—"

"Mom, I'm moving on. I *will* find someone, and you will have grandkids one day. Chelsi, most of the women you are talking about have more in common with unicorns than they do with me. The others are married. And Dad, please don't grunt. Nobody knows what that means," Brady shot back.

For long moments, no one moved. If the sudden outburst had come from Chelsi, it would have been expected. Understood. But not from Brady . . .

He turned his head and sneezed again, then coughed. His mother stood. "I'm getting you something for that," she said, then left the room.

"Tell you what," his father said once she'd gone, "let's eat, open our gifts, and then, son, you'd best get home and get some sleep. Unless you want to camp out in your old room."

Brady glanced up at his dad, eyeing him sideways, knowing that—somehow, some way—his father understood. "No, sir. I'll fight this at home."

By lunchtime, Brady crawled into his own bed in his own room. The curtains were pulled tight, keeping light from filtering in. With any luck, he could stay right there under the mound of covers for as long as possible.

Moments before he fell into drug-induced slumber, his eyes rested on the picture frame that lay shattered on the floor. Eventually, he would get around to cleaning it up, just like eventually he would get around to *moving on*. His last thought before drifting off was how similar his heart was to the frame, broken and fragmented.

The shattered pieces of the frame would be easily cleared away, but his heart and his life would take much longer to put together again.

Months later, the maples downtown began to bloom as spring announced its arrival, and, in keeping with them, Brady pressed for a new season in his life. The mourning that had dragged through the deadness of winter began to give way to the hope of new life.

But would it be a new life for Brady?

Chapter 30

SARAH BATTLED WITH THE INVITATIONS for the wedding. She longed to avoid the awkward but also knew that not inviting Brady was just *wrong*. Maddie was her matron of honor, just as Sarah had served as maid of honor for Maddie, so the obvious thing to do was to call her. Get her advice.

The phone rang twice before Maddie answered. Sarah didn't spend needless time with questions about life or the happenings of the week. Instead, she cut right to the point.

"Should I invite him?" she asked.

"I don't know, Sarah."

Sarah paused to choose her words carefully. "I mean, I *want* him to be there. Brady has been a huge part of my life. But I don't want it to be awkward, not on my wedding day."

"I'm sure Brady's not going to do anything to make it awkward."

Sarah picked up a nearby pen and doodled on the envelope her electric bill had come in. "I really don't know what to do."

"Why don't you call Todd? I'm sure he can tell you the right thing to do. I mean, this is a weird situation and knowing Todd, he'll probably take care of the issue for you."

"Yep. Calling Todd," Sarah agreed, almost hopeful that Todd *would* take care of the issue for her or at least give some guidance to help navigate the murky water.

"What does Peter say about Brady coming to the wedding?"

Sarah hoped to end that line of questioning quickly. Although Peter had met Brady, there were some aspects that had been left unsaid. "He doesn't care one way or the other."

"*Really?*"

"Yeah, well, I didn't exactly tell him *everything* about Brady."

"Why not, Sarah?"

"Because I didn't think it would help anything." Sarah drew a square, put a smiley face in it, then added sprouts of hair as Maddie sighed from the other end of the line.

"Sarah, I love you, but you are rolling the dice on that one. What if Peter finds out that Brady has been in love with you all these years? I mean—okay, let's just get real here—what if he finds out that there is a part of you that will never let go of Brady because, deep down, that's who you *really* want to be with?"

Heat rose in Sarah and she slammed the pen down. "That is not true, Maddie."

"Sorry."

"I moved on. I have. Besides, I can never be who Brady wants me to be."

Okay, so, yes . . . Brady was waiting for her. But Brady was worthy of someone far better than she. And when she looked in the mirror each and every morning, she saw someone nearly worthless. She had made compromises, and there was no turning back on those decisions. She had made mistakes, ones she kept to herself, ones for which there could be no forgiveness.

"Sarah," Maddie began, her voice quiet. A single word with a lifetime of meaning between them. Maddie was her best friend. Always had been and probably always would be. She knew her like the proverbial book. And Sarah knew the next question before Maddie spoke it. "Who do you think Brady wants you to be?"

"He expects perfection, Maddie. The prom queen who is everything you see in a movie, but no one can live up to in real life."

"When has he ever said anything remotely like that?"

"He doesn't have to," Sarah answered as she sat back in the chair. "I just know it."

"Sarah, if you don't want to be with him, that's perfectly fine. I mean, you need to be with whoever it is that you want to be with. But whatever you do, don't shut him out with the wrong perspective. I'm telling you, you're completely wrong about what you think he wants or what he expects of you."

Sarah had no retort. Rather than carry on the conversation and risk a slipup in explaining what had happened in the years since she and Maddie spent every day together, she shut down the conversation. "Maddie, let's just forget it. I'm happy. He's happy. No need to make a mess of things. Look. I'll call you next week and we'll go over everything for next month."

At first Maddie didn't answer and, for a moment, Sarah wondered if they had lost connection. But then, Maddie answered with, "Sounds good."

Sarah laid her phone on the desk and turned to the computer again. She had work to do but as she sat there, she couldn't drown out Maddie's words or the question that remained unanswered: should she invite Brady?

She rose from her chair to stare out the window for a minute. Truthfully, she wanted him there. What she didn't want was the awkwardness she knew she would feel. She walked back to her desk and called Todd, hoping that the youth pastor who had given her insights earlier in life could give her the answers or an out altogether.

"Hey, Sarah," the friendly voice of the pastor greeted as he answered the phone.

"Pastor Todd," she responded, her worry in her voice noticeable even to her. "I don't know how to handle a situation I've got."

"Okay. Well, hopefully, I can help," Todd answered. The sound of a car door shutting revealed to Sarah that Todd was about to drive somewhere.

"I'm getting married."

"I heard. Congratulations," Todd said. "He better treat you right or Melanie and I will have to step in." Todd laughed and Sarah laughed with him, appreciating the protectiveness from someone who'd been there for her after her father had left. "So, what's the problem?"

"I don't know what to do about Brady," she said.

"Okay. I'm sorry, but I'm not sure I know what you mean."

Sarah was hoping to hint around, allow Todd to say what the problem was without her saying it so she could eventually feel like she was not the only one thinking it could be an issue.

"Well, Brady and I have a history, you know?" Sarah explained.

"Okay," Todd answered, giving no insight as to what he knew or didn't know.

"I mean, we've never really dated or anything like that. I mean, we're close. We're like really close to each other."

"Okay," Todd said again, as if he was prodding her to talk it out and expose what was truly bothering her.

She picked up the pen and, this time, scribbled on her desk calendar, wishing the words would come out. "I just don't know what to do. Should I invite Brady to the wedding or not?"

The pause that came seemed to last an eternity. "I'm not sure I can answer that."

"If I invite him, I'm afraid it will be awkward. If I don't, then I might hurt him again." Those words brought a tear to her eye. *Hurt him again.* She had done it before. She didn't want to do it again.

"Again?"

"I think I hurt him before, Todd, and I don't really want to do that again."

"How so?" Todd asked.

What could she say? How could she answer without telling Todd about the promise she'd made Brady? The promise they'd made each other. "We got close. I pulled away. I think he has fallen deeper in love with me than I ever felt for him and honestly, Pastor Todd, as much as I feel for him, I could never be the perfect girl he wanted or deserved. The prom queen grew up, and she's been anything but an angel."

"You know, Sarah, I think you are quite mistaken about Brady."

"I think he wants me to be who I was at eighteen and it's all changed." Sarah could hear the strain and frustration in her own voice and, even though she wanted to control it, she couldn't. The dam had burst and the water now gushed through her words. "I can't be that girl again. Life has changed. *I* have changed."

"I think you're wrong on that."

"How can you say that?" she asked.

"Because, Sarah, I think you have projected on to Brady everything that you think everybody else wants from you. Some of it may even be the expectations that you have of yourself. Brady's different. Always has been. He just wants people to be who they are."

"Believe me, Todd. I am *not* what he wants. I'm not good enough for him."

"I wish you could see things differently," Todd replied. "*Yourself* differently."

"So . . . should I ask him to come?"

"Can you handle him being there?"

Sarah stopped for a moment. There it was, the question that made her face her fear. What would she do if he came? How could she stand there, facing an altar and a preacher, Peter by her side, knowing that somewhere in the congregation Brady sat staring at her? "What do you mean?"

"You're marrying another man. If Brady is there, will it take your attention off the man who should have your attention—all of it—for the rest of your life?"

Sarah knew then what she could not do. There was no way she could invite Brady. Though closure was needed on a relationship that had no definition, inviting Brady was not going to bring closure, only distraction, and further pain.

"I understand and truthfully, Todd, I appreciate how you said that. You're absolutely right."

"Hey, can you call Melanie and tell her what you just said? You know, that part 'you're absolutely right'?" Todd chuckled, Sarah knew to lighten the burden of the answer.

"No can do. Melanie needs me as reinforcement against you," Sarah said with a laugh. "Todd, thank you again. You have always had a way of helping me to see things more clearly."

"No problem at all."

They said goodbye and Sarah continued with her day. She was indeed relived that she had a reason *not* to invite Brady, but even so, a niggling of sadness taunted her.

Why?

Because she wanted him there, that's why.

But . . . *why?* That, she didn't know. But knowing someone loves you, she reasoned, gives a desire to have that person there. For everything.

And one thing Sarah knew . . . she knew that Brady loved her.

Chapter 31

MADDIE AND LUKE DIDN'T HIDE where they were going as they packed up and headed toward Asheville that Friday. Brady's invitation had never come and, as he noted to Luke and Maddie, "At least I didn't have to make a decision as to whether I was going to go or not. That decision was made for me."

After hearing of the wedding and the obvious omission of his name from the guest list, Brady had called and asked Todd to meet him for lunch. If Maddie and Luke were heading to Asheville for the following day's wedding, then he'd treat his pastor to a meal.

They settled on Blackjack's and, once there, they both ordered a burger, fries, and a Coke. As they waited for their meals to come, Todd folded his arms and rested them on the table between them. Then, leaning in, he asked, "You okay, Brady?"

Brady shrugged then waited to answer because their server had returned with their drinks. Once she'd moved away, he said, "I guess so. But to be honest, I am a little hurt by what happened. I mean, she didn't invite me at all." He stared at his Coke, watched the fizzing around the ice, then pulled the paper from the straw left next to the glass, and jabbed it in.

Todd repeated the same motion but took a long swallow of his drink. "I get it, man," he said then. "But look, sometimes it's best to keep yourself away from things that could only make it worse."

Brady rested back against the seat and sighed deeply. "Maybe so."

Todd wrapped his hand around the glass and turned it in a small circle. "Do you want to talk about something else?"

He did. And he didn't. What he wanted—what he needed was—

"Here you go, fellas," the server said as she slid two plates of steaming food before them. "Burgers all the way with an order of fries. Can I get you anything else?"

Brady eyed the ketchup bottle on the table, then looked back up and smiled. "No. I think that's it. Todd?"

Todd nodded. "We're good. Thanks."

Todd offered to bless the food and Brady let him. After the "amen," Todd reached for his burger, biting into it as though it were his last meal. "Now that's a good burger," he mumbled around a mouthful.

Brady nodded, then reached for a fry that didn't quite make it to his mouth. "Have you talked to her?" Brady kept his eyes focused on Todd, wondering how he would react to the question. After all, Todd's job meant he had to be honest. If he lied as the pastor, the entire credibility of his career could be called into question. But he also had a responsibility to keep whatever had been said between himself and Sarah.

"Yeah."

"Did she say anything to you about it?"

Todd sighed. Noticeably. Brady knew that Todd didn't want to have this conversation. His body language alone revealed that much.

"She did. Brady, you know I can't say much, but I want you to know—I think you *should* know—she was torn as to what to do."

"And what did you tell her?"

"The same thing I would have told you if the roles were reversed."

Now Brady leaned forward. Flipped the top off the ketchup, then squeezed a dollop onto his plate. "And that was . . ."

"I told her that she had to be the one to decide. But I also told her that if she's going to marry that guy, he has to be her focus. If you being there was going to pull her attention off the man she was marrying, she shouldn't invite you . . . or she shouldn't marry him."

Brady sat back again. His initial reaction was irritation at what Todd had said to Sarah. Maybe she would have invited Brady if Todd hadn't said anything. But the more he mulled on those words, the more he swirled a fry around the mound of ketchup like a figure skater on ice, the more he decided not to react but to think about it.

"Look, Brady," Todd continued, setting his half-eaten burger back on the plate. "I would have told you the same thing and I mean it. Marriage is a big deal, man. If you're going to make the leap, then you have to do it without looking back."

Brady looked up, his focus now on Todd's eyes. At that moment, Brady knew, Todd was speaking to him as a friend, *not* merely as his pastor. "You're right," he admitted.

Todd started to say something, but before he could, the server returned. "Is everything good today, guys?"

"It's great," Todd replied.

"Everything's good," Brady added.

She smiled, then went to the next table. For a while, Todd said nothing and neither did Brady. Then, "I'm glad I'm not there," he said.

"I think you're just saying that." Todd picked up his burger and continued to devour it.

"No, I'm serious." He reached for another fry. He was hungry now. And a little bit thirsty.

"Okay. Tell me why."

"Full disclosure?" Brady asked. He wiped salt from his fingertips with his napkin, then started for his burger.

Todd nodded.

"I have gone to the bench every year. She's not there. This year, I let her go. She is not mine. Do I care about her? I do. Will I always care about her? I'm sure I will to some degree. But at the same time, isn't it loving not to hurt someone or put them in an awkward position?" Brady asked.

Todd chewed as he thought. "Yeah, I think so," he answered.

"So, at the end of today, what has really changed? Nothing. And at the end of tomorrow? Nothing. I mean, other than she'll be some other man's wife."

"Nothing," Todd agreed.

"Pretty much. Is this what I want? No, it's not, but so what. Life is life. I wish it was different, but it's not. Nothing I can do will change it." Sheer hopelessness enveloped him. His heart. Because he knew. Whether anyone else did or not was inconsequential. *He* knew. This had not been a teenage puppy love that had carried on a few extra years. This love had cost him. Sleepless nights. Tears. The joy of hope and the hopelessness of rejection. Years had evaporated yet, he also knew, his love for her was the one consistent in her inconsistent life.

"You're not going to do anything stupid like jump in your truck and drive over and try to stop the wedding, are you?"

Brady forced a smile. "There is no reason to."

"Are you sure?" Todd asked, before smiling back. "Because if you are considering it, I have to try to stop you."

"Nothing to worry about, Todd," Brady said. He took another bite of his burger, then spoke around it. "So . . . farmer's market at church? What do you think?"

"I'm good with it. Have you gotten enough people to help?" Todd asked and Brady could almost see the relief on the pastor's face. Another subject would serve them well.

"Yeah. This will run smoothly. No worries," he assured.

After the meal, they stepped out the door and said their goodbyes. Todd made his way to his car and Brady walked down the street to his truck. Inside, he started the engine, but sat for a moment, mulling over the conversation he'd had with Todd. The pastor's words made sense but there was still pain attached to them. At least now he knew that Sarah had not decided on her own to keep him from being there. That fact, alone, kept him from completely shutting her out.

Chapter 32

FOR BRADY, ONE OF THE greatest blessings found in the majesty of the mountains was the peacefulness of the rivers and streams that flowed throughout. Regardless of the circumstances, the chaotic cascaded its way downstream. He needed a reprieve from the troubles of his mind and the river would be the place to wash the turmoil away.

So, as Sarah prepared to walk down the aisle, Brady went fishing for trout on the South Fork of the New River. This place knew him well, although better when he had been younger. He had little time to fish anymore. But today fishing was a priority, although a line of irony kept skipping through his thoughts, telling him that even though he had a pole in his hand, he had missed the catch of his life. As the day went on, he realized the trip had become more about forgetting than about fishing.

Brady sighed, his shoulders straining as he cast his line. He'd left his phone behind in the truck in case Todd got it into his head to call and check on him, so—at least for this time of reprieve—he had nothing and no one to interrupt him. The fishing spot was remote. Overhead a few birds called to one another. The breeze rustled the leaves of the trees behind him. The occasional fish jumping and the rocks upstream rippled the deep blue of the water. But, other than that . . .

He wished he'd never met her.

He knew it was a lie, but it was therapeutic, even if for a moment.

After an hour or so of fishing and catching nothing, Brady found a good-sized rock near the water's edge and sat. He kicked off his shoes and socks, then slid his feet into the cool water while he scanned the beauty of all that surrounded him.

And he remembered.

Meeting her that first time on the bench. All their hours of talking. Going to church. Seeing her after Aiden had hit her . . . the fight that ensued. Dancing with her at prom. The scene from the bench that summer night in August before college crept in a time or two. He could remember the smell of her perfume and her hair and could hear her voice, speaking the words that had changed his life—no, halted it—that very night.

"If neither of us are married after college, we'll meet back at the bench on Christmas Eve, and we'll get married," she had said.

But he wasn't on the bench. He sat on a rock. And it was over. Sarah and Peter were probably at the point of their vows by now, he figured, not altogether sure what time the service started, but figuring he was close.

So, it was over. She was married. And he? He was angry.

Hours passed, but he had no desire to move. He had nowhere to be. At least, for these hours, he was as free as the waters flowing over his feet, meandering downstream. He lay back, crooked his arm behind his head, and closed his eyes. Maybe he could just stay here forever. Maybe he could . . .

"Brady! *Brady!*"

Brady opened his eyes, the azure blue of the sky arching overhead. For a moment, he was unsure as to where he was, but the water licking at his feet reminded him. They'd grown ice cold and he sat up, removing them.

"*Brady!*"

Brady reached for the discarded shoes and socks, then turned to scan the landscape behind him as a lone figure ran toward him. "Todd?" A million scenarios jogged through Brady's mind as he ran toward him. Had something happened to one of his parents? Was something wrong with Chelsi?

By the time he reached Todd, the pastor was bent over, his hands on his knees, his chest rising and falling as he tried to catch his breath.

"What? *What?*" Brady said, bending over as well.

"Where's your phone?"

"Um . . . in the truck." He looked toward where he'd parked, although the truck was blocked by trees and other foliage. "What's happened? Are my parents okay?"

"Yes . . ." Todd panted. "But you have to go. They need you."

"Who? My parents? Chelsi? *What* happened?"

"No, Brady, stop."

"Then what is it?"

"It's Sarah. She needs you."

Brady could feel his initial panic turning to impatience and rage. "Are you serious, Todd? Whatever this is, it's not funny." He started to turn away, but Todd caught his arm even as he caught his breath.

"Brady, Luke's been trying to call you. Maddie's tried to call. I called, but . . . Listen, man. Sarah's fiancé was killed in a car accident this morning on I-40."

Brady took a step backward, stared at the ground beneath him, saying nothing. His emotions swung from fear to anger to grief. Grief for Sarah. Dear God, the pain she had to be feeling.

"Where is she?" Brady asked, never looking at Todd.

"Maddie and Luke are with her at her apartment. Luke said she needed you, so I took off to find you."

"All right. I'm going." He looked toward where he'd left his fishing gear. "Let me get my stuff together. I—I won't even go home." Now he looked at Todd. "I'll touch base with you guys when I get there."

"Oh, no. We're going too. Melanie and I will meet you there. And your parents."

"My parents?"

"They're good people."

"I know."

"Brady?"

Brady answered with silence, the rhythm of his breathing echoing within his chest.

"Go home. Get a shower. Pack some clothes. You can't go like this . . ."

"I—"

"Luke and Maddie are there. Sarah needs you *there*. That means you need to calm down. Drive sensibly."

Brady nodded. "Got it."

But he hurried to his truck anyway, pulled out frantically, then rushed home, showered, shoved a change or two of clothes into an overnight bag, and then shot a text to Luke, asking for the address. After Luke returned with the necessary information, Brady headed to Asheville.

Chapter 33

NOT TWO SECONDS AFTER BRADY knocked on the apartment door, Luke answered. "Come on in. She's in the bathroom."

Brady stepped into the narrow foyer. "I talked to my mom a little while ago," he said over his shoulder. "They're heading this way. Should be here soon." He took a breath, peered into the living room where Todd and Melanie sat on an L-shaped overstuffed, cream-colored sofa with large, inviting pillows tossed on both ends. He gave a brief wave in their direction and they both nodded, saying nothing.

The apartment was small and neat and decorated in varying shades of cream and black, from the massive, framed black-and-white prints hanging over the sofa to the off-white floor baskets filled with throws that spilled from the tops. The scent of vanilla and fresh-brewed coffee hung in the air and invited him to take a step farther in to see a galley-style kitchen where Maddie stood at the sink, rinsing out a coffee cup. "Hey, Brady," she said, her voice barely a whisper.

After Luke shut the door, he gave Brady a brotherly hug. "I'm glad you could come," he said. "She's pretty bad off. Why don't you have a seat in the—"

Just then Brady heard a door open and he turned to see Sarah stepping into a short hallway. Her hair spilled in curls around her shoulders and she wore an old pair of sweats and tee shirt that had seen better days. It also appeared several sizes too big for her. Brady drew in his breath; the shirt had been Peter's. No doubt.

Sarah started down the hall, her feet bare, her toenails painted baby pink, and then, almost as if she sensed Brady rather than saw him, she looked up. Her face, devoid of makeup yet still beautiful, was swollen and blotched. Her eyes and lips puffy. And, seeing him, she whispered, "*Brady.*"

He moved toward her, and she grabbed hold of him, sobbing. He held her, his muscles tightening at the dead weight of her until her knees seemed to go out from under her. They slumped to the floor where she continued to weep. Brady pushed back until he leaned against a wall, carrying her with him, his legs and arms wrapped around her, his hands holding her head against his chest. But he said nothing, all the while never taking his eyes off her.

"Brady," she finally said. "Brady."

"Shhh. I'm here."

"Brady, this *hurts*," she cried out. "This hurts!"

Brady kissed the top of her head as his thoughts reverted to where they'd been earlier. Yes, he had been there the night her father left her mother. And he had been there when Aiden had broken up with her and in the aftermath of Aiden hitting her. He had seen her broken before, but this time . . . This time she was completely shattered.

After a few minutes, after her crying had settled to hiccups, he kissed the top of her head again and said, "Sarah, let's get off this floor, okay? Let's go into the living room."

She nodded. He stood, bringing her with him, then, with an arm firmly around her, he led her to the side of the couch opposite Todd and Melanie. By now Luke and Maddie had walked out onto the adjoining patio, leaving the sliding door pushed wide to allow the evening's breeze into the room.

As soon as Brady eased her onto the sofa, her head rested on his shoulder where it remained until her breathing became rhythmic. Deep. He looked over at Melanie and mouthed, "Is she asleep?" and Melanie nodded.

Brady shifted slightly, more for her comfort than his own, and he noted that—small as she'd always been—she seemed frailer now, almost childlike in stature. "Where are her parents?"

Melanie discreetly cleared her throat, then whispered, "Her father wouldn't come unless he could bring his latest girlfriend . . ."

Brady's eyes widened. "*What?*" he mouthed. "Not even to give her away?"

"No," Todd answered. "Miss Susan is with Peter's mother and father. They—uh—they don't have a lot of family or church support, so . . ."

"We told Miss Susan we'd take care of things here," Maddie concluded. "She'll be by later, I'm sure."

Brady nodded, then glanced down at Sarah, his heart wrenched. This poor girl. Had so little gone right for her?

After a while, Maddie came in and asked if she could fix him a cup of coffee and he nodded. An hour passed and, as shadows filled the room, the doorbell chimed. Sarah stirred in his arms as Todd pushed off the sofa and said, "I'll get it."

Luke and Maddie returned to the living room, Luke drawing the door closed as Maddie pulled a rust-colored drapery across it. "Sarah," Maddie said, "Can I get you anything?"

Sarah sat up straight and shook her head as Brady righted himself. When he looked up, his parents entered the room and Sarah stood. "Oh, my gosh," she said.

"I'm sorry about what happened," Brady's father said as he gave her a quick hug.

"Sarah, honey," his mother added, "we are so sorry. And we are here. What can we do to help?"

Sarah stepped into her arms. "Nothing at all," she said. "I can't believe y'all drove all the way down here."

"Well, you're pretty special to all of us," his mother assured her.

They made small talk then, everyone settling into their place. The sofa. An occasional chair. But Sarah returned to him, laid her head against his shoulder again. Brady noted his mother's expression. His father's concern. And he knew this wasn't just for Sarah. This was for him, as well.

After a while, Todd stood, Melanie alongside him. "We'll get going," Todd said.

Brady looked up. "Where? Are you going back to—"

"No," Melanie answered. "We got a hotel room down the road a ways."

"Where?" Brady's father asked. He also stood, Brady's mom with him.

"Country Inn."

"We booked there, too." He looked at Brady, who started to stand, but Sarah grabbed hold of him.

"You're not leaving, are you?"

"Ah—" He looked at his father who said, "Brady, you can bunk with us if you'd like."

"No," Sarah said, her voice nearly begging. "Luke and Maddie are staying here. You can too." Her eyes met his, large and pleading and, once again, filling with tears. This time he looked at his mother. He needed some distance. Sarah needed him.

"Sure," he said. "I can stay."

His mother sighed. "Brady," she said, keeping her voice low and steady. "If you change your mind, just call us."

He smiled at her. "Thanks, Mom."

"Why don't we all meet here for breakfast in the morning," Todd suggested.

"Good idea," Brady's mother said. "Don't worry, Sarah. We'll bring everything."

❄ ❄ ❄ ❄ ❄

A short while later, Sarah's mother arrived, looking as worn out as Brady had imagined she'd be. She and Sarah retreated to Sarah's bedroom, then returned after a short while, Miss Susan excusing herself for the rest of the evening. "I'm going back to the hotel and try to get some sleep," she told them. "My daughter has insisted on it." She gave Sarah a quick hug, then added, "I'll see you all in the morning." She gave Brady a weak smile and he wondered if he alone had perceived it. Almost as if she had let him know that she was quite aware that she was leaving her daughter in the hands of those who loved her beyond circumstances or choices.

By eleven, Luke and Maddie headed to bed, Luke declaring that he was worn out from the day. Before turning in, Maddie asked Sarah again if she needed anything.

Sarah shook her head. "No. Brady's here if I do."

And then they were alone, and, for the first time, Brady worried about what to say. Offering whispered assurances in a roomful of people was one thing, but this . . . this was different. They were in her home. The home she may have been planning to share with Peter. There was a sanctity here, a silent understanding between friends. But there was also an awkward silence. The reality of what had taken place that day collided with the distance of a year and a lack of an invitation.

Sarah curled up near him on the sofa, keeping a respectable distance. She tucked her feet under her before asking, "Are you angry with me, Brady?"

His eyes found hers. "Angry? No. Not angry."

"Hurt." It wasn't a question.

"Yes. Hurt."

"But do you understand why . . ." She pulled her hair over one shoulder, then rested against the back of the sofa.

"It's not important," he said.

"I honestly did not mean to hurt you."

"Sarah," he said, then shifted to see her better. "That's really not a problem. At least not one we need to talk about now. I'm here because I'm worried about you. Okay? I hate you're going through all of this."

Her eyes glistened with fresh tears. "Yeah, me, too."

For long seconds they stared at each other until Brady broke the silence with, "Have you talked to his parents? Peter's?"

"Yeah," she said, then looked down at her hands. "I have to meet them at the funeral home tomorrow morning at eleven."

"Want us to go?"

"If y'all don't mind. It would help to have all of you guys there."

"Then, that's what we'll do," he said with a smile of reassurance to her and she smiled in return.

Brady glanced toward the television—a flat screen mounted on the opposite wall. "Want to watch a little television?"

"As long as it's mindless," she said, then reached into a wicker basket under the coffee table and pulled out a remote. She handed it to him, pulled one of the throws from a basket, then settled in close to him again. "That button right there," she said, pointing to the red PWR button.

Again, she laid her head on Brady's shoulder as he scrolled through channels until he found reruns of *Friends*.

"How's this?" he asked.

"Perfect," she said. Then, "Oh, this is the one where Phoebe has the babies. I like this one."

Brady nodded, grateful that, at the very least, it wasn't the one where Ross married Emily but said Rachel's name at the altar.

Within a few minutes, Sarah's body slumped against his and, without having to ask, he knew she'd fallen asleep at the end of a day that had extracted the last ounce of energy her body had to offer. Though he was anything but comfortable, he didn't move. If she was comfortable and able to forget everything for at least a few hours, he would gladly stay in that position. All night, if necessary.

Brady turned the TV's volume to low, pulled the throw closer to her shoulders, leaned his head against the back of the sofa, and closed his eyes, his last thought being that, once again, he was there when she needed him.

Chapter 34

THOUGH A NEW DAY HAD dawned, the reality of the previous day's tragedy had not changed. Pain still existed. As planned, everyone returned for breakfast at Sarah's, Brady's father and mother toting large bags that emitted delicious aromas.

Brady joined his parents in the kitchen where his father poured orange juice into small glasses and his mother set packets of jam next to fat, steaming biscuits that appeared to have already been slathered in butter.

"Hey, Mom . . . Dad . . . thanks," Brady said.

"You're welcome, son. Wish we could do more."

"This is—" he nodded toward the food—"enough. And coming here."

"Brady," his father said, and Brady turned toward him. "Are you okay? With all this?"

"I'm fine, Dad," Brady answered, knowing he had just lied to his father, but knowing, even better still, that his father knew it. Knew it and understood.

"Well, then," his mother interjected. "Chelsi called last night. She's coming in today and staying at the hotel with us. We are all going to stay through the funeral if that's okay."

"Absolutely. I know Sarah will appreciate it." Brady grabbed two plates and started for the small dining area off the kitchen, then stopped. "We're headed to the funeral home at eleven. I called Todd and Melanie earlier and they said they'd go too. Do you guys want to drive behind Sarah and Miss Susan and me?"

"No, honey," his mom answered as she handed two of the plates to his father. "I think, if it's okay with Sarah, I'm going to stay here and cook. Your father and I will get some groceries and make everyone a late lunch/early supper."

"Mom, you're awesome," Brady said, then stepped over and kissed her cheek.

"Don't tell her that, Brady," his father said. "I'll have to hear about it all day long."

✳ ✾ ❋ ✾ ✳

The only one not eating was Sarah, who'd been in her bedroom nearly the entire morning. When she finally emerged, she'd dressed and fixed herself up, enough to make Brady stare for a moment.

"Sarah, honey," Brady's mother said, "I saved you a biscuit. I can warm it up for you."

"No, thank you," she said, then, noting the concerned looks surrounding her, said, "I'm just not hungry right now, guys."

Sarah and her mother rode with Brady to the funeral home and, on the way there, Sarah explained the plan for the day. When they arrived, Brady helped both ladies out of his truck, then met the rest in the parking lot. They stood for several moments, none seeming to know what to do next, until Sarah took a deep breath, sighed, and said, "Well, let's go on in."

Peter's parents were waiting inside the elaborate parlor of the funeral home, both standing beneath a chandelier that, to Brady's estimation, weighed more than him. Sarah approached them, introduced everyone as quickly as she could, beginning with Brady and concluding with Todd. "He's my pastor," she said, then added, "Or, he was."

Todd slid an arm around her shoulder and said, "Always."

"Well," Peter's mother said, her hands clasped low in front, "I have asked, Sarah, that there not be an open casket. I hope you understand."

Brady watched as Sarah's face drained before she answered, "Of course. Whatever—whatever you want."

A man, tall and broad-shouldered, joined them then. "Folks, I'm Jim Thompson, director here." He motioned to a door behind them. "Would you like to follow me into the conference room?"

And, with that, they all followed behind, each finding a seat around a massive cherry table with craftsmanship Brady couldn't help but notice. Within the next two hours the details were worked out. Todd was asked to officiate the funeral as neither Peter, nor his parents, had a home church. Peter would be buried in the city cemetery of his native Asheville, while the funeral would be held in the chapel of the funeral home. Peter's parents were gracious but were understandably devastated. Todd wrote down what they wanted said about Peter at the funeral to make sure it spoke of the life he'd lived. Brady looked on at Todd with awe, watching and listening as he asked all the appropriate questions, pausing only when the director, who obviously knew his business, interjected. "We need to expect a good-sized crowd," he said. "Peter was well known. Well loved." His focus then went to Sarah and to Peter's parents while, inside, Brady felt a knife sliding into his gut.

Brady also noted that Sarah said little, letting Peter's parents decide nearly everything. Though she had been a part of Peter's life for nearly two years and was about to be married to him, she told Brady on the way back to her apartment, she never felt like she was a part of his family.

"There was a disconnect there," Sarah explained to her mother and Brady. "Even Peter was somewhat distant from them. They were nice to me and all, but I never felt . . . included."

Brady nodded, but said nothing.

"Their son seemed to have a lot of business and social connections," Miss Susan interjected, "but I got the sense last night that his parents are not overly outgoing." She paused and Brady wondered if she was done. But then she added, "I really felt for them last night." Her voice cracked. "I just cannot imagine losing my only child."

Brady nodded again, but still said nothing.

After a few moments, Sarah said, "You're awfully quiet, Brady."

Brady flexed his fingers on the steering wheel. "There's not a lot I can say, Sarah." Then, to ease the sting of his words, he glanced over at her and added, "That was nice of you, considering everything, that you invited his parents back to your place."

Sarah shrugged. "I knew they wouldn't come."

Brady's parents had the table set, ready for the group to eat. Fried chicken, ham, green beans, rice, rolls, and salad had been dished up. Once they sat, Todd was asked to pray. "Father, though we do not understand everything, we turn to You today to give strength, to give comfort, to bring peace to the soul. Bless this food and the hands that prepared it and be with Sarah at this time. We lift her and Peter's family up to You in the days that are to come. In Jesus' name we pray, Amen."

Each voice around the table echoed the "Amen," and Brady noted that while there was pain in the room, there was also a presence. Then, not long after they began filling their plates, Chelsi arrived, hugged Sarah, then made her way to say hello to everyone at the table.

"You didn't have to do all of this," Sarah said. She looked at her plate, a plate barely filled with food.

"We wanted to, honey," Brady's mother said.

"At least let me pay you for the groceries."

"Absolutely not," his father interjected. "This is something we can do for you and want to do for you." He pointed to her plate. "You better get you something to eat, and more than that."

"He's right," Maddie said. "Remember, Sarah, we are here to help take care of you."

Later, Todd, Brady, and Luke stepped outside to the patio. Brady slid the door closed behind him. "How are you going to preach this one?" Brady asked as the three sat around the outdoor table.

"Have to use what they tell you and go from there," Todd responded before taking a sip from the tea he'd brought with him.

"This is why I would never want to be a pastor," Luke commented. "This is the absolute worst-case scenario."

"Depends on how you look at it."

"What do you mean?" Luke asked.

"You're right that this is a tragedy, it's gut-wrenching, and truthfully, it is hard to preach the sermon of someone you hardly know. But the fact is, at this funeral, I'm betting there will be a large number of lost people. So, here's my one chance to tell those people about Christ," Todd explained.

"Didn't think about it that way," Luke said.

"Still wouldn't want to do it," Brady noted.

Chapter 35

SARAH STOOD IN LINE AT a funeral on a day when she was supposed to be in Europe with her new husband. The four-o'clock visitation was set for a two-hour window before the six-o'clock service. The line stretched out the door by three-thirty, guaranteeing an exhausting experience for the family and especially for Sarah. Each person who came through the line meant well and offered words of comfort and encouragement, but few could understand the devastation of the hearts affected.

Brady stood off in the distance with everyone else, making sure he had clear sight of her at all times in case she needed him. Then, after the guests had found their seats in the pews of the chapel, Peter's family led the way down the aisle, followed by Sarah, her mother, Maddie, and Melanie. Sarah had asked specifically that they walk in with her and sit with her so she wouldn't be alone. Brady, his family, and Luke sat near the back so that when they came back through, they could join the rest easily.

"I couldn't even imagine," Luke whispered to Brady.

"Me either," Brady said, his eyes focused on the back of Sarah's head.

From the front of the room, a man played *Amazing Grace* on a bagpipe.

No matter how many times Brady heard the song, when played on bagpipes, chills ran down his spine. A couple of artist friends spoke in memory of Peter. They tossed around the words "gifted" and "creative" while sharing nights of galleries and shared interests. They spoke of what they saw in his work. Then Todd shared the stories as they were told to him. Some brought laughter while others, a few tears. Speaking on the brevity of life, this being the proof that too many believed the Scriptures had no relevance to them until that moment comes. From the looks of all those in front of them, Brady realized Todd had, indeed, connected with all who were in the chapel that day. Todd also reminded everyone that the time given to each is a gift and to make something of each moment, realizing that the next breath is anything but an assurance. He implored each person to live for something more than the here and now.

As the time came to close the service, he spoke on Psalm 23. "'Though I walk through the valley of the shadow of death,' David wrote. For a shadow to be there, light must be present, for without light a shadow cannot be cast. Today, we may feel as if we are in the darkest moment of our lives. But there is still light, and that light is Jesus. He's here and has promised to be with us." He gave the plan of salvation and closed in prayer before the family made its way out the door, followed by a swarm of people.

Because a private burial had been scheduled for the following day, people stood inside and out, talking for nearly two hours as the night grew longer.

"God must really be with you," Maddie said to Todd.

"He is," Todd replied with a solemn look upon his face.

"You did great, man," Luke acknowledged.

"Hey, how long are y'all staying," Todd asked.

"I think until Wednesday," Maddie explained. "We have to get home by Wednesday night. Miss Susan has planned to take off the whole week."

Todd turned to Brady. "How about you? How long are you going to stay here?"

Brady wasn't sure. He wanted to say, "As long as she needs me," but that would just open more doors. Doors he didn't even want to think about. "Probably another night. I guess I'll go to the burial tomorrow then head back home."

"Well, since she has you guys, we are probably going to head back to West Jefferson tonight," Todd explained.

"Y'all be careful," Luke commanded as they exchanged hugs and said goodbye.

Melanie and Todd made their way over to speak to the family and then to Sarah before leaving for the late-night drive up to Ashe County. Brady's parents had already returned to the hotel with plans to leave in the morning, while Sarah's mother returned to get her things so she could transfer them to Sarah's.

But Brady, Chelsi, Luke, and Maddie waited on Sarah. When she finally broke away, she declared that she was starving and then asked who wanted to go to her favorite pizza place in downtown Asheville. Everyone raised their hands and declared, "Me."

"So, when do you go back to Southport, Chelsi?" Maddie asked as a server placed several large pizzas in front of them. Overhead the music was loud. Around them, chatter rose to a fevered pitch.

"Tomorrow, unfortunately," Chelsi said over the din. "I've got a lot of work to do on Wednesday. I wish I could stay longer to help." She pulled a slice of the pie from the whole, then lifted it carefully to her lips.

"How far of a drive is it to Southport from here?" Sarah asked.

"Umm . . ." she said as she swallowed, covering her mouth in the process, "it's about six hours."

"You need me to drive with you?" Maddie asked. "I could definitely use a few days at the beach."

"Nice try, dear," Luke interrupted before any plans could take shape that included him going to Southport to pick up his wife.

"Come on down," Chelsi welcomed Maddie before turning to Sarah. "Sarah, if you want to get away, you can come with me."

"Think I'm going to go home for a few days. Thank you, though," Sarah replied.

"West Jefferson?" Maddie asked. "I thought your mom was staying with you."

"She was," Sarah said, folding a piece of pizza in half and aiming it toward her mouth. "But when I get back to the apartment, I'm going to insist that we return to West Jefferson. Like, tomorrow after the burial."

"Okay . . . well. We were going to stay here until Wednesday if you needed us to, but that works."

Sarah sat for a moment, as if frozen in a thought. "I just really want to get away. What do you think, Brady?"

Brady nodded. "You know what's best for you," he said.

Chapter 36

THE SAD THING, BRADY THOUGHT at the graveside, was that Peter's life was now contained in a dash. His and Sarah's hopes and dreams, buried like a time capsule, one that would never see the light of day again.

Maddie had been asked to read a poem at the graveside service, Brady to give a prayer, which he hardly wanted to do, but did, and a friend of Peter's sang "You Raise Me Up." The casket was lowered into the ground and, for a moment, a misty mountain rain fell.

By noon, everyone was on the road headed back to West Jefferson. Brady just wanted to get home, get to his workshop, and begin work on some project. Which project? He didn't care. Any project. Anything, if it was vastly different from what had been the last few days.

He needed the smell of sawdust to replace the smell of her perfume. He needed the joy of finishing a toy chest or a cutting board rather than the sorrow of an unexpected death. He needed to build again, not just a project, but the rebuilding project he had been assembling before the tragedy struck—his new life. He felt a bit remorseful, as if his need to get away from the situation was selfish, but he had been beginning to heal and healing was necessary for a life that previously lay in ashes.

Brady drove straight home and unpacked. The workshop was calling his name and though he was drained from the previous days, he made his way out to the shop and resumed working on a chair he'd started before leaving for Asheville.

Be there for her but don't fall for her again.

The words echoed over and over in his mind. Knowing she was

in town, mere miles away, only placed her closer to the forefront of his mind.

Meticulously, he sanded the chair again, carefully smoothing the imperfections by hand, taking pride in the smoothness. The feel of the wood would dictate the comfort of the rocker. His chairs weren't mass-produced. They were rustic, unique, and carefully crafted.

His hope of being swept away by his work was proving to be false. Worry crept in as he wondered how she was feeling. Pain shot through his system; he hurt for her. Love beat in his heart. She was his dream, but he had to keep that love at a friendship level, for her sake. For his. The aggravation of it all proved too great, the turmoil too troublesome, so only an hour after he started, he quit for the night. He walked to the house, took a shower, and decided to watch a movie on television before going to bed.

The movie played, but he wasn't watching it. More than anything he wanted to reach out to her. If not a phone call, a text. Then again, maybe she was asleep. Or, if not asleep, perhaps she needed some space. And, even if he called, he didn't know what he'd say.

Besides, if she needed him, she'd call. She always had in the past.

He just wanted peace. The incessant movie dialogue began to get on his nerves so rather than sit and slowly go insane, he decided to go downtown for a walk, hoping it would clear his head. Help him relax. On the way, he called Luke.

"Y'all home?" he asked after Luke answered.

"Yeah," he replied. "What's up, man?"

"Y'all heard anything?"

"No. And I'm giving Maddie the phone. You are about to ask questions that I have no good answers for," Luke said, then called Maddie and handed her the phone.

"Hey, Brady."

"Hey, Maddie," he replied. "What do we do?"

"Nothing," she replied. "I think we let her come to us. She's with her mom and to be honest, she probably needs some room from all of us to catch her breath and adjust."

"You're probably right. I just don't want it to be said that I wasn't there."

"It won't, buddy," she said. "You were there, as you have been all along . . . when she needed you the most."

"All right. Y'all have a good night."

"You, too. Hey, Brady?"

"Yeah."

"Are you okay?"

"I'm fine. A little bit tired but I'm fine." He sighed. "I just hate it for her. I'll help if I can, but I'm like you, let her come to us when she needs us or wants us to be around."

Brady hung up the phone and continued to drive downtown. The stores were all closed, so only a few people would be out. Brady found a place to park easily, then walked down the streets and tried to forget. But as he approached the bench, as he knew he would, all he could do was remember.

He sat down on the very bench that had led to so much disruption. Had he not been passing by all those years ago, he wouldn't be where he was now. He stared off into the distance, his eyes focused on the nothingness beyond the buildings. Such was the direction his and Sarah's lives were headed in, he reckoned.

Again.

Chapter 37

TWO THOUGHTS ENTERED SARAH'S MIND as she pulled up to the sprawling house. One was how the sprawling house was the dream of her mother and father but stood only as a reminder of dreams shattered after her father left. Even after all the years had passed, she hadn't quite adjusted to his absence there. He'd filled every room then and, like a ghost, continued to do so. Even when he wasn't there, he was.

Her second thought was how alone her mom must have felt in such a large house every night since. Especially after Sarah had left for college. She hadn't considered her mother's loneliness until she was in the grips of it herself.

Life has a way of doing that, she figured. No one understands another's problem until they experience the same. Sarah now knew what her mom had experienced for years, and though the cause for the loneliness was different, its pain was surely identical.

Sarah locked her car by habit, then walked to the front door. Halfway there, it opened, her mother's silhouette outlined within. "You made it," she said. Sarah stepped into her mother's embrace, inhaling the scent of her, which brought comfort she'd not expected. "Hungry?"

Sarah shook her head. "No. Just tired."

Her mother took her face in her hands. "Why don't you go on up to your room? Rest a while. We can get your luggage later on."

Sarah's old bedroom had remained primarily undisturbed since the days when she roamed the halls at Ashe County High School, a notion that made her both wince and smile. She closed the door and, for a moment, imagined that she was sixteen again. Her and Maddie giggling on the phone for hours. Going to church with Brady. Aiden . . .

As if dating Aiden had not been difficult enough, what life had taught her in the years since was a lesson in hurt, pain, and broken dreams. She had run from this place to find a new beginning but here she was again. She had retreated to it when she needed security again.

The corkboard hanging over her old desk drew her, and she walked over to it to look at the pictures still pinned there. She smiled at the images of brighter days and happier moments. Voices echoed as she relived those moments.

"Honey, can I get you anything?" her mother called from the other side of the door.

Sarah turned as though she'd been slapped. "Ah—no thanks. I'm going to lie down for a while if that's okay."

"Of course it is, honey. I want to take care of you and help you, Sarah, but I don't want to suffocate you. Just tell me what you need. The worst thing I can do is make all of this worse."

Sarah sighed, picturing her mother standing on the other side of the door, one hand pressed against it, a look of worry on her face. She crossed the room and opened the door slowly. "I know, Mom. I just really want to sleep. No matter how much sleep I get, I stay exhausted."

"I understand." Her mother entered the room almost timidly, then sat on the bed. She crossed her legs and clasped her hands in her lap. "Do you remember when your father left?"

"Can't forget it." Sarah turned toward her mother.

"All I wanted to do was sleep. When I was awake, him leaving us was all I could think about. When I slept, I escaped, if only for a few hours. So, Sarah, I know . . . your body needs rest right now. What you are going through is a lot worse than what I went through."

A lone tear slipped down Sarah's cheek. "Thank you, Mom."

"One thing I know. Time may help one to breathe again, but time cannot and does not erase completely what happened."

The tears came more freely now. She moved over to the bed and instantly her mother's arms found her as hers found her mother. "Does it get better, Mom?"

"It doesn't go away. It just becomes manageable."

The answer had not been one Sarah wanted to hear, but at least her mother was honest with her. If she expected that in a week or a month or even a year the pain would simply vanish, she may be disappointed when time didn't bring the relief. "Thanks, Mom," she said after several long minutes. "Okay, I think I'm going to lay down for a while. I just can't even think right now."

"Tell you what," her mom said as she rose from the bed and wiped away her tears. "I'm going to go and make some supper. If you get up, we can eat together. If you don't, it will be in the fridge for you when you do."

"Thanks. Hey, if anybody calls or comes by, tell them I'm in bed and will call them later."

"Sure thing, honey." Her mother closed the door behind her.

Though Sarah wasn't sure if she would go to sleep, what she was certain of was that she needed some time to herself, with the comfort of knowing that someone was accessible if she needed them. Since the accident, she had been surrounded by so many. And, for that, she was grateful. She would not have made it without them. Now, though, she needed space. She had to process what had been and where to go from here.

Sarah rummaged through a drawer until she found an old nightgown. She held it up and smiled, then went to the adjoining bathroom and started a shower, hoping the warm water would ease the tension in her shoulders. If nothing else, it might help her to sleep afterward. She noted immediately that her mother had stocked the shower caddy with her favorite shampoo and conditioner as well as coconut-scented body wash and a sponge loofah. She made a mental note to thank her.

After drying off and putting on her pajamas, she made her way to the bed. As soon as her head hit the pillow, exhaustion won. The sun was still up but her day had effectively ended.

Chapter 38

SARAH SLEPT UNTIL AFTER ELEVEN the next morning. She blinked several times, the sunlight spilling into her room nearly blinding her. For a few moments, eyes wide, she took in the room, not fully sure as to where she was. Or the day. And then, she remembered she was in her childhood home, in her childhood bed . . . and she remembered why.

She yawned as she made her way downstairs to the kitchen, her hunger at war with a feeling of nausea. She didn't want to eat but felt she should. She didn't want to breathe, but she knew she had to. "Mom?" she called out.

She received no answer, nor were any other sounds coming from the house. As she rounded into the kitchen, she saw a note on the counter, so she read it before making coffee.

> Had to go to work for a little while.
> I'll be back home as soon as I can.
> Love you, Mom.

Sarah put a pod in the Keurig, then looked for something to eat. She spotted the plate from supper in the refrigerator, peeled back the foil, and frowned. A pork chop, baked potato, and asparagus spears weren't exactly breakfast food. She settled on an orange, a banana, and a cinnamon raisin bagel, all of which she balanced on a plate. Then, after preparing her coffee, she padded into the family room and turned on the television, determined more than ever that today she'd do nothing more than veg out. Binge watch all day if she wanted to.

She placed the plate and coffee on an end table, then ran back upstairs for her phone in case her mother called before settling in to watch episode after episode of *The Golden Girls*.

Throughout the day, texts came in, but she ignored all of them except the ones from her mother. Maddie sent three, Luke sent one, Todd sent one. Nothing from Brady. If she needed him, she was going to have to call or text. She knew that but had still hoped she'd hear from him.

Melanie sent a text about midafternoon saying she'd made supper for Sarah and her mother and was sending Todd to deliver the meal. Within minutes, Todd rang the doorbell, but Sarah ignored it. She couldn't handle the questions and she was tired of sympathy. In fact, she was almost at a point of rage.

When she was sure Todd had left, Sarah opened the front door to find a couple of paper bags, their tops rolled down. The aroma of a homemade dinner wafted upward, and her stomach grumbled. She brought the sacks in and placed them on the counter.

Not long after making her way back to the sofa, Sarah heard the garage door rise, then close. Within a few minutes, her mother found her.

"How did it go today?"

"Fine."

"Are you sure?"

"Yeah. I just sat here and watched television."

Sarah knew her mother was studying her. Watching her. Reading her. Finally, she said, "*The Golden Girls*, huh."

Sarah smiled up at her. "They always made me laugh."

Her mother sighed. "Well . . ."

"Oh," Sarah said, veering away from the subject, "Todd came by and dropped off some food for supper. I put it on the counter."

"That was nice. I will have to thank Melanie," her mom said, now dropping her purse on a nearby chair and turning on a table lamp. "How was Todd?"

"I don't know."

"What do you mean you don't know? He dropped off the food, didn't he?"

"Yeah. I didn't go to the door. I just couldn't . . . As you can see, I haven't even bothered to get dressed."

"Oh, honey, I understand, but honestly, staying away from everyone, especially the ones who love you, is only going to hurt you worse in the long run." Her mother laid her hands in her lap. "Can we do something together tonight?"

"I guess."

"Okay. Did you get your luggage out of the car?"

Sarah sighed. She hadn't even thought about it. "No."

"All right. I'll go and get your luggage, then you go get ready and we will eat, then leave."

Sarah dragged herself back upstairs to get ready and, a few minutes later, her mother pulled her luggage into her room. Forty minutes after that, when she descended the stairs, she felt ready to eat and then do whatever her mother would suggest, not knowing what but knowing she was about to play her part again. The bed sounded like a better option but maybe Mom was right.

Melanie had sent fried chicken, green beans, corn, and cornbread and Sarah admitted how good it was. How hungry she had gotten. Then, after finishing their supper, they got into her mother's car.

"Where are we going?" Sarah asked.

"You'll see when we get there."

They drove in near silence. The destination was only a few miles down the road but for Sarah, it seemed an hour away. She stared at the trees, so full of life, as she dealt with death, near and personal. When they passed through downtown, Sarah decided she would walk the area before returning to Asheville. She loved the peacefulness and the way she could lose herself along those streets. The air was pure and the atmosphere relaxed.

When her mother finally slowed, Sarah realized they were pulling into the church's parking lot. "Wait. Mom, I don't really want to go to church tonight."

Her mother turned the car off and turned toward her. "I understand you might not want to, but I really believe you need to."

Then, without waiting for an answer, her mother opened her door. Sarah sat a moment, rolled her eyes, sighed, then followed. In silence, she and her mother made their way to the door, Sarah wondering all the while just how great an idea this was. Then again, maybe this was where she was supposed to be rather than lying in bed.

Chapter 39

TODD HAD CHOSEN TO SPEAK on Job that night and, in conclusion, he said, "Though everything crumbled around Job, his faith gave him strength. Such should be our attitude when everything in life is unraveling. In those moments, we hold tighter to the faith." He paused, then added, "Do we have any prayer requests or praise reports for tonight?"

Brady fidgeted in his pew. He finally stood and spoke. "Todd, I think we need to have a special time of prayer for Sarah Ashford and for her family and the family of her fiancé, Peter."

Without thinking about what he was doing, he walked up to the altar. He knelt at the altar, a place he had knelt on many occasions for a wide variety of reasons, but on this night, he was drawn there like never before. He bowed his head and in a couple of moments, the rest of the congregation made their way to Brady.

"Show her how deep Your love is for her, Lord," Luke prayed aloud from nearby. "Please let her know that You care and please help Peter's family."

"Lord, give her strength. Help her get through today," someone else said.

"Father, let her feel Your presence. May she know You are with her every day," another prayed.

"Lord, comfort her. May You use us to help her in any way we can. Let her know that You are here and be with the family. Also, please be with Peter's family. Though we do not understand these things, we know that You do. In Jesus' name we pray, amen," Brady prayed in closing.

As everyone dispersed to make their way to their seats, Brady caught his first glimpse of Sarah and her mother on the back row. He turned toward Luke and Maddie; they'd seen them, too. Rather than return to their pew, they walked to the back to sit with the Ashfords. Sarah laid her head on Maddie's shoulder and sobbed as the service continued.

After a few more requests, Todd closed the service and immediately made his way to where the group was assembled at the back.

"Thank you for supper," Mrs. Ashford said to Melanie, who had walked with Todd to the group.

"That's why we are here," Melanie assured her.

Sarah looked over to Todd. "Sorry I didn't come to the door. I just . . ."

"I understand completely," Todd said with a warm smile. "How long will you be in town?"

"Just a few days. Think I need to get some rest and try to get my mind off everything."

"If you need anything, let us know," Melanie said as she leaned forward to hug Sarah. "If you need us, we are here."

Brady returned home and went straight to his workshop. Todd stopped in to see if he needed anything, observing for a few moments as Brady worked on a bench, but saying nothing. Finally, Brady looked up and said, "What are you thinking, Todd?"

Todd leaned against the workbench, then drew circles in the sawdust with his finger. "I'm just thinking . . . you work to craft something beautiful out of ordinary wood . . ."

"The way God crafts something beautiful out of ordinary people."

"Mmm. Well, you asked what I was thinking, Brady, and here it is: just as you are at work crafting the bench out of wood, the Lord is at work, crafting a work of beauty out of a tragedy."

"That's what you were thinking?"

"That's what I was thinking."

Chapter 40

THE SUN HAD RISEN BEFORE Brady went into the house to go to bed. Though being self-employed had some disadvantages, this was a definite advantage. He had nowhere to be and he had completed more than enough work for the day. He crawled under the covers after drawing the blackout blinds and drifted off. He had been awake for twenty-four hours at that point and he had nothing left to run on.

But a little after noon, a knock on the door woke him.

He grunted under his breath but rolled over and grabbed a T-shirt, then stumbled toward the door half asleep to see Sarah standing on the porch.

"Were you still in bed?" she asked, blushing.

"Yeah," he said, combing his fingers through his hair. "I was up until seven this morning."

"Doing what?"

"Working." He opened the door wider and stepped aside. "Do you want to come in?"

"Maybe I should let you get back to bed. I should have called first."

"No, no. Come on in."

She followed him to the couch, sitting at the opposite end from him. "So you worked all night?"

He cracked a grin. "I do my best work at night. You know me . . . it's always been that way."

"Oh, well . . ." She glanced around and he realized what a mess the room must appear to her, especially after being in her apartment where everything was color-coordinated and set perfectly in place.

"Forgive the house. Like I said, I've been working a lot and . . . well, forgive me that I look like I just woke up." He laughed.

"You did just wake up." She also laughed, and, for Brady, the sound was like music.

"You thirsty?"

"Nah. I'm good."

"Do you mind . . ." He pointed toward the kitchen. "Do you mind if I get some water?"

"Brady! Why would I mind?"

He stood. "I'll be back in a minute," he said, and he was, gulping on a bottled water to cure the dry mouth he had woken with.

Sarah sheepishly smiled at him, the awkwardness of the moment inescapable. He sat again and she turned toward him and asked, "Are you hungry, Brady?"

"Yeah," he said. "I could eat. But I—" He pulled at his tee. "I have to shower first. I don't think I need to go out looking like this. Do you care if I—?"

She shook her head.

"I'll be right back." He stood. "Make yourself at home." He smiled again. "Hey, clean the place up if you'd like."

And again, she laughed.

He walked down the hall to his bedroom, retrieved some clothes and made his way to the shower fully aware that as soon as the shower turned on, Sarah would tiptoe down the hall. She'd want to know if the photo of her still had a place next to his bed.

Brady turned the water on, then moved to the door to listen for footsteps. Sure enough, within seconds, he heard her quietly moving toward his bedroom. Brady hung his head, keeping his focus on the tiles beneath his feet, and wondered how she'd feel when she saw that the photograph was gone. She wouldn't think, of course, that he'd thrown the frame and that it had shattered. She wouldn't know that the pieces had been tossed some time ago into a trash bin. She couldn't guess that the photo itself had been tucked into the small drawer of the nightstand because the last thing he could do—would do—was throw that away.

He managed to shower and dress in less than a half hour. "What are you hungry for?" he asked her.

"Want to get a sandwich at Subway and go to the river? It's nice out today."

"Sure," Brady said, then reached in a closet to retrieve a blanket. "All right, let's jump in the truck."

They drove to the Subway, ordered their sandwiches, then headed on out to the river. He had little to say, partly because he was so tired but mainly asking her how she was doing seemed ridiculous.

"You are the only person I know," she said, finally turning away from the window, "who orders a BLT without the T." She chuckled, her fingers fidgeting with themselves.

"Not a fan of tomatoes, but I do love me some bacon." He turned his face to grin at her.

"But you grow tomatoes in your garden."

"I grow them for people who like them. I give every one of them away . . . no lie."

"Sometimes you don't really make sense, but then again, when you don't, it seems like you have a reason for not making sense."

Brady chuckled. "I'm sure if I dissect that sentence, it'll make sense somewhere."

Brady turned off the main road and pointed the truck toward the river. He found the clearing where he'd parked only a few days previous when Todd had found him and told him about Peter, then put the truck in park. "I'll get the blanket," he said. "You bring the food."

Minutes later, they had the blanket spread in the filtering shade of towering pines. They both sat cross-legged, opposite each other, their meals tossed out between them, which Brady immediately wolfed into. An occasional breeze brought relief from the building heat and Sarah commented on it.

"Mmm," he said. Then, "You're not eating."

Sarah held up her sandwich. "I'm eating . . ."

Brady studied the top of the sandwich as though it were a lab specimen. "You're nibbling."

"I'm nibbling," she admitted. Then she pointed to what was left of his BLT-without-the-T and smiled. "You're inhaling."

He swallowed, then took a long sip of sweet tea. "I'm hungry." But he smiled at her and she returned it. "You're also fidgeting."

"Am I?" she asked, then placed her sandwich onto its wrapper and laced her fingers.

"Are you nervous about something, Sarah?" he asked, then took another bite, mainly out of his own nervousness.

"I *wanted* you to be there," she blurted, "but I was scared that it would be awkward."

Brady's head dropped, he continued to chew, then swallowed. "Wow. Okay. Well, that came out of nowhere. Look, I understand, but—really—I—"

"Brady, I just need you to understand. I was afraid it would hurt you to be there."

"Look, Sarah. It's fine. I understand why you did it and I am not mad." He wadded the rest of his sandwich in the wrapper and tossed it in the sack the food had come in. "So, let's just drop this, okay?"

"You sound mad."

"I promise you, I'm not."

"Brady, look," she started again.

"Sarah," he interrupted, "it's just not important now. You're going through the worst experience ever. Let's be honest. The fact is, how I feel or how I felt doesn't matter now and it will never matter. All of us are worried about you. You don't have to explain anything and truthfully, now is not the time for that. I mean . . ." He spread his fingers wide, palms up, toward her. "I do appreciate it, but the focus should not be on me right now."

She looked toward the river, watched it for a few moments, then turned back, her mouth open and ready to speak.

"Sarah," Brady said before she could. "You want to fix it. But I want to drop it." What he wanted to say but couldn't, was that while she was performing maintenance on their relationship, he was maintaining a practical distance because of the inevitable mileage that would come soon enough.

"Fine," she said, then looked toward the river again.

He watched her. The jutting of her jaw. The rise and fall of her shoulders and chest as she breathed in and out, in and out. And the guilt came. But if he couldn't be honest with her—especially now—then even their friendship was at stake.

"Hey," he said, and she turned toward him. "Tell me about him. Tell me about Peter."

Her face softened and she smiled. "He was an artist, and his life was his artwork. Some of his work I understood, but to be honest, there was a lot I didn't understand at all." She chuckled.

Brady grinned and chuckled at her truthfulness.

"We spent a lot of time in galleries. He was well known in Asheville as you probably gathered from his funeral, so we spent time with other artists, influential people, you know? That was his thing . . ." Her eyes grew sad. Reflective. "It wasn't mine."

"Wouldn't be my kind of thing either," Brady added.

"He was serious a lot of the time, but he had a way of being funny and sweet. He loved me and gave me as much of himself as he had to give." Her eyes filled with tears and, in that moment, Brady hurt for her in a new way. A different way. "We had some great times together."

Brady picked up the remains of their meals and placed them beside him, then shifted so they sat side by side. His arm slipped around her and she, in turn, laid her head on his shoulder. Words no longer were necessary. It felt good to hold her. To be needed by her in the place of serenity and of the water running downstream. Because sometimes, there just aren't words and this was one of those times.

"So, what's next?" Brady asked on the way back to his house.

"I don't know. I have to try to renew my lease on my apartment. Hopefully I can, or else I'll be looking for somewhere new to live. We had planned to move me into Peter's townhouse after the honeymoon, but I don't even want to think about that. I spoke to his parents and, basically, since we weren't married or anything, everything is theirs.

They are putting the townhouse on the market."

"So, they are taking everything?"

"Yeah," Sarah answered, "but I really just don't care at this point. I'm tired. I really have nothing left to give and don't want to fight."

"People are crazy," Brady remarked, "and selfish. This is why I have my own business and my own workshop. I can deal with people only from a distance."

She chuckled. "Well, I *am* keeping the bread maker. We got it at one of the wedding showers and it's at my apartment."

"I don't blame you," he said, shooting another smile her way. "There's nothing like warm homemade bread."

Chapter 41

WHEN FRIDAY MORNING CAME, BRADY woke unsure of the time and less sure of the day. He glanced at his cell phone to check the time and date. He had slept more than twelve hours.

He groaned. Once a month, he and Luke met with Todd on a Friday for breakfast and to just hang out. Today was that day. Which meant, groggy or not, he had to get up, get dressed, and get going.

By the time he reached the café, his eyes were alert, his mind focused, and the cup of coffee he ordered with pancakes and bacon, he figured, would take care of the rest. By the time he had half a cup in him, Todd had moved the conversation from his omelet order to the boxes for the raised-bed garden Luke and Brady had completed. "The boxes look good," he noted. "I really appreciate you guys working on those."

"Yeah," Luke said, grinning. "I *let* Brady do most of the construction since wood is kind of his thing." He raised his hands, his gaze now on Brady. "But don't worry. I'll do the planting because my garden is always better than Brady's."

"You really think so, Cool Hand Luke?" Brady joked.

"*Cool Hand Luke?* Seriously, where do you get these names?" Luke asked. He looked irritated but his voice told a different story.

"I googled it," Brady admitted.

"Dude, you need to get a life. And I am not just saying that. I truly believe that all the silence of living by yourself and working by yourself, well, it's getting to you. You need to get out more," Luke chided.

"Speaking of a different life, have you guys talked to Sarah since

Wednesday night?" Todd asked.

"Maddie talked to her yesterday morning," Luke said.

"I saw her yesterday," Brady admitted, not looking at Luke. "She came by the house."

"How is she?" Todd asked.

"Hard to say," Brady acknowledged. "I don't know if reality has really set in yet."

"She came by your house yesterday?" Luke asked.

"Yeah," Brady answered. He glanced at Luke for a moment as he twirled his coffee mug in a slow circle on the table. "She just showed up. I didn't sleep Wednesday night, so I was still in bed. I heard someone knocking, I got up, and there she was at the door."

Luke took a drink of his orange juice before questioning further. "What did she want?"

Brady returned his attention to the coffee, then picked up the mug and took a sip. "I guess to just talk. I don't know. She tried to explain why I wasn't invited to the wedding and I didn't really want to get into it, so I turned the subject to Peter and let her talk about him."

"So, you don't want to know why?" Todd asked.

"No. With all that's happened, it's not important. At this point, who cares if I was invited or not invited or why. I turned the conversation to Peter because I figured that at some point, she needed to talk about—"

Brady stopped when the server returned with their meals, then asked if they needed anything. "More coffee," Brady said. "Todd? Luke?"

Both replied that they were good, then Todd said grace and they reached for their silverware almost in unison.

"So, what you're saying," Luke said, cutting into his breakfast ham, "is that y'all spent the day together?"

"Not the day." He poured maple syrup onto the tall stack of pancakes, sliced a small triangle with his fork, and speared it. "The afternoon. She left right after we got back to my house so she could eat supper with her mom last night." He looked at Luke as he wrapped his lips around the pancakes.

Luke had a look on his face Brady knew well: *Here we go again.*

"So, did it seem like it helped her to talk about Peter?" Todd asked. He had added a decent amount of pepper to his omelet along with a long squirt of ketchup and was now ready to dig in.

"I guess so," Brady answered, going for his second bite. "I mean, I don't know. It was worth a shot."

"Well, maybe the Lord pushed her to come over there so you could be helpful and get her to talk," Todd said.

"Maybe," Brady mumbled. "At any rate . . ." The door to the café opened and, almost as if on cue, Sarah and her mother walked in and, as Brady figured they would, right up to their table.

"Hey guys," Miss Susan said as they stopped at the table.

"Hi," the three answered.

"Hey," Sarah said, her smiled forced if Brady's guess was correct.

"How's it going today?" Todd asked, his tone genuine.

"Sun came up, so I guess it's all good," she replied, and Brady winced inwardly. He hurt for her; anyone would.

"Would y'all like to join us?" Todd asked.

"No, we better not interrupt y'all's time," Sarah answered a little too quickly, but then added, "Are y'all busy tonight?"

Brady deferred to Luke to respond to the question.

"Ask Maddie," Luke replied with a grin. "She is my scheduler. She tells me what I'm doing most nights."

Brady and Sarah both burst out laughing. Even Todd uttered a hearty chuckle.

"Okay, then. I'll call Maddie," Sarah replied. "You know I'm going to tell her what you said. What about you and Melanie, Todd?"

"Nope," he said. "We do have plans and . . ." he grinned at Luke, "I don't have to ask my wife to know it."

Again, everyone laughed—everyone but Luke, whose frown was meant for Todd.

"Brady?" Sarah asked. "Are you busy tonight?"

"I'm free as far as I know," he said, looking at Luke to gauge a reaction.

"What about a movie at the Parkway?"

Luke turned his attention back to his half-eaten ham. "Ask Maddie."

"I will. Todd, it's good to see you. Brady, *Lucas*, I'll see you guys later tonight."

Brady had just taken a sip of coffee and nearly spewed it across the table.

"Oh, that's *rich*," Luke said. Then, looking at Brady, asked, "Did you put her up to that?"

The conversation turned to small talk and church plans before someone finally looked at the time and they left to go in separate directions for the day. Before walking out, Brady turned toward Sarah and her mother, who waved. "Call you later, Brady," Sarah called out and, although he wished it hadn't, his heart smiled.

After pulling out of the parking lot, Brady hurried to his workshop to work on a table for Audrey, who owned The Third Day Gift Shop. Her farmhouse had a unique feel to it, rustic and simple, and Brady had worked hard to capture the feel of her home with the table. He had planned to work until late in the night again until . . . Sarah. He adjusted the ball cap on his head with the growing knowledge that he had become all too accustomed to his plans being derailed by her.

By early afternoon Sarah had lined up the night, texting everyone about dinner and the movie. Brady slid a piece of sandpaper over an edge of the table and wondered if she was immersing herself in the company of comfortable before she returned to Asheville where she would be haunted by the sounds of silence. If he were a betting man, he would probably make a killing on it.

Either way, he was in the shower by five o'clock so he could meet everyone at six.

Chapter 42

THE FOURSOME MET DOWNTOWN TO eat at the Hotel Tavern. The lights on the back porch gave a feel of Christmas even though summer knocked at the door. "Should we eat outside?" Sarah asked, her face bright with hope.

"Sounds good to me," Maddie said. "Guys?"

"Like we have a choice," Luke muttered, which brought a playful sock in the arm from his wife.

"A sense of history and charm with the picturesque Buck Mountain as a backdrop," Brady said after they'd settled at one of the picnic-style tables and placed their orders.

"What?" Luke asked.

Brady felt heat run to his cheeks. "Something I read about this place online one night while I was . . ."

"Googling *Lukes?*"

Brady started to chuckle, his eyes catching Sarah's who had pressed her lips together to keep from laughing herself. "Maybe," he admitted.

"Man, I am *really* starting to worry about you," he said, then asked, "So, what movie are we going to see tonight?"

"*The Avengers,*" Sarah responded. "*Endgame.*"

"What?" Luke responded, wide-eyed and grinning.

"I was as shocked as you are," Brady noted. "Of course, I knew it a few hours ago."

"Whose idea was that?" Luke asked.

"Mine," Sarah answered. "I figured you boys would like that a little better than sitting through a chick flick . . . and honestly, I don't need anything sappy right now."

Luke put his hands together and bowed his head toward Sarah. "Thank you!"

"You act like you never watch anything but romance movies, Luke," Sarah teased.

"Well, my dear wife isn't a big fan of the action movies," Luke noted.

"Whatever, Lucas," Maddie shot back.

Sarah and Brady laughed as Maddie looked at Luke with an eyebrow raised nearly to her hairline.

"I'm getting my name changed," he said and everyone laughed again.

"He can't change his name. His mother would kill him," Brady said, not thinking of what he was saying or the company he was in when he said it. "Oh, crud . . . I'm so sorry . . . I didn't think about . . ."

"It's okay," Sarah replied.

The table grew quiet for a moment until Sarah said, "So, Luke and Maddie, how many babies are in the future?"

"Six," Brady smirked, knowing Luke's trepidation about having kids.

"I don't think so," Maddie shot back. "Maybe two. Or three. I mean, I've already got one in Luke so maybe I can raise one or two more."

Luke rolled his eyes as the group again laughed at his expense.

"I think you'll have four or five," Sarah added.

"Don't you put that one on me," Luke demanded, smiling and pointing his finger at Brady and Sarah.

After supper, they began to walk down the street to the Parkway Theatre, Luke and Maddie walking ahead of Brady and Sarah—Luke and Maddie hand in hand while Brady and Sarah remained feet apart. Silent.

"Hey, Sarah," Brady said as they crossed the street, "I'm really sorry about that comment earlier. I wasn't thinking . . ."

She looked up at him. "Brady, let it go."

"I really feel bad about it."

"It's just a saying. I know you didn't mean anything by it."

"I'm still sorry. Sometimes, I am just an idiot."

"Brady." She stopped as they reached the sidewalk. "Please let it go."

Brady bought Sarah's ticket to the movie and they each got a popcorn and something to drink. Maddie, evidently trying to protect all parties involved, sat beside Sarah, putting herself and Luke between Brady and Sarah.

"I figure the boys need to be together and the girls could talk instead of actually watching this," Maddie noted.

But Sarah shrugged, sat in the seat Maddie had assigned her, and took a bite of her popcorn. During the previews and even after the movie began, Brady noticed her occasional glances his way and even caught himself trying to overhear the conversation between Maddie and Sarah.

After the conclusion of the movie, they stood and talked as a group for a few moments outside the theater. Then they returned to the restaurant where their cars were parked, said their goodbyes, and headed in their own directions.

Chapter 43

THE SUN ANNOUNCED ITS PRESENCE early on Saturday. Too early. Brady never set an alarm for Saturdays and, on this day, he didn't need one. His buzzing phone, which he had set to "vibrate" the night before, was an alarm in itself. He reached over to the nightstand and brought it near his face to find a text from Sarah.

TY 4 everything. I'm headed back 2 Aville. Call U soon.

He tossed the phone back on the nightstand. Rolling over, he hoped to go back to sleep but his mind refused to shut off two obvious questions: *A text message? She couldn't even call?*

And although he knew he needed to let it go, he was put off by her casual and disconnected goodbye. He also knew that if he kept thinking about it, it was only going to derail him. She was going through a lot and she'd call soon. There.

He picked up the phone and texted back, telling her to be careful, and that she could call him anytime.

Over the next couple of months, they talked a few times each week. Perhaps this was a new reality for their relationship. She never talked about the struggle of going back to Asheville, and from what Brady could tell, she had thrown herself back into her work. May turned to June and though she had not returned to West Jefferson, she called Brady and Maddie to arrange a weekend together at the Christmas in July event the town held annually.

The Saturday of the festival came, and Sarah met Brady and Todd and Melanie at the church's parking lot. "Hey Sarah," Melanie said as she got out of the car and hugged her. "How are you?"

"I'm good. How are you guys?" She pulled her sunglasses to the top of her head.

"We're doing good," Melanie answered. "When was the last time you came to the festival?"

Sarah thought for a minute. "You know, this is the first time I've been here since my senior year in high school. Aiden and I came over that year for like thirty minutes, so it's definitely been a long time."

Brady jerked at the mention of Aiden's name but smiled despite the emotions that surfaced. "Well, it's about time you came back to the festival." He stepped closer and lowered his voice. "You okay?"

"I'm *fine*," she said then gave him a hug to soften the tension in her answer.

"Brady, you're not selling your stuff this year? I mean, this is like a big money day for your woodwork, isn't it?" Todd asked.

"Yeah, I'm selling some pieces. Mom and Dad had nothing to do today so I had asked them last week if they would man the booth and they agreed. I got here and set up everything around seven this morning."

Todd grinned and shook his head. "You better thank God *every day* for your mom and dad."

Brady smiled easily. "I do, Todd. I do."

After Luke and Maddie arrived, the group walked around the downtown area and looked at what the vendors had to offer while soaking in the celebration. The variety was wide. The Christmas tree contest caught their attention and the vendors each had a talent on display. Woodworkers, potters, and arts and crafts booths stretched down the street, as did the line of people. Brady guestimated that several thousand people had come that day.

Early on, Luke and Brady made a bet. "I bet you," Luke said, pointing at Brady. "that I can outeat you."

"Name it," Brady said, rising to the challenge.

"We each have to eat one of everything deep-fried."

"Oh my gosh," Maddie said with a roll of her eyes.

"What are the stakes?" Sarah asked.

"Whoever gives up first is the loser and owes the other a Dr Pepper."

Now Brady pointed at Luke. "Oh, you are so on . . ."

"Todd," Maddie said, "I nominate you as the impartial judge."

Todd's eyes grew wide. "Why me?"

"Because you're a pastor. You *have* to be impartial."

Luke rubbed his hands together in anticipation. "Where do we begin?" He looked around until he spotted a food truck offering blooming onions, the aroma heavy in the air. "Blooming onions!"

"Does that *really* fall into the category of 'deep-fried'?" Brady asked. Everyone looked at Todd.

"Yep, it is, in fact, deep-fried," Todd ruled. He placed one fist on his hip while pointing toward the food truck. "I'm calling ten minutes between eating a different deep-fried food. Let the challenge begin."

They stood in line, got their onion, and began the first leg of the daylong challenge.

"I can't believe you guys are doing this," Maddie commented only moments before deep-fried Twinkies were up.

"I might throw up for them," Sarah joked as Brady wrapped his mouth around the sweet cake. Part of him continued to feel confident that he could beat his lifetime best friend and another part of him wanted to throw up. "Brady," she said, and he cut his eyes toward her. "You'll make yourself sick." She looked at Maddie. "Are all men this stupid?"

"No," Todd said. "I'm a man and I'm the smart one because I am the judge."

"Let's go look at pottery booths," Sarah said. "I cannot watch this another second."

Brady frowned, watching them go, then looked at Luke. "Should we join them?"

"And stop all this?"

Brady smiled at Todd. "We've got—what—nine minutes?"

Todd nodded with a chuckle.

The men walked up from behind the girls who stood at Mr. Bridges' pottery booth admiring a set of coffee mugs.

"Mr. Bridges, how much are the coffee mugs?" Sarah was asking.

"Oh, those are ten dollars, hon," he commented as he wiped down another piece he planned to set out for sale.

"Done any fly-fishin' lately?" Brady asked Mr. Bridges.

"Nope. Been too busy working on the pottery," he replied before asking, "How about you?"

"Been too busy getting pieces ready myself. I've been wanting to go fishing but just can't find the time," Brady acknowledged, as he pulled a hundred-dollar bill from his wallet. "Here's a hundred. Can I get six of the mugs for my friends here, but I need them in separate bags."

Mr. Bridges smiled and began to wrap the mugs in paper before placing them in separate plastic bags.

"Thank you, Brady," Todd said, thankful for the nice gesture.

"No problem."

"Yeah. Thanks, man," Luke said.

"You didn't have to do that," Sarah noted, "but I do love that mug."

Mr. Bridges continued to wrap the mugs. The group noticed the smile on Sarah's face and Brady couldn't help but be thankful. Sometimes, he noted, the simplest things in life made all the difference.

"Hey, boys, it's been ten minutes." Melanie looked around. "And there's the funnel cake," she added with a nod.

"Bring it on," Luke said.

"I'll join you on this part of the stupid bet," Maddie said. "I do love funnel cake!"

"I'm in, too," Sarah said.

"Me, too," Melanie mentioned, looking at Todd.

"Don't look at me. I've got to lose some weight," Todd said, pinching his stomach fat. "Besides, I'm the judge. I don't need a sugar high."

Chapter 44

THE GROUP AMBLED OVER TO Brady's booth to see his parents and to check in on sales.

"Well, look who's here," his dad commented when he saw Sarah. "How are you, sweetheart?"

"I'm doing okay, Mr. Jameson."

Brady pulled on his ball cap. There was something about her reaction to the question that caught his eye. "Am I a millionaire yet?" Brady asked his mother.

"You've had a good day so far," she assured. "We sold a table, some cutting boards, three jewelry boxes, and a rocking chair."

"Son, these people cannot get enough of your woodwork," his dad said with a smile of pride on his face.

Melanie looked around at Brady's product. She told him often how amazed she was by what he could do with wood and now an ornate footstool caught her eye. "Todd, honey, how much am I worth to you?" she asked.

"Figuratively, a trillion dollars. Literally," he said as he looked through the cash in his wallet, "about a hundred and fifty bucks."

Everyone laughed.

She picked up the stool and hugged it to her. "I need sixty of that for this stool," Melanie commented.

"Melanie, I am not charging you for that. You can have it," Brady told her.

"Oh, no, Brady, we're buying it. It's our way of supporting you and what you do," Todd said as he handed Brady's mother three twenties.

"Can I leave it here for now?" Melanie asked, handing it back to Brady's dad.

"Sure. In fact, I'll drop it off at y'all's house later on."

"Dad's angling for a part-time job as a delivery man," Brady joked. "And, by the way, Melanie, our drivers aren't allowed to accept tips for delivery."

"Well, thank you, Larry. I appreciate it," Todd replied.

Brady smiled, then looked over at Sarah who stood to the left of everyone else. She stared at Brady's handwork intently. A shadow box caught her eye. She picked it up, admiring it, as Brady walked up behind her.

"You're staring at that shadow box pretty hard," he said softly.

"Yeah, I've been looking for one for a while. What's amazing is that this one is exactly like the one I envisioned but never could find."

"It's yours," he said.

"Oh, no, Brady. I couldn't."

"Sarah," he said, taking the box and placing it in her hands, "it's yours. Really. I can make more of these. I want you to have it if it's the one you really want."

"Thank you, Brady," she whispered, her eyes never leaving the box.

"Hey," Luke said. "Let's keep this party going."

After saying goodbye to Brady's parents, the group meandered through the festival. Along the way, they encountered friends and church family and, as they did, Sarah endured questions on how she was doing, if she needed anything, and was told she was being prayed for.

Sarah tried to smile her way through, but with each encounter, Brady could see her resolve wearing down.

"Hey, guys," Sarah said as they neared the parking area, "I'm going to head back to the car and go back to the house."

"Is everything okay?" Maddie asked.

"Yeah, I think it's just the heat," she answered. "Heat wears me out—" Her voice cracked, and the group froze.

"I'll walk you to your car," Brady said.

"No." Sarah raised a hand to stop him from coming closer. "No, you guys have fun. I'm just going to run to the house and get some rest." She smiled, but her lips wobbled in the effort.

Sarah turned and slipped down a side street, Brady's eyes never leaving her until, eventually, she was nothing more than a shadow, a shadow that seemed to disappear, leaving Brady with the sense that, with that shadow's disappearance, every trace of her presence in West Jefferson had been erased.

Chapter 45

"Do you think she's all right?" Melanie asked.

"It doesn't seem like it," Todd answered. "Hey, Mel, maybe we should go and talk to her . . . at least check on her."

They turned to make their way to the parking lot until Maddie spoke up. "Hey, guys, wait a minute," she called out. "I know her, and I can tell you this for sure. If she doesn't want to talk about anything, she really doesn't want to talk about anything. If you catch her, it will only make things worse."

They stood quiet for a moment until Luke said, "Maddie's right. Sarah has always done things Sarah's way, on Sarah's time."

"Did y'all hear that?" Maddie asked, then pretended she was having a heart attack. "Luke just said that I was right." Her humor eased the atmosphere, if only a little. "So, let's continue to enjoy the festival," she suggested.

"Maybe she will be at church tomorrow morning," Todd noted as they walked along.

"Maybe," Melanie said with her mouth, but her facial expression revealed doubt.

Maddie pointed out the next deep-fried delight. "Hey, fellas, the bet is still on, you know. Time for some fried pickles." She laughed.

"Hey, guys," Todd pointed at the sign and called out, "do you see all the things you're going to have to eat?"

Luke's eyes grew large. "Deep-fried Oreos, deep-fried Reese's, deep-fried cookie dough, and . . . oh, sweet Jesus, help me . . . deep-fried alligator."

"You aren't man enough, Lucas and Marcus?" Brady challenged.

Luke stopped. "Who?"

Brady shrugged. "I dunno. Some dancers."

"Googled it?"

"Yep."

They ordered the pickles and devoured them as the rest of the group paused in the shenanigans to watch a juggler on stilts.

Brady took his last bite while Luke had two to go. "You give up yet?" He prayed for a "yes."

"Never!" Luke responded, then swallowed the last of the pickle before licking his fingers in an act of defiance.

"What's next then?" Brady asked.

"Oreos."

After Oreos, cookie dough. By now, Brady wondered if his face was changing colors.

"Is it worth it?" Melanie asked, laughing. "Luke you're going to make yourself purely sick. Tell you what, *I'll* buy you guys a Dr Pepper and y'all can end it."

"Hit me with a Reese's," Luke called, Brady falling in line behind him to do the same.

Brady took his first bite before throwing in the towel. "I can't do it, man. I think I'm going to puke if I eat another bite. You win, Luke."

Luke threw his hands into the air to cement his victory while Brady walked over to a vendor and bought the Dr Pepper.

"I would like to thank those who supported me in this quest for a championship," Luke joked, holding his Dr Pepper as if it were an Oscar. "My opponent was worthy but when it was all said and done, he didn't have the stomach to keep going, the hunger to push through, and it robbed him of the sweet taste of victory." He took a sip of his soda and sighed audibly.

Brady shook his head as Maddie laughed. "All right, you guys," he said, "the loser is going to go check on his parents. I'll see you guys tomorrow."

Later, after the festival closed, Brady took the few pieces from his booth that remained unsold back to his house, placing them in the shop. On his way inside, he checked his phone to see if Sarah might have texted, but she had not. He wanted to call her but fought the urge. No, this time she would have to make the first move. She had walked away again, and he was no longer in a place to continue the chase.

Chapter 46

Sᴀʀᴀʜ ᴡᴀѕ ʀᴇᴀᴅʏ ᴛᴏ ɢᴇᴛ back to Asheville. Maybe not Asheville, but anywhere but West Jefferson. Parts of the trip home had been good for her soul, but the other parts only led to turmoil she had tried to leave behind. She hurt. And the people meant well, but constantly being asked how she was doing after Peter's death only negated the space she had hoped to put between herself and that pain, if only for a respite.

Now, on the way home, she thought about some of the things people had said to her: *Drown yourself in your work. Go on a cruise. Take some time for yourself. Spend time learning something new.*

Her mind raced and the faster it ran, the faster she drove. Maybe with enough speed she could outrun the cloud hanging over her.

Get away.

No. *Stay* away.

Nothing could change what was. She knew that. What she had believed would be her future was now a present that could not be wallowed in. And why? Because of the past. Closure would never come. Not for her, anyway. She had to go on with her life, that much she knew, but she also knew that never would there be a time when all of this would make sense. At least not in her mind. Her purpose now had to be to find a place where she could continue to function, and perhaps even one day *live*, doing something with the time she had left.

The sun had dipped behind the hills surrounding Asheville when she pulled up to her apartment. For long moments she stayed in the car, her head resting against the seatback, her breathing deep enough for her to fall asleep. And she could. What would it matter if she did? Who would know and who would care if she closed her eyes and simply drifted off to sleep?

But the honking of a car's horn somewhere nearby alerted her, and she climbed out of the car, grabbed her luggage, and hauled both herself and it into her apartment. She stored her luggage in her bedroom before seeking the comfort of her living room sofa. She scooped up the remote before plopping down, pressed PWR and, before she could choose what to watch, fell asleep.

Sarah woke the next morning to the sound of her phone notifying her that she had a text message. She blinked several times as her eyes attempted to adjust to the sunlight spilling into the room. She was home. In Asheville. Her television, though nearly muted, was showing an old rerun of *I Love Lucy*.

She had left the phone on the coffee table—something she didn't even remember—so she reached for it and, after wiping her eyes, read the text from Brady.

Call me if you need anything. We're all here and praying for you.

Brady. She had wondered who would cave first—she or he. Apparently, he. And that touched her. However, right then, she didn't want to think about West Jefferson, or anyone associated with it.

Thanks, she texted back, then laid the phone next to her and stretched.

They meant well; she knew that. And Brady was only trying to help. But, right then, she was simply too tired to deal with it, so she closed her eyes and tried to go back to sleep. But her phone buzzed again and, checking it, she found a nearly identical message from Todd.

Moments later, a message came in from Melanie.

Frustration was not the answer, but she could feel her soul giving birth to the rawness of the emotion. She chose not to answer. Instead, she upped the TV's volume and laid a crooked arm over her eyes as Lucy and Ethel concocted some harebrained plan. But after about five minutes, with the sun peeking through the blinds enough to annoy her further, she got up and showered. After, with her damp hair pulled up into a towel, she went to her home office desk and went to work on brochures for the Asheville Tourists baseball team, working ahead on an account she had secured.

As she designed the brochures, she clicked online to see if the Tourists were playing at home that day. Sarah loved sports and baseball was the sport she lost herself in the most. Focusing on all the pieces in motion at a baseball game helped hours to pass and never have a thought cross her mind. Because Peter had not been a fan of any sport, least of all baseball, she had ditched the game for love and hadn't been to any games for over two years.

The website indicated that the Tourists were at home that day; first pitch scheduled for two o'clock. Because of her work for the team, she had free tickets any time she wanted to use them. She jumped up from her office chair, darted into the bathroom, dried her hair fully, then pulled it up in a makeshift ponytail. Within a half hour, she was driving to the stadium. Once there, she grabbed a Coke and popcorn before heading to her box seat behind home plate, the perfect vantage point for the game. She pulled a pen from her purse and propped her program on her knee, ready to keep score.

Sarah closed her eyes and tilted her face upward, the warmth of the sun filling her. *This* was just what she needed. The energy of the crowd and the players, the healthy tension of the game, and the warm Carolina air.

Unwelcome noise jostled her, and she jerked to attention as a group of twenty-somethings descended to her row, filling the rest of the seats. And, as her luck would have it, all men and all young enough to be her little brothers. The scent of the Solo cups they carried filled with frothy beer complemented their attire of khaki shorts and collared shirts.

Great. Frat boys.

Never looking up, she buried herself in the game program, hoping to avoid interaction. She wanted, and needed, to be left alone. She also wanted them to ignore her so she could only be swept away by balls and strikes, home runs and double plays.

But no such luck.

"Hey," a happy voice to her right said. She looked over. "I'm Brandon."

"Sarah."

"Nice to meet you. You like baseball, huh?" he asked.

"I sure hope so. Otherwise, I'm in the wrong place," she said, pointing to the obvious answer to his question.

"Yeah. That was dumb. Sorry. I'm terrible at talking to people when I first meet them." He sipped his beer.

She realized then that he wore a Tourists ballcap and that his shirt held the Tourists logo. His blue eyes caught her attention, as did his goatee. Why the goatee was noticeable, she wasn't sure, but it fit him.

"No worries. But, yes, I love baseball. Is that surprising to you?"

"No, I mean, well, maybe a little. I don't know many women who like baseball."

Sarah worked up a smile. "Well, now you do."

The Tourists fell behind the Charleston RiverDogs five to nothing by the third inning but cut the deficit to two runs by the end of the eighth. Sarah found that, too often, she and Brandon shouted in their joys or frustrations with equal measure, which brought laughter from them both. After giving up a run in the top of the ninth, the Tourists trailed six to three in the bottom of the ninth.

"Come on now," Sarah called out. "Show us what you're made of."

"What we need," Brandon said to her, "is a miracle."

"What we *need*," she retorted, "is bases loaded and a grand slam or four homeruns."

Brandon laughed. "From your lips to God's ears."

A single and two walks loaded the bases before Mike Matthews, the Tourists' first baseman, stepped up to the plate. "Come on, Mike!" Sarah yelled through cupped hands.

"Knock it out of the ballpark!" Brandon added. They looked at each other and laughed.

And then, sure enough, Matthews swung at the first pitch, crushing the ball for a walk-off grand slam to win the game and send the stadium into a state of euphoria.

"You need to keep coming to the games," Brandon told Sarah as they stood. "You're good luck."

"We'll see," she said as she swung her purse's strap over her shoulder.

Brandon pointed to his seat. "Our season tickets are right here so you'll know where to find us."

Sarah said goodbye, then walked the steps toward the exit. She swung through a drive-thru for a burger, then she went home to take another shower, watch a little Netflix, and go to bed. Finally, something had given her space, something had gotten her through a day without it being centered around a tragedy she longed to forget.

Tomorrow was Monday. A workday. A whole new week. And, if she were lucky, the start to a whole new life.

Chapter 47

WINTER HAD COME EARLY, THE fall of the year rapidly overtaken by an early snow and frigid temperatures. Even the majesty of the leaves changing suffered an early exit with the frost that came late in September. Now, the somber gray skies of winter rarely gave way to a cloudless day, assuring this winter would indeed be arduous.

No one, other than Maddie, had heard a thing from Sarah, and what she had heard dated back to August. Sarah's news also didn't sit well with Maddie. She had met some guy named Brandon at a ballgame. They'd started dating and, also according to Maddie who had relayed information to Luke who had then told Brady, Brandon was your typical "user."

"Maddie says he likes being taken care of rather than the other way around," Luke told him one afternoon while visiting at his shop.

"How'd they meet?"

"Baseball game."

Brady only nodded. There wasn't much he could say, other than, "Well, it's her life to live."

Luke toyed with a few wood shavings, then let them slip from his fingers. "Maddie says it's rebound." He looked up. "Or desperation."

Brady hung a chisel back on its place over one of the workbenches. "I guess only Sarah knows that."

Maddie arranged for the group to meet up at the Bistro after church the following Sunday morning. But, that morning, Melanie bowed out. She wasn't feeling well—the start of a bad cold, Todd told them—so he took her home first, then joined the group at the Bistro.

"I want to talk about Sarah," Maddie said as soon as they'd ordered and gotten their drinks. "You need to call her and talk some sense into her, Todd."

Todd took a drink of his water before responding. "I wish I could, but it's none of my business, Maddie." He sat back with a sigh. "Although, I will tell you that her mother is . . . concerned."

Maddie dropped her head. "I know it's not your place, Todd, and I know you cannot say a lot about what Miss Susan has told you, but still . . ."

"But still, what?" Luke asked. "What do you want him to do, Maddie? *You're* her best friend."

Maddie looked around the table, her lips pursed. "I *thought* I was. She's not listening to a thing I say and, well, Todd's about the only one she *will* listen to."

"It's really not Todd's place, honey," Luke said. "She isn't doing anything wrong. Maybe it's not *smart*, but it's still not wrong, at least . . ." He glanced at Brady. "At least as far as we know."

Their food arrived then and, after Todd blessed it, Maddie looked across the table at Brady, who salted his fries before trying them. The Bistro, by his estimation, had a weak hand when it came to the saltshaker. But maybe that was just him.

"Brady, what do you think? Don't you agree that someone needs to reach out to her and help her?"

"Help her what?"

Frustration pinked Maddie's cheeks. "Help her see what is going on?"

"Nothing," Brady answered.

She looked at Todd, then Luke, then back to Brady. "What do you mean?"

"You asked me what I think. I don't think anything," he replied.

The pink changed to a light shade of red. He had made her angry. Not that he meant to. He appreciated the fact that Maddie cared about Sarah. But, for him, this was all just a little too much. "Brady, really? Come on! This is your dream woman we are talking about," she fired off.

Brady set his fork down firmly. "Maddie," he said. "Like Todd, it's *none* of my business."

Luke looked Maddie directly in the eyes. "Maddie, I know you're upset." He glanced around. "All of us are . . . in our own way. At the core, we worry about her, but we can't force her to do anything and the more we push, the more distance she will put between her and us."

Todd nodded in agreement, then looked at Brady as if he expected him to say something.

"Our relationship is nonexistent at this point," Brady pointed out, "so it is truly none of my business. I haven't heard from her in months and probably won't hear from her again until she is in some mess or in some trouble and she needs me." He set his jaw. "Let's be honest. That's about the only relationship Sarah and I ever had. She does what she wants. When it all turns into a mess, she turns to me."

Maddie's shoulders sank. "To be honest, it's been some time since I have heard anything," she admitted. "I mean, I get it. I feel like she only wants us around when she needs us."

Luke grinned at Brady. He'd always said Maddie had one foot in her mouth before she even started any conversation. His raised brow said, "told ya" and Brady smiled, albeit weakly.

"Maddie, if that's how you feel too, like Todd and like Brady, why are we having this conversation?" Luke asked.

Maddie dipped a fry into the mound of ketchup she'd squirted on her plate and swirled it around. "I'm just worried. Probably shouldn't be because she drops us all the time, but I guess this is what I look and act like when I get worried."

Todd cleared his throat. "Look, guys, I don't know that she's using anyone. I mean, she could be, but think about it like this for a minute. It could be that *we* . . ." He pointed around the table. ". . . all bring back some painful memories for her. We were the ones who were there when Peter died and tried our best to get her through it. That being said, just being around us could be painful for her."

"Didn't think about it that way," Luke confessed. "I am the one who pressed Maddie to look at how Sarah was using her . . . us . . . well, everyone. By all appearances, that is what she has been doing for years, but maybe you're right, Todd."

"So, can we stop talking about it?" Brady asked, then smiled. "Can we talk about something else . . . like . . . I dunno . . . the holidays? Or maybe . . . again, just throwing this out there . . . why Luke is just so . . ." He reached over to pop Luke's ball cap off by flipping the bill. ". . .good looking?"

And, with that, everyone laughed.

❄ ❄ ❄ ❄ ❄

December came. With it, a new development, one that brought great joy to Brady and his family. Chelsi was bringing home her boyfriend from Southport. So, for once, the attention was off Brady and on Chelsi.

For once.

Chapter 48

Hours stood between the world and Christmas. Brady's mother's Christmas Eve dinner was both a celebration of the season and a welcome party to Chelsi's boyfriend, Neal. Todd, Melanie, Luke, and Maddie had been invited to join the family for the meal.

For Neal, the evening was somewhat an initiation.

There was the usual stomping off of boots and the shedding of coats and scarves once Chelsi and he finally made it inside. Chelsi made the introductions and Neal, having glanced around the front room of the house, said, "Your home is lovely. Reminds me of a *Southern Living* cover."

Brady had to swallow a chuckle.

Within minutes, Melanie and Todd arrived.

"Wow, smells like Christmas, Mrs. Jameson," Melanie said.

"It's my cookie-scented candle."

"I just smell Christmas *food,*" Todd said with a chuckle.

"Of course you do," Brady said before shaking Todd's hand.

Brady's father walked into the foyer and extended his hand as well. "Todd," he said. "Welcome."

"Larry, it's always good to see you." He glanced into the living room. "Look at that tree, would you, Mel? What is that, Larry? A ten-footer?"

"Nine," Brady and his father said together.

The doorbell rang again. "I'll get it, Mom," Brady said, then opened the door to Luke and Maddie.

"Hey, guys," Brady said as he gave first Luke a hug, then Maddie.

"What's up?" Luke responded.

"Same old, same old, except," he dropped his voice, "this year Chelsi is in there with a guy that is at least six-two."

"Does she look smitten?" Maddie asked as she removed her coat.

"I'd say." Brady closed the door and reached for the coat. "And, he's a former baseball player."

"Hey, listen, I just finished dropping the money off to Mr. Johnson," Luke said. "He told me to tell you thank you for working the lot for him again. You know, his health is really going downhill. I wonder how long he's going to be here."

"Yeah, me, too." He motioned to the living room. "Shall we?"

Chelsi beamed as she introduced Neal to Luke and Maddie. Then, with a look at Neal, she said, "Well, if everyone is here . . ." She held up her left hand to show off a lovely diamond that sparkled on her ring finger. "We're engaged!"

After squeals and hugs and back-slapping, Neal turned to Todd. "Hey, Todd, I know it would mean a lot to Chelsi if you'd perform the ceremony."

"I'd be honored," Todd said.

"And Brady, Luke, of course I've heard so much about you two. I'd like it very much if you would be my groomsmen."

"Of course," Brady agreed.

"Awesome," Luke said.

❄❄❄❄❄

After dinner, the group played Dirty Santa and then, around 10:30, Luke and Maddie, Melanie and Todd said their goodbyes, slipped back into their coats and scarves, and left for their homes. Brady stayed for a little while longer. He hoped for some time alone with Chelsi and Neal but, at the same time, fought an emotion that had niggled at him all night.

Everyone had someone. His mother and father had each other. Todd and Melanie. Luke and Maddie. Now Chelsi and Neal. But for him . . . was there no one? Had he missed an opportunity with someone else along the way?

Around 11:30, Brady hugged his sister with the reassurance that he would see her in the morning. Then he stepped out into the frigid, black, star-filled night and walked toward his truck, his breath a cloud that blew back into his face.

He sat for a moment in the truck's cab, letting it heat up, and playing with the radio until he came across an old version of "Have Yourself A Merry Little Christmas," which he immediately turned off. Could another Christmas alone be merry at all?

Within moments, he drove through downtown and, when he came to where the bench sat as solitary and alone as he felt, he tried to look the other way but found he could not.

She's not going to be there. He knew as much, but the bench knew this visitor would arrive. Crawling out of the truck, he went just to sit.

Why? At this point, there was no explanation other than this was the place he came to on Christmas Eve. Even if she didn't.

The chilly wind cut its way through his coat, freezing his skin and adding another level of ice to his frozen heart. He sat down and stared at his boots before looking across the way toward a grouping of downtown apartments.

At least the town was quiet. At least here he could remember the days and moments from a time gone by and he could hold on to a hope that refused to die. At five minutes to midnight, the last light of the apartments shut off, catching his attention for a moment. No other movement took place.

He bowed his head and whispered a prayer toward heaven, but he felt as if the prayer was getting caught in the tree branches behind him.

"Father, why am I alone? Why doesn't she want me? God, I have tried to leave it in the past, but I can't, and I don't know why. She chooses everything and everyone but me. She comes around only when she needs me, then she disappears again." He rested his elbows on his knees and looked down at his hands, red from the chill. "Won't You help me get over her and get on with my life? I want to feel what everyone else gets to feel. I want to feel complete and have someone to share life with. Year after year, I have come here and year after year I leave here alone. I felt like Sarah and me—and me waiting for her—was Your will, but now, I just don't get it." He sighed as tears moistened his cheeks. "Help me to move on. Bring somebody into my life who will love me. Somebody I can love."

He wiped away his tears as the clock struck twelve. A new day and another Christmas had arrived. He all but hoisted himself off the bench and returned to the warmth of his truck, then drove away, noticing the beauty of the wreaths throughout the city. And, as always, the lights gave a shimmering of hope and the trees resounded a holiness in the atmosphere, even if he was broken.

As he neared the road that led to his house, he chose not to turn, but to drive on. He turned on the radio again, this time to an instrumental version of "Silent Night." Before long, he found himself passing the city limit sign for Blowing Rock. The radio's DJ spoke softly after Mercy Me's "The Newborn Has Come" concluded. "An appointed moment," he said. "An appointed place. God came to earth, His Son taking on the likeness of man. Not a moment too soon or too late, but precisely in the design of redemption that God had for humanity." He paused, and the words wrapped around Brady like the scarf around his neck. Warm. Secure. "Let's listen now to 'O Come, O Come Emmanuel,' and let us remember that God is and has always been in control. His love for people never fades. Even tonight, no matter where you are or what you are going through, His miracles can continue to bless you, if you will let Him in."

"Yes," Brady said into the darkness. "Yes."

And so for Brady, such a miracle had come that night. What had escaped him for nearly a decade now rested within him.

Peace.

Chapter 49

CHELSI AND NEAL CHOSE A date in late May for the wedding, mainly not to interfere with Neal's baseball responsibilities. Chelsi also wanted an outdoor wedding much like Luke and Maddie's had been, specifically at Brady's. The couple came to West Jefferson as often as they could to meet with Todd, the florist, and the caterer.

"Brady," Chelsi said before leaving for home in late January, "I have a favor to ask."

"Anything."

"We're coming back for Valentine's weekend and . . . well, I'm bringing my friend Andrea." Her eyes widened. "She's going to be in the wedding and she's great at wedding planning so . . ."

"So?"

"Well, we—Neal and I—made plans to go out with Luke and Maddie and Todd and Melanie for dinner and I was . . . sort of hoping that . . ."

Brady got it. And he chuckled to ease his sister's pain. "I get it. You want to set up a blind date."

Chelsi chewed on her lip. "Do you mind?"

Brady winked. "Not at all."

The date turned out not to be so bad. Andrea, a small-town beach girl from the Outer Banks—Buxton to be exact—had a personality that fit in well with the rest. Brady found her to be a bit quiet at first. Not that he blamed her. Anyone who dared invade their group was bound to be stunned into silence, at least for a while.

He also found her to be exceptionally pretty, something his little sister had failed to mention. She had fixed up her long blond hair so that it lay over one shoulder of a dress that matched her blue eyes.

Once the group was seated at the restaurant and the menus had been passed out, the basic chatter slowed. Everyone studied the listings as if they were studying for exams. He overheard Chelsi say something about Hawaiian chicken, but his focus was on steak. Just as he was choosing his sides, Andrea leaned over and said, "I really appreciate you taking me out of dinner for Valentine's Day."

"I appreciate you letting me take you out," he replied with a smile. "Have you decided what you want?"

She smiled and Brady noticed the perfection of it. "Well, Chelsi just said something about Hawaiian chicken and that sounds pretty good, so . . . What about you?"

Brady closed his menu. "Steak."

She nodded. "If it's done right, nothing beats a steak."

"You are correct."

She closed her menu as well, then asked, "Are you ready for Chelsi to get married? I know my brother will have a rough time when I do. He already told me I couldn't get married . . . ever."

"I guess so. Still feels a little weird thinking about my little sister being all grown up," he joked. "But—" he stopped as the waiter approached the table, order pad in hand. After everyone had given their order, Brady raised his glass. "I'd like to make a toast to everyone at this table tonight. Each of you are a blessing and tonight is an incredible night. We get to be together. To share Valentine's Day is something I hope we will all remember years from now. Cheers!"

The glasses came together as the group echoed, "Cheers."

Later, as the group enjoyed their meal, Brady couldn't help but feel a certain amount of unwanted attention coming his way—his and Andrea's, to be more specific—from the others, which he tried to play off by engaging her in conversation. The general stuff; nothing heavy. But all the while his own thoughts cut in—*was Andrea the one he had prayed for . . . could he let go of Sarah, even by some degree, to open the door for someone else?*

"So, you guys getting ready for the big day?" Maddie asked Chelsi and Neal, bringing Brady's musing to a close. He sliced into another bite of steak, then aimed it for his mouth, his eyes now focused on his sister.

"Trying to," Chelsi said. "Man, it's a lot of work."

"That it is," Luke said. "There's a ton of decisions to make, then the day comes, and it seems like it's over as quick as it starts." He paused a beat, then realizing everyone now smiled at him, he said, "What? Well, it's *true*."

"Are you sure you weren't the bride, Lucille?" Brady teased.

Luke pointed his fork at him. "Don't go there, Bradford."

Chelsi waved her hands. "You two . . ." which brought a wave of laughter from the group, including Andrea. "Andrea, excuse them. Trust me, it's been a lifetime of this."

"Trust us all," Maddie said.

"Back to *me*," Chelsi teased. "Since I am *the* bride . . . I'm trying to enjoy *all* of it without stressing out too much."

"I think you're doing great," Andrea said. "You haven't gone crazy yet so you're good to go." She looked around at the group. "And I should know. I've been sitting on the front row for many of the decisions."

"She has," Chelsi agreed.

"Well," Melanie added, "make the most of it."

"Hey, Brady," Maddie chimed in, "are you taking notes on all of this?"

Brady frowned as he spoke around another bite of steak. "Not really. Why do you ask, Madalyn?"

"Because you're next. The whole group has gotten married so now, you *have* to be next." She raised her glass of sweet tea. "You better be taking notes, boy."

Brady shook his head and laughed. "We'll see about that."

"Well, I know which direction I am aiming the bouquet," Chelsi said laughing, then pointed across the table at Andrea.

Even in the low glow of overhead lights and the flicker of the table's candle, Andrea's face noticeably pinked. "I can't catch," she said, then placed her palms down on both sides of her plate. "I need to be excused . . ." She started to push back from her seat, but Brady stood and helped. She looked up at him and smiled. "Thank you."

"You're welcome."

"Wait," Chelsi said. "I'll join you."

"Me, too," Maddie said.

Todd glanced at his wife. "Honey . . ."

But she shook her head. "Nope. I'm good," she said, and Brady grinned, knowing that her remaining at the table meant she'd be able to fill the others in on the conversation between the men. And, of course, whatever was said in the restroom would be shared with Melanie by his sister as soon as possible.

"She's into you, man," Luke noted as soon as they were out of hearing range. "You better not mess this one up."

"I don't have to mess it up. There's the distance." He shrugged. "Plus, I don't know her. Sure, she's pretty, but . . . wait a minute. Why am I explaining this to you?"

"Brady," Melanie offered, leaning forward, and crossing her arms to rest them on the table, "don't be afraid to take a chance." Her brows shot up in a peak. "I mean, we all know what's what and we love you. We want to see you happy."

"Yeah, man," Luke said. "Just take a chance."

Brady gave him his best "drop it" look, knowing full well it wouldn't work but was worth the try.

"Look, dude, the preacher's wife just said it and she is *definitely* closer to heaven than you or me. What can it hurt?"

"Can we please just enjoy tonight and not worry about what may be or may not be?" He'd had his fill of his meal, so he placed his fork and knife on the plate. "We all know what you're thinking. Heck, I'm thinking the same thing. In fact, I may be thinking more than you realize. But . . . can we just—"

"I agree with Brady," Todd said "Yes, we all know what and who is on everyone's mind and we all want the best for you, Brady. You know that." He raised his chin. "Aaaaand incoming," he said to denote the arrival of the other ladies as they made their way back to the table.

❄ ❄ ❋ ❄ ❄

After arriving home, Brady started a fire in the house, then began sketching a design for Chelsi and Neal's wedding. Periodically, thoughts of Andrea popped into this mind, but memories of Sarah never allowed him to spend too much time on someone new.

At midnight he decided he'd done all he could do for the day. The night had been a good one and, he had to admit, Andrea's company had been pleasant. Perfect for such a night. Maybe, if he could put all memories of Sarah away—all hopes of her—then perhaps Andrea's company would be pleasant and perfect for more than just one evening.

He all but fell into bed, his phone clutched in his hand.

Happy Valentine's Day, he texted.

He turned the phone facedown beside him and went to sleep.

Chapter 50

BRADY GRABBED HIS BIBLE, HIS phone, then took off for church in his truck. He pulled into the parking lot behind Chelsi and Neal, who waited for him to join them for the walk inside.

"Where's Andrea?" he asked.

Chelsi looped her arm with Neal's as she answered, "She had to leave early."

He nodded. "Oh, yeah, that's right. She mentioned she had a bear of a workweek in front of her."

"Sooooo, did you like her?"

"She's really nice, Chelsi, but you have to know that it may or may not happen. Don't get your hopes up, okay? There's the distance, you know, but no matter what, I think she and I will be great friends. Let's just give it time and see if anything comes of it."

They went inside and found seats near their mom and dad.

After the song service, Todd approached the pulpit with a look Brady had never seen before. Usually, Todd led with a corny joke or funny illustration, but not that morning. He went straight to the heart of the message. "Today, we look at the biblical understanding of love. Today, however, we are going to look back at a time when God taught a man to understand His love for His people. It's the story of Hosea. Please turn there with me."

Shuffling filled the room as the pages of a hundred Bibles turned. Brady grinned. He'd always called it a biblical-page orchestra, and, in his mind, it pleased the Lord.

Todd told the story of Hosea and Gomer, drawing in the

congregation with the message. "Gomer, a promiscuous woman, perfectly depicts how we treat the Lord. Hosea learned the pain of love as the one he loved went astray time after time . . . Hosea, through the pain, through the rejection, learned what the love God has for His people truly looks and feels like. He learned what the Lord *feels* like when we turn away from Him time after time, choosing the *world* over the *Creator* of the world. Gomer was never going to find in the world what she had in Hosea." He paused. "So, we come to two questions. One: how are we loving God? Do we remain faithful to Him or do we look to the world for what we think we need rather than clinging to Him? The second question is this: how are we loving others? So often, people offer love and show love when others do what they want them to do but stop loving when something unacceptable is committed. Remember this. We are all like Gomer. Let me say that again. In our own ways, we are all like Gomer. Yet, we are also called to show the love that Hosea showed, the very love that God shows us every day. Love is so vitally important. So is understanding how to effectively give away such a love. First Corinthians 13 gives us the characteristics of such a love. 'Love is patient, love is kind. Love does not envy, is not boastful, is not conceited, does not act improperly, is not selfish, is not provoked, and does not keep a record of wrongs. Love finds no joy in unrighteousness but rejoices in the truth. It bears all things, believes all things, hopes all things, and endures all things." Again, Todd paused, and for a moment Brady felt as if he were looking straight at him. "'Love never ends.' So, do we *truly* love? We can answer that by looking at Hosea and assessing our love for others through the lens of 1 Corinthians 13."

The congregation rose to sing "Jesus Keep Me Near the Cross" as Todd opened the altar for prayer. Several couples made their way to the altar, praying together, asking God to hold together their marriages or relationships. Individuals joined them, some, Brady supposed, thanking God for His unending love while others prayed to learn to love as God loves.

But Brady remained at his seat, standing. He bowed his head. He felt the furrowing of his brow. As he had on Christmas Eve, Brady called to out to the Lord. An inner turmoil rose between what he had heard—*Love never ends*—and what others thought he should do.

After the song concluded, a prayer was offered to close the service. Still, Brady didn't move. Though everyone around him chatted amongst themselves, he eased himself down to sit as a pillar of prayer. He didn't look up. What he was enduring was not bound by a benediction.

At one point, Chelsi said, "What about Brady?" to which their father answered softly, "Leave the boy be."

A few minutes passed and the noise of the sanctuary became silent. When Brady finally looked up, he realized he was now alone.

He slipped out of the church, then walked to his truck, which sat as alone as he felt in the parking lot. Once inside the cab, he pulled his cell phone from his pocket, turned it on, and dialed the number for Mr. Johnson, who had a cabin in Meadows of Dan, Virginia. "Any time you or Luke want to use it," he had told them both, "it's yours for the asking."

Well, now he was asking. And Mr. Johnson, in his man-of-few-words way, merely answered the request with, "You know where I hide the key."

More than anything, rocked to his core, he wanted to get away, drown out other voices, and listen quietly enough to hear the still small voice of God. He didn't even feel the need to tell anyone where he was going. He hurried home to retrieve some clothes, then headed out of state.

As he neared Galax, Virginia, Brady's phone lit up with a text from Todd, which he read at the first stop sign he came to.

Seems like the Lord was doing something with you today. Hope you are good. Call me if you need me for anything.

He was halfway through the hour and forty-five-minute drive. He had no intention of turning back or talking with anyone who might try to give their two cents, no matter how much he respected them.

A while later, he pulled up to the cabin, then sat in the truck for a moment to embrace the scenery. The tidy cabin with the tilting front porch. The overgrowth. The creek shimmering under the afternoon sun off in the distance and the split rail fence between it and the cabin. He grabbed his overnight bag, bounded out of the truck, found the hidden key, then made his way into the cabin.

"Brrr," he exclaimed as a puff of warm air left his lungs only to hang about like a cloud in front of him. Thankfully, he and Luke had visited in November to cut firewood for the season at the cabin. The forecast called for snow, which was pleasing to Brady. He had his Bible, wood for the fire, and no one was around but himself and God. He dropped his bag onto the sofa of plaid fabric Brady guesstimated to be a leftover from the 1970s, then set about to making a small fire.

With it now roaring warmth into the room, and not wanting to be rude to Todd, Brady finally texted back around 4:30.

Time for me and the Lord to work some things out. Need to know Him more and understand Him.

He set the phone on the counter, then took his bag into one of the two bedrooms, and unpacked.

Later, with the fire now no more than glowing embers, Brady returned to the truck, then drove to Mabry Mill for supper. A plate of breakfast food sounded like the perfect meal, so he ordered "The Hunt"—a spread of pancakes, bacon, and home fries. On the way back to the cabin, he stopped by the food market to get some snacks and drinks. As he rolled to a stop in front of the cabin, snow began to fall.

It only took a few minutes to get another fire burning in the fireplace, but it failed to rival the burning in his heart. He pulled up the Amish bentwood rocker Mr. Johnson had purchased for his wife several years back, opened his Bible, and began to take notes.

For nearly two hours, he studied and jotted notes. The fire began to die down as the midnight hour approached and the kindling within Brady also burned lower than it had earlier in the day. He moved to the bed, turned on the television, and hoped he could fall asleep. As he lay there, the chill of a winter's night was overcome by a blanket that brought an undeniable warmth.

Okay, so his Valentine's text hadn't been answered, but it didn't matter. Brady was learning . . . the focus for his life needed to be on what he did, not on what others did or did not do.

Chapter 51

BRADY WOKE EARLY THE NEXT morning, slipped out of bed, and ambled over to the one window the bedroom boasted. He pulled back the gauzy drapes to see the sun peering over the hills, revealing a transformed landscape from what had been sixteen hours earlier. Brady felt a similar transformation even as a chill ran through him. He hurried to the fireplace to start a fire.

After getting warm, he dressed and stepped outside to look at the beauty of the snow-covered mountains. What was naked and barren on his drive up was now covered in white. And, he noted, just as peace had fallen from the heavens to cover the landscape, peace had begun to cover Brady's soul. He stood and looked, breathing in the cold air, felt it expand within his lungs, and somehow found the reprieve from normal life invigorating. This trip had been wise. The solitude allowed him to think aloud.

The lure of doughnuts and orange juice drew him back indoors. After his less-than-healthy breakfast, he returned to the rocking chair, took out his notebook, and began to answer the questions he had wrestled with.

"Everyone says I'm crazy for still wanting to be with her," he finally said. "Lord, I feel like You want me to wait, like You're telling me to be patient." He paused in his prayer as he rocked back and forth. Back and forth. He then wrote: *What do I do? What do you want me to do?*

He turned to the book of Galatians and jotted down the words he read in the tenth verse of the first chapter. *For am I now trying to win the favor of people, or God? Or am I striving to please people? If I were still trying to please people, I would not be a slave of Christ.*

He sat quietly for a moment and rocked as he stared at the fire. The crackling of the wood served as a peace to his soul, just as did the words he read in Galatians. Did those around him think he was crazy?

Yes, they did, especially Luke. But what was at stake was bigger than anyone else's opinion.

He spoke the words over to himself and the repetition served as his own motivational speech.

After a few moments, he wrote down his next question: *What is love, Lord? What is the real sense of love?* He longed to understand why life had transpired for him the way it had. Maybe a day *would* come where he would get married. *Did* he even understand love, or did he see love solely through the scope of what others had said about it?

He turned back to 1st Corinthians, then wrote down the words from Chapter 13. He imagined for a moment what those characteristics looked like in a life. In *his* life. Patience and kindness. Forgiveness and understanding. He thought about the words of Jesus from a verse he had memorized years prior. He then wrote on paper what had been etched in his heart. *No one has greater love than this, that someone would lay down his life for his friends.*

He had laid down his life for her. They had made a promise—one he'd meant—and his life was placed on hold.

She had his heart.

He'd give up everything for her. Still, when was it time to give up and move on?

He certainly felt the need to move on. This wisdom in it. But his heart had never let go—could never let go—of her completely. However, the love that God has for people and the love he had for Sarah, was unending. He could push it aside, but he would never be able to fully let her go.

Everything that happened in his life left him wondering what it would have been like if she had been there. He often thought of things she had said, finding a feeling of joy in her words. He thought about moments they'd shared and wondered what she was doing most days.

True love cannot walk away, he knew, but giving up on the hope of something more seemed logical.

He turned to Hebrews 13:5, and again scribbled down the words in his notebook: *For He Himself has said, "I will never leave you or forsake you."*

Never. The word stood out. He had been taught *conditional* as a child, but with the word "never," Brady realized the unconditional nature of the presence of the Lord.

What began with a sermon on the book of Hosea had led to a time for Brady to understand how to love. As the day continued, he continued to ask questions and ponder the consistent nature of the God he loved, the God he served, and the God who loved Sarah.

Though he had only planned to stay one night, he decided to stay another. With nothing pressing at home, he could lose himself in a place out of the ordinary. Away from home, his mind could embrace the Lord, his heart could rest, and his life could be redirected. At home, he would deal with the temporary. What was happening on the side of the snow-covered mountain had eternal implications.

Before heading to bed, he knelt before the Lord in the living room, the heat from the fire warming his skin, the nearness of the Lord, his soul. "Father, I am in awe of You and I am overwhelmed by the way You love me. Lord, I don't deserve that. I am completely unworthy of Your love and of the grace and mercy You have shown to me. You brought me here and You have spoken to me here. I get it, Lord. I get it now. I know that I can't love anyone the way they ought to be loved on my own, but if You change my heart and my life, anything is possible. Give me a love for her that You have for her and I pray that You give me a love like that for everybody around me. My life is in Your hands and I pray that You will help me. In Jesus' name, amen."

He rose from the floor with a renewed sense of peace. He ambled to the bedroom, picked up his phone and sent Todd a text.

God has changed my heart. Thank you for the sermon you gave yesterday. That put a lot of things in perspective for me.

Within a minute, Todd returned the text.

Always here if you need me. Thank you for your kind words. When are you coming home?

Tomorrow. Be blessed tonight, Brady texted back before shutting the phone off.

A few more logs on the fire meant a longer warmth. Brady grabbed a blanket folded atop an old hope chest, then returned to the living room and sprawled out on the couch to watch television.

He never made it to the bed that night.

❄ ❄ ❄ ❄ ❄

Another dusting of snow fell that night and as Brady awoke on Tuesday morning, the ground remained covered under the blanket of white. He praised God for the day and the revival of his heart. He took out the trash, tidied up the cabin, and then locked the door, a different man from the one who had only recently unlocked it.

On the way out of town, he stopped at Christmas in the Meadows, then Nancy's Candy Factory before leaving altogether.

But his *situation* had not changed. She never returned the text from Valentine's Day, which could be a sign for what would be. Now, though, it didn't matter. He would do as he felt God leading him to do regardless of what she did in response and regardless of what others thought. A step in his faith began with a change in expectations. He would do what was right and let God do what He can do and what He chooses to do.

The drive seemed to pass quicker than normal and, for a fleeting moment when he pulled in the driveway, it was as if he were coming to West Jefferson for the first time.

Chapter 52

SHE HAD GOTTEN THE TEXT but simply couldn't text back. A return text could start a conversation. A conversation would lead to a revelation. Namely that Brandon had turned out to be exactly who her mother warned he would be. Though it had taken some time, Sarah's eyes finally opened to his true nature. And so it was that on Valentine's Day, the relationship ended. Brandon had left Sarah drained financially, emotionally, and mentally. She paid the last of his bills and saw the last text from another woman on his phone that she would ever see.

Brady's text came in as Brandon took the last of his stuff out of her townhouse. A couple of shirts, some books, his gaming system, and a few other things that fit neatly in a box she had prepared for him. Reading the text only served to hurt her heart more than it already was. She had made another bad decision and knowing that Brady still thought about her only made her feel worse.

She needed change and her life needed redirection. Asheville had become like an old campground fire—no more than the mere ashes of a life she had once dreamed of but would never realize. At that point, the very thought of developing any relationship, even a friendship, sucked the strength out of her.

When spring came, the hope of a seasonal boost to her system proved empty. The temperatures rose daily, but her heart remained cold.

Owning her own graphic design business offered her freedom that most eight-to-five jobs restricted. Her residence could be anywhere. Flexible hours and only herself and her clients to listen to gave her the independence to choose anything. Anywhere. Moving had begun to sound good.

She sat at her desk, doodling the possibilities, then looking them up online when her phone rang. "Hey, Mom."

"What are you doing, honey?"

Her shoulders sank. How was it that her mother always seemed to know when to call her? Or when *not* to. "Not much."

"I don't believe that. I know you. You're always into something."

Sarah hesitated, before answering. She didn't like to lie to her mother, but she also protected her mother from possible stresses by avoiding full disclosure.

"Umm . . . well, I'm doing some research if you must know," she responded, clicking on a link on her computer and laughing at her mother's assertion that she was always into something.

"For one of your accounts?" Susan asked.

Again, Sarah paused. If she revealed her plans to move, even though they were at the beginning phases of a thought, or a whim, she knew her mother wanted her to come back to West Jefferson and would say so. Reluctantly, she revealed the nature of her research rather than delaying the inevitable. "Not really. I'm actually thinking about moving."

"Oh, honey. Are you moving back home? I mean, you are always welcome to move in with me. This house is huge and . . . well, lonely."

Sarah sighed. She had to let her mother down quickly. "No, Mom. I'm looking at other places."

"Oh," her mother replied, her disappointment thick enough that one word started Sarah on a guilt trip.

She shouldn't have said anything. She leaned back in her chair, wishing her mother could understand. In a perfect world, West Jefferson wouldn't be a painful memory, but her world was far from perfect, the shattered pieces barely hanging together. Her reality was made up of stories far removed from fantasy. "Mom, I—"

"So, where then?"

"Maybe the beach? Virginia, maybe? I don't know. I was also

looking at going back to Tennessee. I just started thinking about this. To be honest, I even looked at New York City. I know it's not what you want, Mom, but I'm dying here in Asheville and I just *can't* come back to West Jefferson."

Her mother took a deep breath, which led Sarah to both grimace and smile. Her mother was fighting an urge to lecture her adult daughter. But, once a mother . . .

"Okay, honey. What can I do to help?"

Sarah's mouth fell open in true surprise. Her mother *had* resisted the urge to lecture.

"Honey?"

"I'm checking my pulse. I think I may have died," she teased, and her mother laughed along with her. "Right now, there's nothing anyone *can* do. I'm just looking around. I really just want a fresh start, you know?"

"Well, I'm behind you, no matter what."

Sarah's mirth turned to tears. So much had built up within her and knowing her mother was right about Brandon had devastated her. Furthermore, her unspoken regret of cutting ties with the group in West Jefferson stood in the way of her returning, as did the constant questioning from church members and friends about her mental state. "Mom, that means so much to me. I'll keep you updated." She stood, walked into her bathroom, and pulled a tissue from the box. "Can you do me a favor? Don't tell the people in West Jefferson that I'm moving. I just—I just need to start over."

"Oh, honey. I promise. I won't say a word. I love you, Sarah."

"Love you too, Mom."

After disconnecting, Sarah returned to her research, making a list of the benefits of living in each city as well as the downsides. Cutting the list to three to four served as her first step, then she planned to spend at least a weekend in each city to truly get a feel for each place.

For the rest of the weekend, she stared at the computer and jotted notes. She binged on pizza and Netflix, with the Netflix serving only as background noise. Her mind created dreams and images of what life could be somewhere else and, for once, she allowed such thoughts to be okay. By Sunday night, the list had whittled down to four magical destinations.

Gatlinburg, Tennessee seemed like the most likely. Not too far from home but far enough to be a real home. Her second choice was Southport, North Carolina, which could prove to be a shoreline haven for her soul. She smiled, remembering the Nicholas Sparks book and movie set there.

Her third choice was Williamsburg, Virginia, rich in both beauty and history. The longshot was New York City, a place that offered not only a different *place,* but a new *pace.* She mapped out the month of August as her month to travel and experience what each had to offer.

She booked lodging, then mentally began to decide what she would pack and what she would leave behind.

Chapter 53

BRADY WORKED EVEN HARDER DURING that spring than he had in years past. Chelsi's wedding was the first major project. He built an arbor, much like the one for Luke and Maddie's wedding, but added a kneeling bench for the couple to take communion during the wedding.

On the Thursday before the wedding, Brady drove over to Blackjack's for a bite to eat. Entering, he caught a glimpse of Chelsi and Neal, who had arrived a few days earlier. "Hey, guys," he called as he made his way to their table.

Chelsi sprang from her seat to give her brother a hug, nearly knocking the wind out of him. Neal stood and extended his hand.

"What are you doing here?" Chelsi asked as the men exchanged a handshake, her question drawing a look from both Brady and Neal.

"Umm . . . well . . . getting something to eat. That's what they do here," Brady answered with a grin. "I had to take a quick break from setting up the wedding to eat before I passed out. And, just so you know, everything is nearly done and tonight Luke and I will cook the pig."

"Hey, man," Neal said, "I cannot thank you enough for everything. You are awesome."

"Not a problem. I actually enjoy it, to be honest."

"You want to join us?" Chelsi asked, pulling out a seat for her brother.

Brady shook his head and held up a hand. "Looks like you guys are about done. Plus, like I said, I need to get all this done before tonight so I'm just going to get mine to go."

"Brady, we would gladly stay here with you while you eat," Neal offered.

"It's all good. You guys staying at Mom and Dad's tonight?" he asked as he looked over to flag down a waitress whose attention he couldn't quite catch.

"Yeah. Then Neal's getting a hotel room tomorrow night. Can't run the risk of him seeing me on the morning of the wedding. We don't want or need any bad luck," Chelsi explained with a slight giggle.

"Are you kidding me?"

"What?" Neal asked.

Brady rested his hands on his hips. "Man, you are about to be my brother-in-law. You aren't wasting money on a hotel. You can just stay at the house."

"You sure? I mean, I don't want to get in the way or anything."

"Yes, I'm sure. After the rehearsal, just stay at the house. Bring your stuff and don't forget the clothes you are going to change into after the wedding."

"Thanks, Brady," Neal said, extending his hand again. "That's pretty cool of you to do that."

A server walked up to them then. "The usual, Brady?"

"Yes, ma'am, but I need to get it to go."

"You got it," she said before turning on her heel and heading for the kitchen.

"Are you sure we aren't asking too much of you, Brady?" Chelsi asked.

"Absolutely not. Besides, I'm billing Dad for all of this anyways."

They laughed at the very notion.

"So, everything is good for tomorrow and Saturday? You don't need us to do anything?" she asked.

"Nothing at all."

"You guys have gone all out for us," Neal commented. "And to be honest, I'm ready for the rehearsal to be over so I can eat some barbecue."

"Careful," Chelsi chimed in, her eyebrow raised. "This is about more than food, you know."

"Yes, ma'am," Neal teased. He looked at Brady. "I've only got one thing to say. I'm just glad we don't do this *every* weekend. This is exhausting."

Brady slapped his future brother-in-law on the shoulder. "Come Sunday we'll all sleep."

Chapter 54

BRADY AND LUKE STAYED UP all night cooking the pig. Brady's dad and Neal came by for a little while but left after the older of the two declared that he was ready for bed.

"Dad," Brady said with a chuckle, "it's barely nine."

"And I've got some years on you. Just wait," he said, pointing at his son, "you'll see one day."

After they left, Brady and Luke set up several white canopy tents, then placed tables and chairs underneath. They lined a trail with tiki torches and put others at the four corners of each canopy.

Thankfully, the rehearsal wasn't scheduled until 6:30 Friday night. After pulling the all-nighter, Brady went to bed, not to wake up until around five o'clock that evening. He showered and got dressed by 5:30, then he went outside to meet his mother, who had called out to him in the middle of his shower. When he found her, she was under one of the tents with his father and Neal's parents, whom he'd met only recently, all four decorating the tables with flowers and candles.

"Looks like we're doing this," Brady teased, to which his mother replied, "Goodness, let's hope so!"

Within minutes Chelsi, Neal, and Andrea arrived in one car, Todd and Melanie, who sported the tiniest of tiny baby bumps, in another. Brady glanced at his watch; he expected Luke and Maddie any moment.

He walked toward his sister and her bridesmaid with purpose—to kiss the bride and to welcome her guest. Andrea was as sweet and friendly as she had been months before, and now that the pressure was off, Brady felt more at ease than he had previously.

The rehearsal ran smoothly, the only interruptions brought about by Brady and Luke being Brady and Luke. After two walk-throughs, everyone went to the tents to eat.

Barbecue pork and chicken, baked beans, slaw, rolls, and hushpuppies had been beautifully displayed. Todd blessed the food and as they approached the table, Neal lit up like a Christmas tree, drawing fresh laughter from Brady and Luke.

The crowd ate until they were nearly sick. Laughter filled the air and as Brady took note of Chelsi and Neal, he saw his sister had found a soulmate, a relationship he believed would last and endure all that life threw at them.

After cleaning up, the crowd went home except for Neal, who stayed with Brady.

They made their way into the house where Neal's luggage had already been placed in the guest bedroom. "Make yourself at home, Neal. If you need anything and you can't find it, just ask."

Neal sat on the couch and stretched his legs. "Thanks, again . . . and by the way, the food was incredible tonight."

"Help yourself if you want more. Mom put it all in the fridge," Brady said as he sat in the recliner and reached for the remote.

"Man, if I eat anymore, I won't be able to wear my clothes tomorrow."

Brady nodded in understanding. "The Braves are playing. You wanna watch?"

"You never have to ask me that."

The two talked about baseball for more than an hour. Neal talked a little about his career, but mostly they talked of teams and greats of the past, while Neal shed even more light on his hopes for the future.

As the clock neared the eleven, Brady righted the recliner and said, "Well, I slept all day, but if I don't go to bed now, I won't get up in the morning. And since your bride insisted on a morning wedding . . ." Brady stretched as he spoke.

Neal lifted his hands in mock surrender. "I voted for the evening, but she said she didn't want the guests to have to endure the heat."

Brady handed the remote to Neal, then started for the hallway door. "Good point," he said with a chuckle.

"Hey, Brady," Neal said, calling him back in. "Can I ask you something?"

"Of course."

Neal leaned forward, resting his elbows on his knees and lacing his fingers together. "Are you okay?"

"Umm . . . yeah."

"No, I mean, like . . . are you happy?"

Brady nodded several times. "Yeah, I'm happy, man."

Neal stared down for a minute before looking back at Brady. "I'm sorry, Brady. I'm not trying to be nosy or nothing, but Chelsi worries about you all the time and I never know what to say to her. I mean, I want to reassure her when she starts worrying, you know?"

Brady cracked a grin to ease the tension of the moment, then ran his teeth over his bottom lip. "I know she worries. But honestly, life is good. I found something recently that changed nearly everything."

"What's that?"

"A deeper understanding of faith and a new understanding of what love is." Brady returned to the recliner and perched on one of the armrests. "I went to the mountains awhile back and spent a couple days by myself. It made a world of difference."

"Really?"

"Everything makes more sense now. I came to grips with what was, what is, and whatever may or may not come."

"Well, you seem to be at peace. I hated to ask anything but really, Chelsi gets all stressed out sometimes and now I can tell her that you are all good."

"I am," Brady said as he stood again to leave. "Hey, Neal . . ." he said at the door.

"Yeah?"

"Thanks for asking. I know that's a weird thing to ask but I'm really thankful you did and even for the reason. You obviously love my sister."

"That I do."

Brady made his way to the bed. The next day promised to be exhilarating and exhausting.

Chapter 55

THE GUESTS BEGAN TO ARRIVE at ten o'clock the next morning.

The bridal party made their entrance on cue, then stood in line waiting for Chelsi to enter. Brady stood in line beside Neal's father, who served as best man. Luke stood to Brady's left. Maddie was Chelsi's matron of honor and Andrea served as her bridesmaid. As the music began, Todd asked everyone to rise.

Then Chelsi appeared with their father, this vision of her blurred by the tears that suddenly sprang into his eyes. He swept them away with a thumb before glancing over to see a smile sweep across Neal's face. Brady tried to avoid looking at his dad but found himself as drawn to him as he was to Chelsi. His father, whose face was normally stoic, broke a little more with each step he took down the aisle with his little girl. Brady sent a smile in his direction, hoping to ease the pain and, for only the briefest of moments, the smile was returned. His father had long said that the four hardest words a daughter's father would ever have to say were, "Her mother and I."

A half hour later, as the newly married couple walked up the aisle, Brady caught a glimpse of Sarah's mother seated near the back. His breath caught. Had Sarah come as well? But as he looked beside her, there was no Sarah.

After photos, the wedding party moved toward the tents. Brady walked behind the couple, next to their mother and father.

"Chelsi," a voice called out and he looked in its direction.

"Oh, hi, Miss Susan," Chelsi said to Sarah's mother. "Thank you so much for coming today."

"You look beautiful. I mean, absolutely stunning," Susan said as she hugged Chelsi.

"Thank you so much."

"Look, unfortunately, I can't stay. Sarah couldn't make it today, hon," she said, and Brady stopped, his parents continuing on without him. "She wanted to, and she got your invitation, but she just couldn't make it."

"Oh, it's not a problem. I understand."

Susan handed Chelsi two cards as Brady now drew closer. "She sent this and asked that I get it to you. Here is one from me, as well."

"Thank you, Miss Susan. You guys didn't have to do that."

"We love you. I promise that Sarah wasn't being rude or anything. If she could have been here, she would have."

"I understand. Oh!" She looked up at Neal. "Forgive my poor manners. Neal, this is Susan Ashford, Sarah's mother."

"Very nice to meet you," Neal said as he shook her hand.

Brady cleared his throat and took a step toward a woman he'd known his whole life and now suddenly felt awkward around. "Hey, Miss Susan. Good to see you today."

She hugged Brady and smiled. "Good to see you, too, Brady. Sarah was just heartbroken she couldn't be here today."

"Well, it's a busy time of the year, so I understand that." And he did. What he didn't understand was that Chelsi invited Sarah without even mentioning it. He glanced toward the tents to see Luke waving him over. "I'm really sorry but apparently Luke needs me. Probably can't figure out which fork to use," he said, smiling. "Which means I've got to get over there. It was nice to see you. Tell Sarah we said hello."

For the next several hours, photos were captured on cell phones as well as by the photographer Brady's father had hired as the reception became an all-out celebration. They ate. They danced. They ate some more. Then, as the heat began to rise in earnest, the newlyweds prepared to leave by going inside to change for the honeymoon. "Brady," Chelsi said. "Can you walk with me to the house?"

Brady placed his Mason jar glass filled with sweet tea on the linen-covered table. "Sure thing."

Then, to Neal, she said, "Honey, can you walk on ahead. I'd like to talk to my brother about something."

Neal winked at her, then gave Brady a nod and Brady knew where the conversation was headed. "Look, Chels," he began as they started for the house.

"Bubba, I didn't know what to do."

"About inviting Sarah?" he asked, his focus on Neal's back. He was only a few feet in front of them, so the conversation wasn't exactly private.

"About inviting Sarah, yes," she said, her voice lowering. "I didn't want to put you in an awkward situation by her being here and I didn't want her to feel left out or unwanted."

Brady smiled. "This was your day. You had every right to invite anyone you wanted to invite."

Neal stopped and turned. "Brady, I told her to tell you that she had invited Sarah, but she didn't think it would come up," he explained as Brady and Chelsi made it to where he now stood. "I almost said something last night, but figured it wasn't my place."

"Guys, it's okay that you invited her and there is nothing to worry about. I promise. It was fine that she wasn't here, and it would have been just as fine if she had shown up. Just do me one favor."

"Anything, Bubba."

"Don't ever hide anything like that from me again. That whole situation should not have been on your minds on your wedding day. This is about you guys. Nothing else. Can we agree not to hide anything? From now on?"

"Agreed," Neal said.

"Promise," Chelsi seconded.

"Now, get inside. Go get dressed and enjoy your honeymoon," he said, then gave his sister a hug before giving the same to his new brother-in-law.

❄ ❅ ❆ ❅ ❄

As Brady worked later that evening on the cleanup, he remained silent on the subject of Sarah's invitation. But the "what ifs" ran through his mind as garbage was bagged, tables were torn down, and chairs were folded.

What *would* have happened if she had been there? What would he have said to her? What if he could have talked to her once more, face-to-face?

Eventually the rest of the cleanup crew—Luke and Maddie, Todd and Melanie—said their goodbyes. Night fell and again, Brady was the only occupant in his house. This time, however, he didn't feel alone.

Chapter 56

SARAH'S LANDING SPOT WENT TO Gatlinburg, Tennessee.

Southport offered peace by the sea and she loved the sound of the ocean and its scent that combined with the crashing waves. They seemed to tell her soul that everything in life would be all right.

Her weekend in New York overwhelmed her. Fast-paced and an abundance of offerings made the city alluring, as were the possibilities for business in such a large city. Fulfilling a dream, she took in a Broadway show. The view of the city and the lights almost had her choosing New York. But the cost of living broke the deal. Sarah feared she couldn't afford living there in the manner she wanted. So, New York became only a vacation spot—one she planned to return to—and not a residence.

Williamsburg brought a different sense of joy. Inspiration bloomed with each step she took down the cobblestone roads in the historic districts. While New York had moved fast and futuristic, Williamsburg moved slow and harkened back to a time when life seemed simpler, less distracted. A time when community mattered.

But Gatlinburg presented the mountainous backdrop her life had been built upon. Another plus was that she would live within driving distance to her mother. Not to mention that Gatlinburg gave the allusion of a Hallmark film set. She also liked the way water flowed down the Pigeon River through the town with access points calling out to drivers to stop and rest for a moment. When her Gatlinburg weekend extended beyond the weekend and then into Tuesday, she knew she had made her decision. The time to look for an apartment had come, and hopefully one that matched her personality.

She toured four places before returning to Asheville to ponder the possibilities. Resisting the urge to make any quick decisions, she called her mother as soon as she unpacked.

"Mom, I really like Gatlinburg. I looked and found a few places while I was there."

"Back to Tennessee, huh?" her mother replied with an upbeat lilt that Sarah didn't buy. "Well, I made that trip a few times during your four years of college, so I know how to get there."

Sarah had so wanted her mother to be as excited as she. After all, this *wasn't* New York, and it *wasn't* Virginia. "It's less than four hours from home. Not too far away, you know?"

Her mother didn't answer right away, and Sarah assumed she was choosing her words before responding. "I know. I'm sorry, Sarah. I just wish you were moving home with me or, if not that, to West Jefferson."

Sarah understood her mother was lonely and she had certainly encouraged her to get out there . . . date again . . . find a group of friends to have outings with . . . but she had no interest. When Sarah's father abruptly exited, her mother's world had become Sarah. Sarah's leaving home for college had left her mother dangling.

"You never know, Mom," Sarah said, breaking the silence, "maybe one day I will come back home. But for now, I want to look into other places."

She didn't want to give her mom a false sense of hope, but she also didn't want her mother's reaction to drain the rush of hope she felt about moving somewhere new, a hope she hadn't found for some time.

"Well, at least Gatlinburg is a great place to visit," her mother noted.

Sarah had moved into the laundry room and had started to sort her clothes from the trip, dropping the first load into the basin of the washer. "Yeah, I mean, you can come any time you want and stay as long as you want . . . if I go there."

"So, you haven't completely made up your mind yet?"

"Well, no. I mean, I don't know. I do know I need to get out of here and right now, Gatlinburg feels like the best fit for me." She poured detergent into the cap and then over her clothes before closing the lid and pushing the appropriate buttons.

"What are you doing?"

"Laundry," Sarah answered with a smile before exiting the room. "That never-ending job."

Her mother chuckled. "Then I'll leave you to it."

Sarah said goodbye then ended the call before ambling to her desk and sitting. Pictures of Gatlinburg hung on the bulletin board behind her desk. Yes, Gatlinburg seemed exciting, but she tempered the excitement by reminding herself that there were months between now and the end of her lease in Asheville. As anxious as she was, she simply had to wait.

❄ ❖ ❄ ❖ ❄

Sometimes, time flew past her, but with the nature of everything, now time dragged on. At night, Sarah looked at online brochures of the apartments and daydreamed about what life could be like in the hills of Tennessee. She stared at the layouts of the apartments, determining where she would place furniture and jotting notes about items she needed to get rid of versus the ones she'd need to purchase once she landed there. She had loved her years in college, but as an adult, her perspective was different. Her love for her alma mater also made the move appealing as she would only be separated from the campus at Knoxville by about an hour. She could again attend football and basketball games, experiencing the excitement of Saturdays in fall and the snow-kissed weekends in the winter.

As September ended and October began, Sarah decided to surprise her mother for her birthday. Because that year her birthday fell on a Friday, Sarah made plans to end her workday early on Friday and make the drive before traffic became congested.

Nervousness filled her as she drove closer to town. The thought of

West Jefferson still brought pain, as did the thoughts of running into people she knew. They loved her and she was aware of that, but the shame of pushing them away made accidental interactions upsetting to think about. Hoping to avoid coincidental encounters, she decided to take her mother out of town for their celebration dinner.

As she pulled up to her childhood home, she put on her smile like Marilyn Monroe in front of a crowd, covering the anxiety of the moment. One night. She was doing this for her mother and she only had to be there one night. She wouldn't see anyone, there would be no awkward apologies, and her mother would be thankful.

Instead of using her key, she rang the doorbell, her overnight bag at her feet. Moments later, her mother answered the door. Sarah spread her arms and posed with a loud, "Ta-da!"

Her mother's squeals of her joy wrapped around her almost as quickly as her arms. "Sarah! What are you doing here?"

"It's your birthday," Sarah answered as she stepped back. "I wanted to surprise you. Are you surprised?"

"Aw . . . I am. I am. Come in, honey."

They walked to the living room and Sarah placed her bag beside the love seat. No one ever sat on the love seat. It was the place where purses and mounds of clothes fresh from the dryer landed, waiting to be folded. "Is it okay if I stay here with you tonight?" she asked.

"You can stay here anytime you want for as long as you want, you know that."

"Well, I wanted to take you out to eat tonight if you're up to it. What do you think?" she asked.

"Well, I don't know . . . I was going to warm up a can of soup . . ." She beamed. "Of course I am up to it. I just need some time to get ready."

Sarah playfully looked at her watch. "You have ten minutes, young lady . . ."

Susan laughed before leaving for her bedroom and Sarah carried her luggage up to her old room. She dropped it at the foot of her bed, then walked over to the window and peered out at the mountains.

The leaves, early in the process of changing, provided a kaleidoscope effect with the red, yellow, and orange colors woven together. Their home was less than fifteen miles away from the Blue Ridge Parkway, the very highway people came from hours away to take a drive down during the fall season. What they longed to see was readily available right outside of Sarah's childhood window.

She left the window to sit at her old desk, the one that had supported her through hundreds of hours of high-school homework and stared intently into an old vanity mirror she used as a teenager to get ready for dates and football games. She blinked at her reflection; what happened to the girl who'd stared back at her?

Brady crossed her mind, which brought a frown. She hadn't tried to forget but she also hadn't tried to remember. She'd left the past behind, but she also thought about his faithfulness over the years. She'd leave. He'd stay. She ran away. He waited.

She turned to look out the window again, this time at the driveway, the very driveway where he'd brought her home after the incident at the prom, then back to the bulletin board where a photograph captured a memory from a youth trip.

There he was.

She missed him. His consistency gave her peace, but she had long passed up her chance with him. By this point, he would have moved on. Found someone else. He would no longer want *her*.

"Sarah?" her mother's voice called from downstairs. "Ready."

Sarah stood, ran her fingers through her hair, and made her way to her mother, who had taken a shower, then slipped into a stylish red dress.

"Where are we going tonight, honey?"

Sarah grinned. Her mother had a few preferences in life. Sarah knew most of them and she knew what restaurant assured satisfaction from the birthday girl. "I booked us a table at the Glendale Springs Inn."

Her mother's eyes sparkled in the overhead light. "You know I love that place!"

"I know. That's why I picked it. Are you ready?"

Her mother held up a clutch purse, wiggled it in the air, and said, "Ready."

The drive down Highway 16 provided a picturesque backdrop that they both commented on. Then, Sarah teased, "So, how old are you now, Mom?"

"Stop that," her mother answered with a giggle. "You know how old I am. Fifty years old."

"No," Sarah retorted. "Fifty years *young*." She turned her face long enough to catch the sincere smile from her mother. "What are you hungry for tonight?"

"I'm going to have the blackened salmon. By far, it's my favorite thing to eat there," she answered as Sarah drove the car into the parking lot beside the imposing Victorian home-turned-inn and restaurant. They got out and walked inside where they were immediately seated in high ladderback armchairs that flanked a small table draped in white linen.

"What about you?" her mother asked once they'd received their menus. "What are you getting?"

"Hmm . . . I think it's going to be the beef strip loin," she answered. "No, wait a minute . . ." She pointed to the right side of the menu. "I'm having the ribeye."

"You and your beef," her mother laughed.

"Cows make me happy," Sarah grinned in return as the server approached.

They placed their orders, and the server made his way back to the kitchen after letting them know he'd have their salads out soon.

"So, honey, what's new?" her mother asked, taking a sip from her stemmed water glass.

"Not a whole lot. Working like crazy. I've looked hard at moving to Gatlinburg, which is where I think I'm going to end up."

"Okay." She placed the water goblet back on the table. "So, what's your plan? Are you going to buy a place or rent?"

"Hard to say. I'm thinking about a six-month lease. That way, I can try it and see if that's where I want to be. I also found some more specials on cabins. Wouldn't that be fun? I'll be like a pioneer woman."

Her mother laughed easily. "You'll never be a pioneer woman, Sarah." She motioned to the dark wood glowing in the ambience of muted lights and said, "*This* is about as rustic as you get."

Sarah slipped the white linen napkin to her lap and grimaced. "That much is true."

"But a temporary cabin may be fun."

Sarah nodded. "Then I can make a better decision. I'll know the area better and . . . you know."

"Well, it sounds like you are approaching it wisely."

"Trying to. I know I need a change but making the wrong change would only make it all worse. I have a history of further complicating already complicated matters," Sarah said with a chuckle.

"Well, again, I think it's smart. I really do."

"You do?"

"I do. Try it out. See if it's where you really want to be. If not, then you can look somewhere else. If it is, then you can make that commitment. It's a heck of a lot smarter than signing away a year of your life without being convinced that's where you want to be."

The waiter arrived with their salads. As they began to eat, Sarah felt uplifted by her mother's support. She'd expected discouragement but the opposite proved true.

Later, after their food arrived, her mother took her first bite, then moaned in delight. "You should try this salmon."

Sarah's nose curled. "I'm good."

"You don't know what you're missing."

"I'm pretty sure I don't want to know. I can't eat anything that smells like that," she said, pointing to her mother's plate with her fork. She sliced a single bite of steak before clearing her throat. "We've talked enough about me. How is *your* life?"

"Me?"

Sarah brought the beef toward her mouth, then paused. "Well, we are here to celebrate *you.*"

Her mother dotted at the corners of her mouth with her napkin before responding. "You know me, Sarah. I keep to myself. I go to work, and I go home." She paused. "Most of the time."

Sarah reached for her glass. "Most of the time?"

Her mother blushed in the glow of the room. "I'm taking a photography class."

"Really?" Sarah dropped her hands to her lap. "I didn't know you liked photography."

"I do. In fact, I love it. Before you were born, I spent a lot of time taking pictures. The Arts Council offered a photography class and I happened to see the sign one day as I was getting a coffee at Bohemia. Normally, I would have ignored it, but something told me to throw caution to the wind and do it. It's every Tuesday night for eight weeks. I found something that I had lost over the years and honestly," she smiled, "it makes me happy."

"Mom, that is so cool. Who knew you were an artist?"

"No, honey, *you* are the artist. What I do I would hardly call art," she joked. "It's a fun hobby and one I can do by myself."

Sarah finished her next bite of ribeye before pressing the matter. "Well, since I am staying here tonight, can I see your pictures?" When her mother hesitated, Sarah leaned forward and said, "Oh, come on, Mom."

"Okay. I'll let you see some of the pictures but there is one stipulation. You cannot laugh at them or at me. I have weird taste in pictures."

Sarah "crossed her heart."

"All right then. I'll let you see some of them when we get back to the house."

"Okay. I can't wait."

Her mother took a final bite of salmon. "Delish," she said around it.

"Save room for cheesecake, Mom," Sarah told her. "You know how much you love their cheesecake."

Chapter 57

THEY PULLED UP TO THE house after nightfall and made their way into the house, Sarah excited to see her mother's newfound passion on display.

"Want some coffee?" her mother asked as she walked toward the Keurig.

"Sure, but I can fix my own," Sarah said, even though, as she said it, she scooted onto a barstool next to the island.

"I've got it. I'm standing here already."

Minutes later, her mother brought two cups of coffee along with the creamer and sugar bowl over to where Sarah sat.

"Okay, Mom," Sarah said sliding off the stool. "Don't sit down. I want to see your pictures and I know you are putting it off to see if I will forget."

Her mother sighed as she shook her head at the determination of her daughter. "Okay. We can go to the living room so we can set the pictures on the coffee table. But remember, you promised not to laugh."

"I promise."

They made their way, cups of coffee in hand. Susan placed her mug on the table, then made her way to the study to retrieve her portfolio.

"Here they are," she said, her voice quivering as she handed the albums to her daughter. "Don't forget. I am *not* a professional."

Sarah turned the pages, excited to see a side of her mother she never knew existed. "Mom, I love this," Sarah exclaimed as she looked through the pictures, pausing when she came across an image of an old tobacco barn. "I love the angle on this and that the picture is in black and white. Where did you take that one?"

Susan leaned back on the couch while balancing her cup of coffee. "I was driving one day and saw the old tobacco barn off the road. Thankfully, I had my camera with me, so I decided to stop and snap a few shots. I wasn't sure they would turn out, but I thought they came out pretty good."

"I think it's awesome."

"I liked the rustic look of it. That old barn had been weathered, but it was still standing." Her mother leaned forward again to stare at the picture for a moment. She then joked, "Kind of like me; old and weathered but still standing."

Sarah flipped over some more pages in the book, still in awe of what her mother had captured that others would never have noticed. "You should do something with your photography."

"Like what?"

Sarah paused for a moment to think before replying. Her mind raced as possibilities flowed.

"I don't know. I mean, you could sell your prints in Bohemia. They feature local artists there. You could also try to get some of them featured in a gallery somewhere. You know what else you could do?"

"What?"

"You could compile some of them for a book. People love photography and maybe you could make one for Ashe County or just for West Jefferson."

Her mother grinned at the encouragement from her daughter, but her doubts were seen in her reaction to the encouragement.

"I don't know if they're quite that good, Sarah."

"Mom, when I was with Peter, our whole relationship revolved around galleries. I've seen it all as far as the weird, the simple, and the amazing. I think these could get featured. You need a theme, but yeah, these are that good."

Her mother preened a bit. "I might just do that. Who knew a silly hobby could actually lead to something?" She took a final sip of coffee before saying, "I have to go to bed, sweetheart. I'm a little tired, in spite of all your enthusiasm."

Sarah hugged her mother. "I'll probably be up for a while."

Her mother cupped her chin in her hand. "Not too late. I don't want you sleeping all day tomorrow." She smiled. "I love you."

"I love you, too, Mom."

Sarah spent a while going through the remainder of the photographs before stretching to rise and return the mugs to the kitchen. She glanced at the clock on the stove. It was late, yes, but she wasn't tired. What she wanted, more than anything, was to take a stroll downtown and, with the lateness of the hour, the streets should be empty with little chance of running into anyone she knew.

A breath of fresh air beckoned, as did the desire to bid a farewell to her past. The breaking of dawn meant the ghost would disappear again, this time possibly for good. She was moving. To move forward, however, the doors to what was had to be closed.

Chapter 58

HER HEART DROVE HER TO the place her mind didn't want to go. Or was it the other way around? Visions of the past were not pleasantries, the echoes of those ghosts still haunting her in the present.

She turned onto Jefferson Avenue and drove through town. Not a soul journeyed down the streets, not a single car or truck other than her own dared to disturb the stillness. She pulled up in front of Bohemia—darkened and almost lonely looking—and parked, ready to take a walk and breathe in the mountain air.

The things before her offered a cocktail of pleasure and pain. She remembered moments with her dad as a child, his abrupt abandonment and its effects rippling through her life even now as a woman in her mid-twenties, including his refusal to attend her wedding, to give her away, unless she also invited his current girlfriend. When she'd been a child, he always brought her uptown with him when he had quick errands to run.

As she walked, she glanced back at Bohemia. She and Maddie spent so many evenings there. When they turned sixteen, driving to get coffee was one of the first things on their list of things to do. An *adult* thing to do. Over time, such a trip wasn't such a big deal, but the place was special for so many reasons. There they had talked about boys, school, and what the future might hold. For Maddie, it had always been Luke. But for Sarah . . .

She continued down the street until she reached the end, stopping to look at the church. The recollection of worship songs filled her as she remembered those Sundays and Wednesdays. She leaned against the building and stared for a few moments, remembering the youth group meetings. No longer did she believe, leaving the church after Peter's death, burying her faith alongside her fiancé in a cemetery in Asheville. She attended a few services after the accident, but could only do so a few times, unable to continue following something she no longer believed.

Help me in my unbelief . . . The words slipped into her heart; she must have heard them during one of Todd's sermons.

She turned and walked up the other side of the street. She walked past Blackjack's, where music played but everyone was confined inside. Memories of Friday nights after football games, the twangs and beats of country music, a side of fried pickles, and the company of friends made the place special in such a way that would never change.

Her pace picked up and she ducked her chin to make sure she saw no one. She prayed no one recognized her.

With nowhere to be, now was the time to wrestle with everything inside her. Compartmentalizing her life had helped her exist but if she wanted to live again, she needed closure. Answers. And she needed to deal with things left undone. When she came to Third Day Market, she stopped long enough to peer through the windows, marveling at the Christmas trees and the beauty of miniature lights that pierced the darkness within.

She circled back to her car. Within a hundred yards the place that couldn't be passed by stood like a sentinel, poised to keep watch. Her mind told her to keep going, but her heart wouldn't let her pass by without stopping.

The bench.

The place where her relationship with Brady began. Beneath the lambent light of a streetlamp, she had sat crying twice, and twice he had come to her rescue. She made a promise here, and regardless of desperate attempts to recall the good, shame weighed on her as she knew she had broken the promise. She also knew *why* she had done so.

To protect Brady.

She crossed her arms against the chill that seemed to suddenly permeate the air and looked up at the arch of blue-black sky dotted with brilliance as she lowered herself to the bench and crossed her legs. The seasons were changing. Visual evidence reinforced the truth as what had been green was transforming more by the day. And, just like the year, her life now entered a new season. Her residential move nearly in motion, she now tackled the beast of returning to what was to move into what would be.

She remained at the bench for a while, then stood and walked toward her car with a final glance back at the bench. A silent goodbye.

As morning broke the next day, Sarah spent time with her mother before gathering her stuff to drive back to Asheville. She had to box up more of the old to prepare to move into the new.

"Want some help?" her mother offered after Sarah mentioned the work that lay ahead of her once she got back to Asheville.

"You want to come down?" Sarah asked, surprised by the offer. "Don't you have to work?"

"I've got so much sick time, I could take six weeks off," her mother answered with a laugh. "I don't really use my vacation or sick days anymore."

"Well, sure. I could use your help," Sarah agreed, amazed that her mother wanted to go to Asheville. In the years that Sarah called Asheville home, she had visited rarely, and never longer than a night or two at the most.

"Give me a half an hour to pack some stuff for the week and make a call to tell them I won't be in for a few days."

"Are you sure you won't get into trouble?" Sarah asked.

"Honey, my boss told me last week that I needed to use up some of my time off. I can say that I'm just following orders," she joked as she grabbed a suitcase out of a hall closet. She hurried to her room to pack.

Sarah again looked through the photo album to pass the time. Twenty-five minutes later, her mother rolled her luggage down the hall and closed the door as they left Ashe County.

They drove in separate cars but they were quite the tandem. They stopped along the way to eat, then finished the drive. They made it to Asheville by seven o'clock and, as they stepped out of their cars, Sarah called out to her mother. "Tonight we rest because tomorrow we work!"

"You are a slave driver," her mother joked as she removed her luggage from the trunk of her car.

Sarah did the same as she pulled her overnight from the backseat of her car. Having her mother there felt good. It felt safe.

It felt like home.

Chapter 59

ON A COOL SATURDAY MORNING in October, Brady and Luke revved up the chainsaws to cut wood at Brady's property for the Johnson cabin at Meadows of Dan.

"Any plans to go up to the cabin soon?" Luke asked as they finished sectioning off a tree. "I mean, seeing as you so kindly agreed to help Mr. Johnson with cutting the firewood?"

"Just going up there to take the wood for the season but not to stay. Why?"

Luke wiped the sweat off his forehead with the sleeve of his red-and-black plaid shirt. "Thought about taking Maddie up for a few nights. It'd be nice to get away."

"Well," Brady began, resting his hands on his hips. "I'm going to take the wood up tomorrow." He raised his brow. "That is, if you would finish splitting it, Luke Bryan. But I probably won't go back up 'til January."

"Luke Bryan, huh? Well, at least he's cool," Luke said with a grin. "I'll let you know what we are doing. I better ask Maddie before I commit to it to make sure that's what she wants to do."

Brady pretended to crack a whip.

"Hey, dude, I'm not whipped."

"Oh, okay," Brady said. "From now on, when we want to do something, I'm going to call Maddie first and ask if you can come out and play."

"Whatever." Luke threw his hand forward. "But I'm not whipped. If you think I am, then prove it."

Brady grinned and leaned against the truck. "All right. Do you want to go to the cabin?"

"Yeah," Luke replied.

"So, just decide to go."

Luke started to laugh. "I have to see if she wants to do that before I make any decision."

Again, Brady created the sound of the bullwhip, his laughter now becoming infectious.

"I'm *not* whipped," Luke said, holding back a laugh.

Brady finally sobered. "I'm just messing with you, you know that. You and Maddie have something I want to have one day." He took in a breath, let it out. "Come on. We need to get back to work. And we need to make sure we cut the tree into pieces that will fit on the splitter."

"I know . . . I know," Luke said.

As the day progressed, the temperature rose as quickly as the sawdust flew. Brady had stopped to get a drink of water when his phone rang. He pulled it out of his pocket, looked at the screen, then held it up toward Luke who cut off the chainsaw. "Chels," he said. "What's up, Chelsi?"

"Not a whole lot, Bubba. What are you doing?"

"Cutting firewood for the cabin with Luke."

"Hey, tell Luke I said hey."

"Luke," he called out. "Chelsi said hey."

"Tell her I said hey and ask her if she can move back up here and we will send you to live down there," Luke joked as he made his way to the water cooler on the back of the truck.

Brady shot his friend a silent "ha-ha." "So, what's up?" he asked.

Chelsi hesitated for a moment, then said, "Well, Neal and I wanted to do something but wanted to check with you before we go any further with it. I mean, like, if you don't want to do it, we understand and it's perfectly fine."

"Okay . . ."

"We wanted to know how you would feel about having Christmas here this year. What do you think?"

Now Brady hesitated. The tradition had always been to have Christmas at his parents' house. And though it may have seemed trivial to some, Brady treasured it. There was also the issue of Christmas Eve. And the bench, though with every passing year, he wondered why he kept it up. "Have you talked to Mom about it?" Brady asked.

"Yeah. She said it was okay with her and Dad, but that I needed to talk to you about it."

"Okay," he responded, wondering what he could say, really, that wouldn't be a complete disappointment to the whole family. Then, realizing there were no words, he answered, "I guess it will be Christmas at the coast this year."

"Awesome," Chelsi exclaimed. "We'll get all the details worked out as we get closer to the holidays."

They ended the call, then Brady shoved his phone into his back pocket before staring off in the distance for a moment. After a few minutes, he moved the wood over to the splitter where Luke waited for him.

"Christmas at the beach?" Luke asked, and when Brady raised a brow, he said, "I overheard."

"Yeah, evidently," Brady said as he rolled a large piece of wood onto the splitter. "Can't believe my mom went for it."

"Me either," Luke noted. "Your mom has always seemed to love doing Christmas, at least that's how it came across."

"Yeah, I know. It's going to be weird celebrating Christmas somewhere other than West Jefferson."

Brady pulled the lever to send the blade through the wood. The noise gave pause to the conversation.

"Maybe it will be a good thing," Luke added after. "Sometimes, new is good."

"Maybe," Brady said, tossing aside the pieces of split wood. "Let's get back to work."

"I getcha."

Sometime later, Luke left to go home and Brady went to work in his shop. Building a new piece occupied his mind while he struggled to deal with his sister's phone call. He understood. She wanted Christmas in her new home. And he didn't blame her. But as much as he didn't blame her, he also didn't much care for life's changes. Especially when it came to . . .

Then again, maybe this was God's way of stopping it. Keeping him away from West Jefferson. Keeping him from going to experience the yearly disappointment.

Time would tell. Things were changing, that much was for sure.

And sometimes, change was a good thing.

Chapter 60

HALLOWEEN APPROACHED AND SARAH KNEW it was time to call the rental company to assess her options for renting a cabin. She knew she had cut it close and she cared little about appearance as it was only a forty-eight-day trial run to see if she could live there. But the non-negotiables were cleanliness and affordability.

"Yes, ma'am," she said after her call was answered. "I wanted to see about renting Bear Haven for an extended period of time."

"What dates are you looking for?"

"I'd like to check in on November fourteenth and stay until New Year's Day."

There was a short pause before the woman answered with, "Okay, well, it *is* available. Give me just a minute to put in the codes for discount stays." The clicking of computer keys filled the space. "There is a promotion of buy six nights, get the seventh night free. Since you will be there for about . . . seven weeks, we can give you one full week for free."

Sarah's eyes grew as large as her smile. "That would help."

"The weekly rate is normally four-fifty, but they are offering a monthly rate of a thousand dollars." Sarah waited while the woman continued keying in the discounts. "With another discount I can put in there . . . I can keep this around fourteen hundred for your entire stay."

"Are you serious?"

"Yes, ma'am," the woman answered, and Sarah could almost see the smile across her face. "These owners are different. They aren't trying to make a ton of money. They bought the place ten years ago and said they wanted it to be a blessing to other people."

Sarah did a quick calculation in her head. With having no utilities, cable, or water bills, she would actually *save* money during the trial run in Gatlinburg. "This is incredible," she said, fumbling in her purse for her credit card. "Here . . . I can give you my credit card number. Please go ahead and charge the full amount."

This must be the right thing to do. It has to be because everything is falling into place.

"I will send you a confirmation email, as well as the code to retrieve the keys from the lockbox. In the email, there is a list of emergency contact numbers. If you need anything, do not hesitate to call. Again, my name is Martha."

"Thank you so much."

Sarah's downsizing began. Decluttering her life seemed a logical step as she didn't want to make multiple trips and could buy new stuff after she bought a new place. By selling much of her possessions online, she rid herself of nearly all her furniture by the week's end. She'd sold her bedframe but kept the mattress and box springs, so they served as her new bed. She ate supper sitting on the floor each night and, before long, fell in love with the simplicity her life had taken on.

On moving day, she loaded the last of her things in her SUV, turned in her keys, and turned a page in life.

Five minutes into the trip, she called her mother. "I'm on my way, Mom."

"Great, honey. Are you excited?"

"I am. It's something new and it's cheaper. Hopefully, things are turning around."

"I think they are."

"When are you coming?"

"Well," her mother began, "I was thinking we could do Thanksgiving down there."

"*Really?*"

"Yeah, really. I could spend a few days with you, and we can do some shopping. What do you say?"

"Perfect! Oh, my goodness. That's next week! Okay," she laughed. "I can get things settled before you come down."

"I'll come down Wednesday."

"Sounds like a plan," Sarah exclaimed, the excitement of spending Thanksgiving with her mother rising.

Within twenty minutes, Sarah was out of Asheville, headed toward Tennessee. She drove on autopilot, her eyes and mind taking in the changing of leaves—from green to gold or red or orange. Everything was changing. Brilliant and majestic. She was alive, she told herself, and life was going to go better now.

Her heart soared with the opening of the door to the cabin. A view of the mountains stood unavoidable out the front windows. The wraparound porch beckoned her, so after unpacking the car, she made a cup of coffee and rushed to it. She rested her backside in a rocker, her feet on the porch railing, then breathed in the scent of coffee beans, crisp clean air, and—somewhere off in the distance—smoke from a fireplace chimney.

This was it, she told herself. This was her life now.

For days, she shifted and sorted until she settled in and had set up the cabin in a manner that brought her order. By the time her mother was due to arrive, Sarah would have put the final touches on the cabin, and she would be ready to celebrate the holiday with her mother.

Her mom arrived just before noon on Wednesday. After a quick tour, she put her stuff away, then found pen and paper to write down the rest of what was needed for the following day.

"So, can we go out? I needed to get cold stuff but was afraid it might go bad before I got here," she asked.

"Sure. Let me get my coat," Sarah said as she hurried upstairs. "Where do you want to go?"

"Just need to go to a grocery store . . . and maybe get a coffee."

"Perfect," Sarah said, descending the stairs as she put her coat on. "I'll drive."

They drove down to the village, first to get coffee, her mother taking in the decorations. Sarah smiled; they were as breathtaking for her mom as they had initially been for her. Still were. An overcast sky with temperatures in the lower forties said that autumn was close to giving way to winter and the coffee they purchased warmed their bones, shaking off the shivers of a cool November afternoon.

"Can we look around for a little bit?" her mother asked.

"Sure. What do you want to see?"

"Let's go to the candy store over there and get some chocolate," she said, pointing to the Ole Smokey Chocolate Factory.

"Mom, I need to lose some weight."

Her mother raised a brow while taking a sip from her coffee. "You weigh about as much as a feather. I think you need to gain some weight."

"Well, hey," Sarah said, patting her middle, "it is the holidays. Let's do it."

Chapter 61

THE SATURDAY BEFORE CHRISTMAS, SARAH'S phone rang. A glance at the caller ID told her that her mother—who was due to arrive soon—was calling. Eagerness swept through her; she was putting up a tree for the first time since Peter's death and had found healing in the hanging of ornaments and the stringing of lights. She couldn't wait for her mother to see it. To revel in it as she was doing now. "Hey, Mom. I'm getting everything ready. Wait till you see the tree," she said.

"Umm . . . Sarah . . . this is Carla, from Third Day Market," the voice on the other end of the line said.

"Carla?" Panic replaced her enthusiasm. "What's going on?"

"Sarah, your mom collapsed in our store a little bit ago. She was rushed to Ashe Memorial."

Sarah blinked several times, telling herself to breathe. *Breathe.* "Please tell me she's okay. Please."

"I don't know anything yet. I'm at the hospital with her, but they have her back in the emergency room. I got her phone from her purse and—where are you?"

"I moved to Gatlinburg last month." Sarah looked around the room as if in search for something she couldn't find. Wouldn't find. "Look, I am on my way." She unplugged the tree lights and headed into her bedroom. "Please call me if you hear anything. I'll be out of my house in fifteen minutes and I will get there as quickly as I can."

"Well, you be careful—oh. Hold—hold on a second. A doctor is coming this way."

Sarah tried to overhear what was being discussed as she pulled clothes from her closet and threw them across the bed.

"Okay, Sarah?"

"Yes. What is it?"

"Susan had a heart attack. They have her stabilized, but the doctor feels sure they'll need to do surgery."

"I'm on my way," she said, now darting into the bathroom for her toiletries. "Call me if you hear anything. If anything changes."

Nearly four hours stood between the cabin and the hospital. Four hours where anything could go wrong. She shouldn't speed, she told herself as she drove out of the driveway, but she had to hurry. She couldn't be too late. Couldn't—

She should have moved back home. Should have listened to her mother. She should be there, at the hospital, by her bed. It should be her talking to the doctors, helping to make decisions. Instead, she was driving to get there.

She had to stop to get to get gas, her tank only a quarter full, then continued to West Jefferson. Just before seven, she pulled into the parking area of Ashe Memorial Hospital. She called her mother's cell as she walked toward the building and Carla answered. "Where are you?" she asked. They had talked more than an hour earlier, Carla relaying that the doctors were doing "some sort of surgery."

"I'm in the waiting area of the lobby. If you walk straight in, I'll see you."

The doors whooshed open and she entered the holiday warmth of the lobby. She spied Carla, who stood from one of the occasional chairs dotted about. She hadn't seen the woman in years, but she recognized her immediately. The chestnut-brown hair that curled away from her face, the dark, unblemished skin, the full lips that always seemed to be smiling even when, in times like these, they were not.

They met halfway across the lobby. "Any news?" Sarah asked after a brief hug.

"She's upstairs," Carla told her. "And she's fine."

Sarah felt the weight of the world lift from her shoulders, but they sagged at the news. "What did the doctor say?"

Carla turned her toward the elevators. "That as soon as you arrived, to have him paged. He'd explain everything. The only reason they kept me informed as much as they have is because your mother was able to tell them it was okay. HIPAA laws being what they are."

"Oh," Sarah said, "Yeah, of course." The elevator doors closed behind them and she clutched her purse close to her belly. "Carla, I am so thankful you were there today. I don't know what—"

"Don't go there, now," Carla said, her voice instructional. "Susan scared us, that's for sure."

"I only know that y'all saved her life. Has she let on that she wasn't feeling well?"

"Not to me she didn't."

"She was coming to Tennessee to—" The elevator jerked to a stop and the doors opened. "—to see me."

Carla guided Sarah to the nurses' station and then they were led by a student nurse to the consult room. "Just have a seat in here," she said, motioning to the room lined by chairs surrounding a low-sitting coffee table strewn with magazines. She closed the doors behind her as she left, and Sarah crossed her arms. "I can't sit," she said, her eyes taking in the wallpaper, the artwork, and the escape instructions framed and hanging beside the door.

"May as well," Carla said as she lowered herself into the nearest chair. She crossed her legs and placed her purse in her lap.

Sarah acquiesced but stood again when the door opened and a doctor—balding and wise-looking with half-moon glasses that rested low on his nose—walked in. After introductions, the doctor slid his hands into the deep pockets of his lab coat and said, "Your mother had a mild heart attack, but nothing to be taken lightly."

"Okay . . ."

"After running some tests, we decided that the best course of action was *not* to crack her open but to go in and insert heart stents. Are you familiar?"

Sarah *was* familiar. While in college, a friend's father had had the same surgery. "I am, actually."

"All right then . . ." he said, then continued with how things would progress over the next few days. "Right now, your mother is still in recovery, but we'll have her in a room soon enough." He started for the door. "I'll have someone come get you shortly so you can be there when she arrives."

Sarah stayed beside her mother's bed all night burrowed beneath a starched, white sheet and too-thin blanket and stretched out as best she could in the room's recliner. She only slept intermittently, the nurses waking her every couple of hours when they came in to check on their patient. "How is she?" she asked each time and each time she received a, "Looking good."

The next morning, she opened her eyes to see her mother staring at her.

Sarah pushed the covers aside and went to the bedside. "How are you feeling, Mom?"

"I've had better days," her mother answered, her voice raspy. But she smiled all the same.

"You gave us quite a scare."

Her mother nodded, then ran her tongue over her bottom lip. "I'm thirsty," she said.

"Let me call for the nurse," Sarah said. "Mom?" she asked while they waited. "How long have you felt sick?"

"Since Thanksgiving," she said, then swallowed hard. "I just thought I had a virus or something. I didn't tell you because I didn't want you to worry."

Sarah tried not to cry but hearing her mother struggle to speak and seeing her so weak tugged at her heart. Wanting to lift the moment, she smiled down at her, then brushed errant hair from her mother's forehead. "Look. If you wanted to do Christmas at your house, all you had to do was ask. You didn't have to go to extremes to get me here."

The nurse stepped into the room with a smile. "Look who we have here," she said, as though they'd come to a party. "How are you feeling this morning, Miss Susan?"

"Thirsty."

The nurse looked at Sarah. "I'll get her some water and call down for a breakfast." She looked at her patient again. "We've got to get you energized like a bunny so we can get you home in time for Christmas."

Sarah smiled as the nurse left the room, then said, "I think I like her."

Her mother sighed. "So, I had a heart attack, huh?"

"Yes, and now you have to take it easy. You have to get some rest." Sarah walked back to the recliner and began folding the blanket and sheet. "And eat breakfast so you can be energized like a bunny." She looked over her shoulder at her mother who smiled in return.

"As long as I'm home for Christmas."

❄ ❅ ❆ ❅ ❄

Sarah had asked Carla not to say anything to anyone about her mother, so there had been no visitors at the hospital and no casseroles waiting for them when they returned home a couple of days later. The kitchen was fairly well stocked, so—at least—Sarah didn't have to go into town. There would be no one to face. No one to make small talk with.

While Christmas Eve was not what Sarah had thought it would be, it *was* a celebration of survival and life. She and her mother enjoyed the day by watching Hallmark movies while sipping hot tea. Around eight o'clock, her mother threw in the towel by saying, "I don't think I can stay awake much longer. I'm going to bed."

"Good," Sarah teased. "The sooner you get to bed, the sooner Santa can come down the chimney."

Her mother chuckled, then leaned over and kissed the top of Sarah's head. "Goodnight, sweetheart," she said.

"Night, Mom."

Left alone on the couch, Sarah sat with the next in the lineup of movies playing, but she paid little attention to it. She wasn't supposed to be in West Jefferson, she kept telling herself. She was supposed to be in her cabin, with her mother, drinking hot cocoa and pretending to hear reindeer on the roof.

    Instead, she was back home. On Christmas Eve.

    Again.

Chapter 62

THE PLANS TO GO TO Southport with Neal and Chelsi hit a last-minute snag. The newlyweds had bought a rambling historic home near the shoreline shortly after they tied the knot. They'd spent countless backbreaking hours restoring it, getting it just like they wanted, when—in the second week of December with less than fifteen days to Christmas—an electrical fire destroyed much of the kitchen. By the grace of God, Neal happened to be home and put out the fire before it spread throughout the house. The damage, however, was substantial enough to shift the family plans back to West Jefferson.

"At least you don't have to drive all the way down there," Luke noted as they wrapped up the last of the Christmas Eve sales at Mr. Johnson's tree farm. He sipped at a cup of coffee he cradled between his gloved hands. "You know, I never understood people who wait till the last minute to buy their tree . . ." he muttered.

"For some people it's a tradition," Brady said, staring down at his own cup of cocoa. "For others, it's just cheaper."

"Maddie'd die if I said, 'Let's wait till Christmas Eve.' She's gotta have the house all done up from Thanksgiving on."

Brady laughed, then sobered. "Hey," he said. "Don't say anything to Chelsi but I'm not so unhappy we are having Christmas here. I didn't want to hurt her feelings when she suggested us coming down there but, you know me. I am a traditionalist when it comes to Christmas. It would have been weird not being here."

Luke rested his backside against one of the tables inside the small shed. "Have you heard anything from Todd and Melanie?"

Brady checked his phone in case he'd missed anything. "Not since lunch when they were heading to the hospital. Her contractions were getting closer together."

"You think it's a boy or a girl?" Luke asked.

"Ten bucks says it's a girl," Brady wagered.

"Oh, you're on. It's going to be a boy. However, when you pay me, I would like that ten bucks broken up into two fives if you don't mind."

"Whatever," Brady said, looking out of the shed to see if anyone was approaching for a tree and pleased to see that there wasn't.

"Think we ought to start loading the trees up?" Luke asked.

"Yeah, man. Let's get to it."

Seven trees remained. They stacked them on the trailer and with one tree left to go, Brady's phone chimed. He read the incoming text, then said, "Dude, grab that last one. Baby is coming. Todd just texted. Call Maddie and let's just go over to the hospital."

Luke hurried to get the last tree then jumped in the truck with Brady, calling Maddie on the way who met them a few minutes after they arrived. Together, the three friends found the maternity ward waiting area where they sat for roughly twenty minutes before Todd, decked out in hospital gear, emerged with a smile on his face. "It's a girl!" he said.

"Yes!" Brady air-pumped his fist before turning to look at Luke. "Ten bucks."

Luke shook his head and reached for his wallet. He handed Brady a ten, which Brady in turn handed over to Maddie. "Traitor," Luke said to his wife who grinned and stuck the cash in her pocket.

"Details," Maddie said.

"Six pounds, eleven ounces. All fingers and toes accounted for."

"What about the name?" Brady asked.

"Hope," Todd explained. "That way we can say that 'Hope was born on Christmas Eve.' We thought it was pretty cool, you know?"

Todd pointed toward the doors. "I've gotta get back. Luke and Maddie? Do you guys want to come back first? They only allow two people to come back at a time."

Maddie and Luke didn't have to be asked twice. They disappeared behind the double doors with Todd while Brady called his mother with the news, letting her know that he'd see her and the rest of the family in the morning.

Ten minutes passed before Luke and Maddie returned. They spoke in passing before Brady made his way to the back where he found Melanie looking no worse for the wear. In fact, she was downright resplendent. "Want to hold her?" she asked.

"Best not," he said. "I haven't showered since being outside all day at the tree farm." But he leaned over the bed and took in the tininess of her. The chubby cheeks and the full head of dark fuzzy hair.

"Do you guys need anything?" Brady asked after straightening.

"I don't. Mel, do you need anything?" Todd asked.

"I think we're okay. We've got what we need," she responded as she stared down at her daughter.

"Thank you for coming over here. We wanted you to be a part of this night," Todd said.

"I'm glad I was able to be here. You know, we were supposed to be out of town this year," Brady reminded Todd.

"I know," he said. "Makes you wonder if the Lord didn't keep you here this year for a reason. I'd like to think He did it so you could be here when Hope arrived."

Brady grinned and put his arm around Todd's shoulder. "When will they let you go home?" he asked.

"The day after Christmas," Melanie answered. "Which means we get hospital cafeteria food tomorrow." She smiled.

"Nothing doing," Brady said. "I'll come back tomorrow with plates for the two of you."

Todd looked toward the window on the far side of the room. "It's snowing," he said. "Isn't that just about perfect?"

Brady nodded. "I'd say so."

He left the young family to themselves, then headed back home. He intended to build a fire, then stretch out and watch a little television, but his stomach growled before he could even make it to town, so he decided to stop at the Waffle House, one of the few places open. A pecan waffle and hash browns sounded like the perfect meal for the evening.

Inside, Brady chose a booth on the far end of the restaurant where someone had left a copy of Charles Dickens' *A Christmas Carol* on the seat. He'd always wanted to read the novel, telling himself year after year that he'd buy a copy and do so. But, so far, he never had. When the waitress came to take his order, he asked about it, but she only shrugged. "No idea," she said. "If you want it, it's yours."

Brady smiled. "Good deal," he said, then slouched in his seat and opened the book to the first page. Time passed and before long he was lost in a story he knew from the retellings. While the waitress kept his coffee cup topped off, he ate slowly, all the while devouring the classic work of literature. When he ate the last bite of waffle, he checked his phone to see that it was eleven thirty. He laid a ten-dollar tip on the table and, after paying his bill, trekked across the snow-covered parking lot, the book tucked under his arm, and into his truck.

Makes you wonder if the Lord didn't keep you here this year for a reason.

The words echoed around him. He blinked several times as he started the truck and adjusted the heat to his liking, hoping to push his thoughts far enough away that, when he drove out of the parking lot, he would simply head for home. Watch TV. Fall asleep.

Maybe this will be the year.

He had witnessed hope earlier in the form of a child and, thinking on her, a new hope rose within him.

She's not going to be there. The only hope you'll see this year is that newborn. Don't waste your time.

He took a deep breath. Held it. Exhaled, a puff of white forming around him. He turned off the truck's engine, got out, and rushed back inside the restaurant.

"I need two cups of hot chocolate to go," he told the waitress.

Minutes later, he turned out of the Waffle House and headed downtown. Maybe she would be there. Maybe she'd finally realize how much he loved her. Maybe . . . maybe . . . maybe.

God had stopped him from being in Southport for Christmas; maybe Sarah was the reason why. After all, as always on Christmas Eve, he had everything he needed.

Just in case.

Chapter 63

Midnight approached. Brady sat on the bench, waiting, his eyes trained on the lighted Mary and Joseph kneeling at the manger across the way. Was it the coldness of the night or the situation that left him numb? Perhaps a little of both. Too much exposure to elements or disappointments can rob one of the ability to feel, he reckoned.

But in an instant, the pain grew even more intense than before, because he knew this had to be the end. This year would be it. He couldn't go on like this. Tormenting himself with what would not be had proved unproductive.

But would he continue to love her? Yes, with every fiber of his body, he would.

A tear rolled down his cheek. Still, he was at peace within himself.

He pulled his phone from his pocket. Eleven fifty-nine, it read. And then . . . the digital numbers shifted.

Midnight.

I thought this is what You wanted, Lord. I thought this was what You were teaching me through the story of Hosea. How could I have been so wrong?

He shook his head slowly as the snowfall persisted. The lights all around him continued to shine, but, within the deepest part of himself, the hopes and dreams he'd held on to for far too many years died. They had frozen to death in the very graveyard of a place where they fought for life for the previous half decade.

He needed to get up. He needed to go home. Yet, he struggled because this was the completion of it. It was over. He'd never come here again. Not like this. Never like this.

"Just breathe and get up," he whispered to himself. "You'll get through this."

A sigh. A last prayer. Now, a motion toward the warmth of something real, a trip back home would begin thirty feet from where he sat.

"I don't know why you want me."

Brady sat still. For a moment, he thought perhaps he had imagined the voice. *Her* voice. And even though he longed to turn around to know for sure, he stayed facing forward. "I always have. I always will."

"Brady . . ." she said, her words calculated. "Do you realize how broken I am? I'm not the same girl you fell in love with a decade ago."

For a moment he didn't know whether to laugh or cry. But he managed, "Sarah, I'm in love with you. Not because you were a prom queen or anything like that. I'm in love with *you*. The perfect parts of you and the imperfect parts."

She hesitated. He wondered if she would come around to face him, but it was as if they were as frozen as the ground beneath their feet.

"Why are you here again?"

The question caught Brady off guard and his eyes widened. "What do you mean?"

"You've been here the past five years. Every Christmas Eve."

"Who told you?"

"No one," she said after a moment. "I saw you."

Brady thought back. No one had been around those nights, at least not to his immediate recollection. Then, the flashes of what had been ran over him like a train. The car that passed that first year, the sleigh in the distance the second, the person walking down the sidewalk . . .

"That was you?"

She walked around, finally, to face him and he took her in. She looked tired. And too thin. But she was beautiful. Beautiful beyond words. "I was here Brady. I was watching, but . . . I never felt like I was worthy of being . . . loved . . . by you. There were so many times I wanted to . . . but, I was in relationships that broke me and— and though I could see you year after year—" Her voice cracked, and his heart ripped in two. More than anything he wanted to stand up, gather her to himself. Hold her and never let go. But he waited until she said, "I couldn't figure out why you would want me."

And then he stood, his arms wide open. "Come here," he said, and she willingly stepped into his embrace. His lips found her ear. "I will want you forever," he whispered.

Beneath the glow of the streetlamp, in front of the very bench where it all began, she tilted her face up to look at his until his lips met hers.

Time stopped. Then, when they broke apart, he hugged her tight, silently thanking God for the lesson he had learned. He knew better how to love her now because of what had happened over the years. Some promises simply required a longer period of time before they can be fulfilled. Some blessings are a little belated but the journey to the blessing makes it even more fulfilling.

"Sarah?" he said, then led her back to the bench. He picked up her cup of hot chocolate and handed it to her.

She laughed, her face lighting in a way he hadn't seen in years. "Thank you," she said, then took a tentative sip. She laughed again. "It's a little cold."

Brady slid his hand into the right front pocket of his jeans, his finger finding the treasure that he'd tucked into its recesses earlier in the day. When he removed it, he looked over to Sarah's face. To her eyes, which had widened. "Brady . . ."

Brady eased himself down on one knee. "For five years I've brought this ring here with me," he said, moving it so the diamond caught the light.

Sarah touched it lightly with her fingertip. "It's—it's *lovely.*"

"It was my grandmother's. I asked my dad if I could have it and—and he gave it to me. Said it was mine anyway. Nana always wanted me to have it so I could, one day, give it to my bride."

"Oh, Brady . . ."

He captured her eyes with his own. "Just say yes."

"Yes," she said without thinking. "But only on one condition."

His brow rose. "Name it," he said, because whatever she wanted . . . whatever she needed . . .

"You'll kiss me one more time."

Brady chuckled as he slid the ring on her finger, as his heart's smile matched the one on his face. "I think I can handle that," he said, then gathered her into his arms again.

Chapter 64

Morning came. Brady rolled out of bed, exhilarated by the night before. His phone buzzed as he went to the shower.

I've always loved you, her text read. *Merry Christmas, Brady.*

Brady hurried to text her back, wanting to get ready as quickly as possible.

Be there in thirty minutes. Love you forever.

He then added. *Remember, don't say anything to your mom.*

He showered, dressed, then grabbed the gifts he needed to take with him. Sarah had told him the night before about Miss Susan, and he hoped he could convince both mother and daughter to go to his parents' house with him for the day.

The drive to Sarah's seemed to take forever, his excitement uncontrollable.

Once he pulled up, he all but ran to the door.

"Come in," Susan welcomed him at the front door. She was dressed in sweatpants and a long-sleeved Christmas tee. Her hair had been brushed but her face was devoid of makeup. Brady couldn't help but note that his fiancée's mother looked much paler than he had expected. "You'll have to forgive the way I look," she said as if she read his mind.

Brady gave her a kiss on the cheek. "You look just fine, Miss Susan."

"And," she said turning back to go inside. "You'll have to forgive Sarah. She's been trying to get ready but can't settle on what to wear." Brady stepped inside and waited as Susan closed the door. "Let's go in the family room."

Brady followed her in. For the next few minutes, they talked about Susan's "brush with death," as she called it and how, providentially, it had brought Sarah back to West Jefferson. "But you're doing okay?" Brady asked her, leaning forward to rest his elbows on his knees. Overhead, the sound of Sarah's footsteps brought a rush of happiness and he wondered how much longer he could sit and make small talk, no matter how critical.

"I'm fine," Susan assured him. She looked up to the ceiling and smiled. "I'm telling you, Brady, she will take a year to get ready," Susan added with a chuckle. "She got it from me."

"She doesn't have to worry. I love her just the way she is." Brady felt heat rush to his cheeks. He hadn't intended to say anything remotely close to that. Now, in some ways, the proverbial cat had left the bag.

"I hope you mean that," Sarah called as she descended from the upstairs and rounded into the family room. She spread her arms wide, then let them fall to her sides. "This is my third choice of outfit for today."

Brady stared. He couldn't help it. She had settled on a pair of dark jeans and a white button-down shirt, the cuffs folded back to expose her slender wrists. Her dark hair lay over one shoulder, the other boasted a small red purse. Other than pearl earrings, she wore no other jewelry.

"You look beautiful," he said as she approached. "Have you said anything?" he whispered.

"Only that I love you," she whispered back, then gave him a quick kiss before he turned toward her mother, his smile wide. "Susan, will you come with us today?"

"Oh, no. I better let you guys have your Christmas with your family."

"No—um—we, Sarah and I and my whole family, we want you there," Brady assured her.

"Mom, listen to Brady. Please," Sarah pleaded.

Susan sighed. "Guys, I'm not dressed or anything. I would be holding you up."

Brady grinned. He could tell they were wearing her down. "Amazing thing is, well, it's Christmas all day long, so I'm pretty sure you've got enough time to get ready."

Susan had no defense. She gingerly rose from the couch and made her way to her bedroom. "I'll try to hurry," she said.

As soon as her bedroom door closed, Brady looked down at Sarah and said, "Come here, you."

She giggled as she stepped into his arms and lifted her face for a kiss.

"Where's the ring?" he asked, keeping his voice low.

She held up her purse. "Tucked away for safekeeping."

"Good deal," he said, then kissed her again.

❋ ❋ ❋ ❋ ❋

"Sarah, oh my goodness, give me a hug," Brady's mother said as she spread her arms to hug Sarah.

"Dad! Chels!" Brady called out toward the back of the house. "Look who's here."

When Chelsi laid eyes on Sarah, she squealed. "I haven't seen you in forever," she said as they hugged, rocking back and forth.

"Lauri, you might want to take their coats, you know," Brady's father said.

"Oh yes, yes. Let me take your coats. Susan, it is so good to see you. Brady told me you'd had a scare. Do you need anything?"

"Just to sit and relax," Susan said as she shrugged out of her coat.

"Well, I'm just so glad you're here. Here, let me take that."

"You are always welcome to be here with us," Brady's father noted as the family walked into the living room where the Christmas tree dominated a corner of the room. "At Christmas or anytime."

"Well, Dad," Brady said. "I'm glad to hear you say that . . ." He looked at Sarah, who pinked.

"What's going on?" Chelsi asked. She looked at Neal who shrugged.

"Don't look at me," he said. He lowered himself to an armchair, then pulled his wife down to his lap.

Brady extended his hand to Sarah. "Want to go fishing in your purse?"

Sarah grinned as she slowly opened first the purse, and then a small compartment within it. She removed the ring and placed it in the palm of Brady's hand.

"Oh . . . my . . . goodness," Chelsi said before wrapping her arms around her husband's shoulders. "I cannot believe this is finally happening."

Brady turned to his family and held the ring up for a moment, then slid it over Sarah's left ring finger. "I asked Miss Sarah last night if she would marry me and . . ." He cocked one brow.

"And I said *yes.*" She grinned up at him as their families clapped and cheered.

"I love you, Sarah Ashford."

"And I love you, Brady Jameson."

Brady's dad clapped him on the back. "Looks like love won the day," he said.

"Yes, sir," Brady returned as he slid his arm around Sarah's waist. "Took a little longer than I expected, but . . ." He looked down at her and winked.

"But I was worth the wait?" Sarah teased, her eyes sparkling in mischief.

"You bet you were," he said. "You *are* more than worth the wait."

THE END